Ring of Diamonds

Sharon Stevens

Library of Congress Number:		00-192007
ISBN #:	Hardcover	0-7388-3530-7
	Softcover	0-7388-3531-5

This book was printed in the United States of America.

To order additional copies of this book, contact:
Xlibris Corporation
1-888-7-XLIBRIS
www.Xlibris.com
Orders@Xlibris.com

To Danielle, Catherine, Denise, Nicole,
Steve, Roland, Linda, and all of our
other readers, for their suggestions,
encouragement, and enthusiasm.
Thank you.

Prologue

November, 1963

The sun beat down on the roof of the Studebaker as Margaret Drummond drove her seven-year-old daughter Lilly along the mountain road from the school in Springbok. The Cape Town newspaper she'd picked up in town was a week old, and the news in it was even older. The American president, Kennedy, had been shot in a motorcade in Dallas. That all seemed very remote to her, here in South Africa. They said it was dangerous here, but she'd never felt particularly threatened, and couldn't imagine such a barbarous act as an assassination happening in the regimented society of South Africa's diamond mining communities. Of course things could be pretty rough if you were Coloured. But she and Charles had built a fairly nice life for themselves and Lilly, isolated from all that nastiness. It was a privileged existence they led, she knew.

She looked over at her daughter. It was two weeks before Christmas, and Lilly was full of excitement about the holidays. The child straightened the beret on her head, then scrambled onto her knees and reached over into the back seat for her school bag.

"Sit back down Lilly, this is a dangerous road," cautioned Margaret. The child turned back and began rummaging through her papers.

Glancing into the rear-view mirror, Margaret noticed the large, black automobile behind them drawing closer. She slowed a little, and waved her hand out the window, indicating to the driver to pass. It was the only straight stretch on the treacherous road.

They had been behind her for several minutes, and she had begun to get worried. Charles had been concerned of late about Winston's erratic behavior. He'd warned her to stay away from his unscrupulous partner. Not that she'd needed much urging. She'd never gotten along with the man. She'd never trusted him.

The driver of the other vehicle sped up, but instead of passing her, he suddenly rammed into the back of her car. Lilly screamed as she was hurled forward onto the dashboard of the car.

"Lilly, my God, are you alright?" said the frantic woman, attempting to gain control of the vehicle.

Before the child could answer the black automobile hit them again.

Margaret swerved out of control. The edge of the road came rushing up toward them. Beyond that edge was open air, and then a 500-foot drop, to the base of the mountain.

She was still spinning the wheel in a futile effort to regain control, as the vehicle plunged over the edge.

*   *   *

The orange South African sun was setting behind the scrub-covered hills of North Cape as Charles Drummond stood at the roadside, looking into the abyss. In his hand he clutched two pink roses, his daughter's favorite color.

The car had been removed, and his wife and daughter laid to rest in the village cemetery. Still, he was drawn to the spot where it had happened.

Gouges in the dirt border of the road marked the place where the car had started its plunge. Bark was torn off the huge tree as the car had crashed past, leaving deep scratches in the trunk.

The police said that it wasn't an accident. The car had been hit from behind, more than once.

They said that there were no leads. Perhaps that's what they'd been told to say, he didn't know. But he did know who had done it.

Winston.

Only Winston could be so heartless.

Perhaps he should go kill the man, right now.

But if he did, he couldn't be sure that the secret wouldn't come out.

Not the secret about the diamonds. That was his to take to the grave.

The other secret.

The boy.

Was revenge worth endangering the last remaining person that he loved?

Perhaps there was another way.

He watched the last sliver of sun die, and shivered even though the air wasn't cold.

Time was on his side. He could destroy Winston, perhaps with time alone. And if not time, a trap. He would set a trap that would destroy his hated rival. Even if it took more than a lifetime, he would make the man pay.

He opened his hand and watched the two pink roses settle silently into the abyss.

Chapter 1

The Present

The wet pavement had begun to seep into her shoes as Jessica Farrell hurried through the thick London gloom. It was cold for November, but not quite freezing. The heavy rains had come to an end, but there were deep puddles everywhere. Neon lights from the shops, and the bright headlights and red taillights of the passing cars were reflected in the road, filling it with light, so that it was hard to know what was real and what was illusion.

She was thinking about the mysterious note she had received. What had it meant? She was most curious about its brief reference to the ring. No one in the entire world knew about the ring—except Edward. And she had not seen Edward now in nearly five years.

No, six. No, it *was* five. It had been such a long time. And yet . . . she quickened her pace.

Jessica pulled the ring from her pocket and looked at it. The gold band gleamed in the subdued glow of the streetlight. A row of small, brilliant diamonds encircled it. Jessica turned the ring around in her fingers, remembering the day it had been presented to her. The tiny diamonds caught the light and refracted it back a brilliant indigo.

Just then a dark sedan with smoky windows swerved close to her and almost mounted the curb. Horns blared. She heard people yelling at each other, swearing at each other. The driver ran down his powered window and looked at her. He looked like a foreigner.

"Are you all right, miss?"

Jessica looked down and saw that she had been splashed with dirty water from the street.

"Yes," she said, coming back to her senses for a moment, "Yes, just splashed a bit. That's all."

"Sorry, miss. But you really oughtn't walk so close to the curb, miss. It could be dangerous on a night like tonight."

Dangerous, she heard the man say, but by then she was walking onward, through the wet streets.

Her thoughts drifted back to that day in Paris, five years earlier. She had played that day over in her head a hundred times since. The walk through the galleries of the Louvre. The impromptu picnic in the Tuileries. Kissing on the quays along the Seine with the towers of Notre Dame rising up above them. It had been like a dream, that day. And it seemed so long ago—a lifetime ago. That had been the last day she had seen Edward.

She remembered the tightness around the corners of his mouth as he waved to her. His face had been set in stony impassiveness, as he stood on the platform of the Gare de Lyon. She'd craned her neck as the train began to move, watching him recede to nothingness.

She felt a fluttering inside her, a renewal of feelings she had long suppressed.

Jessica sighed inwardly, replacing the ring in her pocket. As hard as she had tried, she had not been able to settle the matter of Edward. Maybe this night would give her the chance to bring things to a satisfactory conclusion, in a way she had not been able to manage five years before.

How many failed relationships had she been through since then? Two had been utter failures from the start. The third . . . well, that was a different story. In other circumstances, in an earlier time and place, she and Jack might have made a go of it. Jack was kind to her always, and it seemed they never, ever argued with each other. Unfortunately, Edward's handsome face always loomed in front of her whenever Jack tried to get too close. Jack was still Jessica's friend, though. Her best friend. It was obvious that he wanted more from her. And she'd been close to opening up to him . . . but now.

A spray of cold water snapped her back to London, and the present. She stepped farther from the curb and brushed a lock of damp auburn hair from her face. She knew that many men found her attractive. There was certainly no problem finding potentially interested suitors. She had always felt that her lightly freckled skin and slim build made her appear somewhat childish, but Jack said they were the perfect accompaniment to her beautiful hair.

Jack. Poor, devoted Jack, whom she'd strung along for so long now. Too long. She needed to be fair with him, stop kidding herself—and him. It was time to get things back on track, and just be friends. With so few friends, she didn't want to lose Jack altogether.

Late at night, when she lay sleepless in her bed, she knew there could have been something more to her life. Something she'd been so close to, once, and then lost. And then she'd stare at the ceiling as the clock ticked off the hours until daylight.

Sometimes she felt so alone in the world. It had been a little more than ten years since her parents had died in that horrible car accident, yet she still thought of them often. Losing them both at seventeen had been very hard on her.

But why was she filled so much with the past? There was business to attend to. *Now.* There had been the note, and she had been invited, and what was the address she was looking for?

Across the street Jessica saw a row of houses, their dull brown facades stained with the rain. The signs on the doorways bore small brass numbers. As she passed the third house she could just make out "22" when the numbers caught the glow of passing headlights.

She glanced at her small silver watch. Two minutes until 9 p.m. She swallowed nervously. She'd give almost anything to be back at her flat, door securely bolted, a glass of sherry next to her computer as she worked on her architectural drawings. But the note had made it sound urgent . . .

She'd examined it, when it arrived in her mailbox. There was no return address—no postage even. Just a simple two-line message: "I need the ring back, urgently. Please meet me." Then the address and time. Was it Edward's handwriting? She couldn't be sure.

She approached the unlit doorway and raised her hand to the knocker, then stopped, startled, as the door began to open of its own accord. She squinted, trying to make out the face that then appeared, cloaked in deep shadow. She knew that face, or at least she thought she did. It seemed so long ago.

Jessica drew in her breath.

"Come in, Jessica" the man said. "We have things to discuss."

"Edward, what is this all about?" she said, stepping out of the chilled night air and into the dry warmth of what appeared in the dim light to be a foyer, lined on one wall with a rack of coats.

She looked exactly as she had that last day. The warm glow of the living room lamp reflected in her eyes as she brushed away a wet tendril of hair. Edward felt his heart skip as he watched her fingertips trace a line across the creamy skin of her forehead. Five years and she looked the same. She'd been on a train, running away, from what he didn't really understand. Her eyes had locked on his, and he'd held them knowing she'd be back. And then, as the train pulled out of the Gare de Lyon, she'd looked away, and he'd suddenly known that she wouldn't be back.

So he'd come back to London to try to carry on. But he'd really been waiting. Waiting for the phone to ring, or the door to open, and for her to be there again. But it never happened. And then things got bad, and he knew she wouldn't want him. And somehow, without understanding it, he'd known that he would never see her again. Not in that life, anyway.

And here she was, in another life, and he could reach out and take her in his arms and it would be like it had once been before. And yet, looking in those beautiful eyes, he realized that that would be exactly the wrong thing to do. Because he didn't understand. And until he did, he couldn't risk losing the chance at another try.

Jessica stepped into the hallway, and waited anxiously as he closed and locked the door. "Here, give me your coat," he said, and she slipped out of it and handed it to him.

He hadn't changed much in the five years they had been apart. His eyes were still as bright and as entrancing as she remembered. There was a hint of gray to his hair, but strangely it did not make him look older but more handsome. Those dark eyes, and the handsome angles of his face could still twist her heart. He was dressed in a charcoal suit with a thin stripe, the kind he was known to wear, but it seemed old, and somewhat worn, which puzzled her, because she remembered accompanying Edward to his tailor on Saville Row, and Edward had been a perfectionist when he purchased his clothes. What happened to the Edward she knew, who purchased new suits twice a year?

"Through this way," he indicated, pointing to a small, unevenly decorated sitting room.

Jessica sat in an overstuffed chair, clutching her bag. She looked around the room, trying to balance the tacky furnishings with the educated and cultured man she remembered.

"Can I get you a drink?" he asked, walking to the sideboard. When she shook her head he retraced his steps, then turned again. She felt that she should say something, but it was Edward, after all, who had arranged this meeting. Surely he would speak first.

Edward paced back and forth, his eyes avoiding hers. He was making her more nervous than she had been when she arrived. Was he nervous, too, or was he just trying to unsettle her? This was even harder than she'd imagined. She felt herself withdrawing farther into the overstuffed chair, wishing she was anywhere but facing Edward again.

A shock of neatly trimmed brown hair lay across his forehead, bobbing as he turned at the end of each short circuit across the small room. His hands were clenched behind his back, and Jessica could see that he still had the strong muscular build that had felt so wonderful, pressed firmly against her each night.

Again, she surveyed the room. Victorian furniture, an assortment of tacky knickknacks, crocheted throws coating the under-stuffed, uncomfortable-looking sofa. This was not how the Edward that she remembered lived. Her Edward had been rich. His family had been rich. Hadn't that been one of the things that had bothered her? So why was she so disturbed now that he stood in a room that was obviously not home to the rich or famous?

Even as she discovered herself becoming irritated at his silence, she found herself saying, "Edward, whose place is this?" It came out more harshly than she'd intended.

He stopped pacing.

"Mine," he replied.

"Yours? What do you mean? What about the manor? Why aren't you there?"

He settled into a chair facing her, then leaned forward. "It's gone," he said.

"Gone?"

"I've lost it. And all the money that went with it."

Jessica shook her head in disbelief as she looked around the room. It wasn't possible. Did he really live in this . . . dump? She swallowed nervously.

"Actually . . ." he said.

"Yes?"

"This isn't really my place. Or at least I don't own it. I'm renting it from an acquaintance who has gone on some excursion in the Amazon. Still, it is true that I have seen some hard times of late."

Does she realize what this means? he wondered. Is it what she wanted? Or might it be a case of one needing to be careful what one wishes for? When the truth of it really sinks in . . .

A droplet of water lay upon her skin in the V of her neckline. As he watched it rise and fall with her breathing, the edge of the fabric touched it and it was gone.

Is he toying with me? Jessica wondered. *How could he possibly have lost all that money? And he doesn't seem all that upset about it. He's nervous, yes, but not upset. And the way his eyes follow my every move. After what I did to him, he should be furious with me. Yet even after five years, in some ways it's as if I'd just gone out for a walk around the block . . .*

She sat back in her chair and looked at Edward skeptically. "How could you possibly have lost all that much money? Surely you're joking."

"I'm not, Jessie. You know an investment banker uses his money to make money. But I was just getting started, when I came back after the service. I'd made a few good decisions, before we met, and it seemed easy. I guess it was, for a while. But the expenses of keeping up the estate were always a strain, and then I made some bad decisions. And there were other demands on my financial resources . . ." He waved his hand vaguely, as if to brush away the line of thought. "Anyway," he said, gesturing at the room, "Here I am."

Jessica looked at him, poised there as if waiting to see which way she would move. And which way should she move? Frankly, this was all so surprising, she barely knew where to begin. Best to let him do the talking. She cleared her throat. "Edward," she said, "what is this really all about? Why did you want to see me? Why are you being so mysterious?" And where is Sarah, she wanted to ask, but couldn't. For it would mean more than she wanted it to mean.

Edward rose from his chair and walked to the fireplace, his back to her. The silence grew, like a balloon filling the room. After a long time he finally turned and spoke.

"Five years ago, when you came into my life, I was looking for nothing more than a nanny for my child. But she, and I, came to love you. I so loved you that I proposed marriage to you. And you turned me down. I have tried very hard to comprehend what possessed you to leave, but I'm afraid I have failed miserably. The first year after you left was wretched for both of us."

She opened her mouth to speak, but he held up his hand and continued.

"I was prepared to forget you forever, as painful as such forgetting might be. But, unfortunately, circumstances have dictated that I seek you out, to ask for your help."

Jessica looked at Edward in puzzlement. What help could she possibly give to him? He was rich . . . well, he had *been* rich. Could it really be true? And his friends. He had rich friends—had he lost them, too?

She was now an architect who was gaining a solid clientele, in spite of the field that becoming fiercely competitive in recent years. She was comfortable, yes. But the real money hadn't started to roll in yet. If he needed money, why come to her? Surely his other friends could help out in a more ample way.

She decided directness was the best course of action.

"Edward, I don't pretend to know what this is all about. As for my reasons for leaving . . . I think you can guess some of them, at least. I believe I made it clear how uncomfortable your position and money made me feel at the time, especially given the circumstances of how we came together. We talked about this, Edward. Many times. It's not that I didn't . . ."

She stopped, afraid of what she'd been about to say. "You know, I don't really have any money if that is what you need from me."

He stared at her, his eyes dark, and intense. They'd always been intense. Once they'd been filled with love. But now, they seemed empty, and sad.

"I don't need your money," he said coolly. "Yes, it's true that I don't have the resources I once had. But that isn't why I called you here tonight." He looked at her so intently that she found it hard to meet his gaze. "I need the ring I gave you," he said.

"You want to take back your engagement ring?" After five years, the exchange seemed ludicrous. And yet, for a moment, when she'd mentioned the word "engagement" it was as if nothing had changed, and Edward was as he had been on the last day she had seen him. "Of course I'll return it," she said quietly. "I should have returned it years ago. I only held onto it because . . ." *Because why?* She asked herself.

Because you wanted to believe that it wasn't all over, you silly ass. Even after you left him at that station like so much unclaimed baggage.

"Something has happened," Edward said softly. "Something extraordinary."

She looked at him quizzically.

"I've received a letter. It was postmarked from South Africa."

She remembered something about South Africa. A story Edward had told her once.

"As you know," he continued, "the ring is one of a set of three rings that were made by my Uncle Charles. He made them shortly after he returned from South Africa. You may recall my telling you that his wife and daughter had been killed in a tragic automobile accident? Well, that was in the early sixties. When Charles died a few years later, the rings were passed on to Charles's brother, my father, and then at my father's death they passed to me."

Jessica nodded. She remembered vaguely having heard this story before. Edward's Uncle Charles had been a partner in a diamond mine in South Africa, north of Cape Town, near the largest field of diamonds in the world. Charles's father had started the mine. Jessica had always assumed that this was the origin of the family's wealth, but she knew also that Charles had surrendered his interest in the mine when he had returned to England after the accident.

"I'd never attached much significance to the rings," Edward continued. "As family heirlooms, I passed one on to my sister Emma, and I gave another to you, when I asked you to . . ."

His gaze grew distant, and he swallowed before he continued.

"Anyway. I recently received this letter from South Africa. A most peculiar letter."

He paused and then stroked his chin thoughtfully. "The letter indicates that the rings lead to a treasure of some sort. Yes, I know—a 'treasure.' It sounds like a childhood adventure story, doesn't it? But given my current financial needs, I feel I owe it to Sarah—as well as to my uncle—to see if I can locate this 'treasure' and reclaim it for the family. That's why I need your help, Jessie. And the ring."

No one had called her Jessie in five years. It made her heart flip flop, but she pressed on. Now he was looking at her expectantly and she forced herself to return his gaze. Those eyes. Those eyes could make her do most anything. But she couldn't let old emotions to get the better of her. "Who was the letter from? How could someone write a letter about the rings? Who would even know about them after all this time? It's been almost thirty years."

"That's what is most peculiar about the letter, actually. It arrived in the mail this week, but it bore a recent postmark and South African postage. It was not addressed to me but to my father. As you know he's been dead now for quite some time."

"Obviously the person who mailed the letter doesn't know that. Lucky for you the postman even delivered it. I'm forever having problems getting my mail delivered properly."

"Hold on, Jessie. I haven't even gotten to the odd part yet," he said.

"It's not odd enough that a letter was written to a dead man?"

"No. You see, the letter was written *by* a dead man, too."

Jessica arched her eyebrows.

"Yes," he said, "The letter was from my late Uncle Charles."

* * *

It was after midnight when Jessica returned to her flat across town. She bolted the door, kicked off her shoes, and plopped down on the couch, staring into space. What a night!

Had she done the right thing? She had to admit, it had been nice seeing Edward again, after all these years. It had awakened something within her that she'd forgotten she could experience. Still . . .

To continue to see him to help him solve the puzzle . . . that was dangerous. Dangerous for her emotional well-being. She still wasn't sure if she could handle spending time with him. She had so many unresolved feelings.

Edward had sensed her reticence and had promised that their relationship would be strictly business, that the emotional ties that had once bound them together would not come into play. That was easy for him to say. But could she be as cool about it as Edward? And did he really mean it? There'd been something about the way he looked at her tonight that stirred feelings deep within her. Was she imagining it?

She hadn't even told him that the ring was in her coat pocket. She had coyly lied, saying she'd just missed the bank, that it was in her safety deposit box, and she would get it in the morning.

She wasn't sure why she'd done that. Caution perhaps? Or just reluctance to give it up? Or perhaps just an excuse to see him again?

She didn't know.

With a sigh she got up from the couch and went into the kitchen, and put the kettle on to boil.

Edward was still as handsome as she remembered. Possibly even more so. Some men just seemed to improve with age. She knew every line, every glimmer of his eyes, every mannerism. His body, finely toned by his years in the army was still trim, and athletic, despite the passing years.

And, to her considerable annoyance, he still made her feel weak at the knees.

She poured the boiling water into the cup and watched as the warm amber glow of the tea spread throughout the water. She leaned down to smell the bergamot. The smell of her Earl Grey tea always seemed to have a relaxing effect upon her even before she had brought it to her lips.

Why did Edward still have such a strong hold on her? She had already told him no. Long ago. Why was that not the end of it? Forever.

She returned to the couch, fished the remote out from between the cushions, and clicked on the television. She hardly noticed what she was watching, but she enjoyed the noise. It distracted her. At least at first. But as she began to drink the warm tea, it was as if its sweet taste was a potion that drugged her. She closed her eyes, not in sleep but in peaceful meditation, and remembered how she and Edward had first come to know each other.

The pursuit of love had been the last thing on her mind.

* * *

Jessica Farrell had been a bright, ambitious girl of twenty-two, from a drab town in the Midlands. She was alone in the world then, after the death of her parents, but she had friends and she had dreams, and she seemed to be moving toward her goals much faster than many young women her age, despite her adversities.

She had never considered working as a nanny, though she had an aunt who was a governess to three children in Mayfair. She had babysat for several neighbors in her high school years, and knew what it entailed to care for children. But she had not really come to the Drummond home by choice, but more by necessity.

She needed money.

The architectural firm in Battersea where she had been working had just laid off half its staff, mostly the youngest and the least experienced designers, and this hit Jessica on both counts.

She still had a year of further study before she could obtain her license, and the insurance money was running low. There was no one helping her any longer. She had to do it all alone. So why not work as a nanny for a while? It might give her the flexibility she'd need to finish up her studies. The advertisement had said, "experience necessary," and she knew she did not have the credentials wanted, but that had never stopped her before, had it?

The underground squealed to a stop at another station, and the lighting changed from the warm glow of the train to the bright fluorescent glare of the platform. Four stations to go, she counted.

Although she'd lived on the outskirts of London all her life, she'd rarely been into the center of the city, and certainly never found a reason to take the underground to the High Street Kensington station. Oh, her parents must have taken her to Kensington Gardens when she was little, but if it had made any impression on her, she didn't remember it. Certainly she hadn't spent any time contemplating whether real people might actually live in such a place.

And *were* they real? She flipped upon the magazine she'd checked out of the library and leafed through it until she found the picture of Edward Drummond. Not a half bad looking chap. Perhaps a bit too lean in the face, or was that just a stern of expression he put on for the photographer? He was, after all, supposed to be some sort of war hero. The article wasn't very well-written, a jumbled up mess of facts, really, but she felt lucky to have found anything about him. Somehow, she thought that if she did her homework it might help her with the interview.

Apparently the Drummond family was a wealthy one, but with a Kensington address that didn't require strong deductive powers. What was surprising was that the article spoke mostly of Edward Drummond's military career. Apparently he knew how to fly a helicopter, and had actually seen some combat, rescuing several crewman of a downed helicopter behind enemy lines.

She wondered if his family had gotten him the placement as an officer, but decided that it probably required more than a little ability to fly combat helicopters.

Two subway stops to go, she noted as the car came to another stop.

She skimmed through the article looking for any mention of what he did for a living. There was some talk of investment banking, whatever that was. It sounded like the sort of thing a rich person would do. But a curious quote in the article had him talking about the cost of keeping up a large estate, and made it seem as if he didn't find it an enviable position. Of course it was easy to say that if you were already rich.

On the whole, the article seemed pretty flattering. Perhaps that was just the way it was written, but the magazine had a reputation for digging up dirt, and there didn't seem to be any dirt on Edward Drummond.

One more stop. She scanned the rest, looking for a mention of his family, but aside from the fact that his father was deceased and his Uncle had spent most of his life in South Africa, there wasn't anything. She wondered how old his children were.

Flipping back to the photo she stared at the picture. He *was* rather attractive.

What kind of a man could be both a successful soldier and a banker? Or did he just have a good press agent? She folded the magazine and stepped out of the underground into High Street Kensington determined to find out.

The house was rather plain on the outside, but within it was as rich as a palace—her two-room flat would easily have fit within the foyer.

She did not know if it was rude or not, but as she waited she wandered about, examining the furnishings and curios. The gold of the organdy curtains imparted a cheerful warmth to the room, and she wondered if the ornate marble fireplace was ever really needed. Atop the mantelpiece was a large collection of elaborate Steuben Glass—tigers caught mid-leap, an elephant, a sleeping dog. Each captured the light spilling into the room as tiny rainbows that shimmered as she moved her head. There were so many pieces crowded together, though, that it appeared more as clutter than collection. When Jessica surveyed the rest of the surfaces in the room she saw why. All of the lower spots had been swept clear of breakables. There were plastic toys, a girl's doll, even a wooden circus train on the carpet behind the couch. She smiled at the thought of what little hands could do to that fragile assortment of glassware.

There was also a photograph on the mantle. A thick silver frame encircled a family scene. The man was tall, and handsome, and a bit older than in the picture in the magazine. He lounged casually in a handsome navy blazer, although the portrait had been taken with them sitting on a formal velvet couch. He was smiling at the little girl sitting next to him, who was gazing at the camera with a mischievous expression. The woman next to them was blonde, severe-looking, and appeared somewhat detached from the scene. It clearly was a family portrait, and yet, something did not seem quite right.

She turned at the sound of someone entering the room. Edward Drummond smiled at her. He was the man in the photograph, yet even more handsome in person. He was tall, and ruggedly handsome, with a strong square chin, and a smile that seemed to originate from his very soul. His silky dark brown hair fell over one eye, giving him an easygoing look. The photograph in the magazine hadn't done him justice.

She swallowed, loudly.

"Miss Farrell, I presume." His dark eyes sparkled as he looked her over.

She had chosen her clothes very carefully. A soft blue silk blouse with a white linen jacket and a short cotton skirt. But not *too* short. The colors contrasted nicely with her green eyes and auburn hair.

She's too attractive for the position, thought Edward. She'll be off and married in no time, and I just have to train someone all over again.

He proffered his hand and she shook it. There was the slightest spark of static that leapt between them. Her grasp was firm and her hand felt warm and comfortable in his.

Still, he thought, it would not be unpleasant having an attractive young lady around the house. If she has a brain, and is good with Sarah. Sarah so needs a mother.

He smiled, and she found that her heart was thudding. "Please, call me Jessica." she said nervously.

"Jessica," he said, as if he were trying the name out. He released her hand and guided her by the elbow to the couch. He settled himself opposite her, and rested his arm on the back of the couch. He seemed at ease with the world, she thought. At ease, yet in control. He smiled again, and once more she felt herself drawn to him. It would be easy to feel attracted to such a man, she thought.

Apart from a high school sweetheart, Edward was the only man who had ever had that affect upon her. She had consciously steered clear of the opposite sex ever since her parents had been killed, cutting off any chance for a relationship. Some small part of her still felt responsible for their deaths. If she hadn't stayed at the dance with her date, her parents might still be alive.

"So tell me about yourself," said Edward, and she found herself saying all of the things she had promised she'd avoid. After fifteen minutes they were discussing the differences between Ionic and Doric columns, and she found that they both shared a passion for good architecture. She found herself hoping that she could secure the position if for no other reason than to spend more time with this interesting, charismatic man.

But how many other things is he equally comfortable discussing? She wondered. While this is all that I know.

And yet when the conversation turned to child rearing, she discovered that she had plenty to say, and Edward was nodding along with her.

She does have a brain, thought Edward. She's really quite captivating.

After a half hour of chatting, Edward rose and excused himself. A few minutes later he returned with the little girl from the photograph. She appeared to be about four years old. She held her father's hand tightly, and stayed shyly beside her father's leg as Edward explained to her who she was. When her father had finished, Sarah politely stepped forward and smiled hesitantly at Jessica.

In spite of her shyness, her big brown eyes were wide with curiosity.

"Hello, young lady," she said, gently taking her hand. "You must be the mistress of the house?"

Sarah giggled at her, but didn't respond. As Jessica and Edward continued to talk, Sarah gradually detached herself from her father, and began a slow circumnavigation of the room. In a short while she was sitting on the couch by Jessica, and the two of them were playing with her doll.

"She's taken a fancy to you," smiled Edward.

There it was again, that smile.

"Well Sarah, are dolls your favorite, or are there other things you like to play, also?" asked Jessica.

The child's face lit up in a smile reminiscent of her father's. "I've got a Noah's Ark and some animals. Do you want to play that?"

Before Jessica could even reply, Sarah had taken her hand and was towing her toward the door,

"Hey, hold on princess. Give the lady time to get used to us," laughed Edward.

His laugh was warm, and full of love.

Sarah walked over to her father, who promptly picked her up and hugged her.

Jessica watched them together, observing the tender way that he held her.

It would be easy to love this child, she thought. But what if I don't get the job? Don't get too close. You might never see them again.

As she was thinking these thoughts, Edward excused himself, and ushered Sarah from the room. She heard him talking to her outside the door.

In a minute he returned, and Jessica looked at him expectantly.

Edward smiled. "We would like you to stay, Jessica."

She beamed at him. "That's wonderful," she said. She didn't want to seem over-eager. "If you're certain. Perhaps I should interview with your wife, also, to make sure that she likes me as well?"

Edward's smile faded. "The child's mother has passed on," he said sadly. "I've been on my own for some time, now."

Oh, gosh, she'd put her foot in that one. "I'm sorry," she stammered.

"Yes," said Edward, shaking off his gloom. "Now, let me show you where your room will be. Sarah's room is right across the hall."

The room was tastefully decorated, with soft pink curtains and white walls. Jessica admired the room, her fingers touching lightly on the furnishings.

Behind her, Edward's eyes followed her about the room. His breath quickened as he watched the grace with which she moved, caught the quickness with which she took it all in, and moved on. She's not used to fine things, he thought. But she fits in well. And good glory, she's lovely. Was that why he'd been so quick to offer the position? He shook his head. No. He'd seen her with Sarah. She was a natural. The two of them would be wonderful together. Not like the poor child's mother. He found himself grimacing.

Jessica fitted into the household easily. Her days became a whirl of walks, stories and the like. At the start, most meals were taken with Sarah alone, but dinners were in the dining room with Edward, and Jessica was asked to join them. Edward often came home early now, and spent increasingly greater time with Sarah. And with her.

Days turned into weeks, and her familiarity with Edward grew. There were moments together when they inadvertently touched, and Jessica felt a rush of emotion. Sometimes, she caught him looking at her intently, and she wondered what he was thinking. She found herself trying to hide her feelings from him. A man of his stature could not afford a romantic interest in someone like her.

But he was so easygoing, so good-natured that she found it impossible not to feel more drawn to him every day. By the time three months had passed, the three of them were like a family, going on outings together, laughing in each other's company.

She learned that Edward had gone into the service to spite his father, who had wanted him to be a businessman. But Edward had craved the excitement of active duty, and he was good at it, rising through the ranks to position of some importance in just a few years. He'd traveled the world and even been involved in a bit of espionage that he still wasn't able to discuss. Then had come Desert Storm, and the hottest action that he'd seen yet. When some allied troops became trapped behind the enemy lines after their helicopter malfunctioned, Edward had volunteered for the rescue mission. Under heavy fire he had gotten them all out alive. It had earned him an award for bravery. But when he got back he learned that his father had passed away.

His sister Emma was beside herself with worry that she was going to lose Edward, too, and be left alone in the world.

And so Edward had taken early retirement, and come home to manage the estate. He found that the finances were far from bountiful, and embarked on a plan to use his assets to make money as an investment banker.

Jessica also learned that an investment banker was someone who used his own money (or borrowed money) to get other people started in business. Edward had had some modest success at it so far, and was hoping for even better things.

Contrary to her early expectations, Jessica found that Edward was by no means a stuffy English gentleman. He was warm, considerate and fun to be with. And he loved his child, making it obvious by the amount of time he chose to spend with her—and with Jessica.

One bright, sunny day a picnic was organized. She helped Sarah to get dressed in play clothes and the three of them assembled in the main hall.

"Come on, my little troop," said Edward, leading the way to the car.

After strapping Sarah safely into the back of Edward's Jaguar, Jessica settled into the passenger's seat beside him.

The countryside was beautiful. Sarah talked excitedly in the back seat, pointing out the cows and horses that they passed. Jessica closed her eyes and smiled, enjoying the warm sun on her face, the wind in her hair.

Edward drove carefully, filling Jessica in on the history of the small villages along their way. He stopped at a turnout next to a luxuriant green dell, and they spread the blanket out under a huge old oak tree. Nearby, a small brook washed its way over the smooth rocks in its bed.

Sarah finished her lunch quickly, and ran around with a rubber ball, calling for her father to hurry and finish. Edward polished off his sandwich, and sighed.

"Duty calls," he said with a grin. He and Sarah kicked the ball around together while Jessica stowed the picnic supplies and got up to stretch her legs. She ambled over to the stream, kicked off her shoes and waded in. It was only ankle deep, and deliciously cool. With one eye on the ball game, she began to stroll down the streambed.

She hadn't gone very far when she spotted something in the water a little further down. It looked like some kind of animal. She picked up her pace, and waded over to it. It was a small fox, still breathing, but badly hurt. It had been attacked by something, and was bleeding into the water.

Loudly she called out to Edward, who came jogging over to her side, with Sarah following close behind.

"It's still alive Edward. We've got to help it."

"Looks like the dogs have gotten to it," he said. "I doubt that it has much of a chance."

"Daddy, you've got to help it. You must," cried Sarah, distressed at the sight of the injured animal.

Edward sent the child back to the car to get another blanket, and knelt down to examine the animal. Its stomach had been ripped open, and the intestines badly perforated. Edward shook his head. "I suspect there's been a hunt, and they didn't bother killing off the poor creature, damn them. We can try to get it to the vet, but it will only prolong things."

"Oh no," whispered Jessica.

He stood up, and cupped her face in his hands.

"Jessie, I think we should put it down. It won't survive the journey, it will just cause it more pain to take it from here."

Jessica blinked. He had never called her that before. She felt a sudden rush of love for him, and for his concern.

Sarah came running back and she took the blanket from her and handed it to Edward. Then she took the girl by the hand and led her back toward the picnic, saying, "Daddy is going to put the fox in the blanket honey, so we can help him. Let's put the picnic basket in the car and get ready to go."

As Sarah led the way, Jessica looked back at Edward. A silent look passed between them. She watched him kneel down to the animal and then she turned away toward the car.

A few minutes later, he returned. Sarah was very distressed to learn that the fox had died. She sobbed into her father's shoulder most of the way home, while Jessica drove.

She felt terrible, yet wonderful at the same time. Sad for the fox, upset for Sarah, excited and nervous about the direction that her relationship with Edward seemed to be taking.

It was late when they arrived back at the manor. Sarah was asleep. Edward carried her up to bed and tucked her in.

"I think we deserve a drink after all that," said Edward, as he shut Sarah's door.

She followed Edward into his study, and watched silently as he poured two brandies. He looked tired; his handsome face was drawn.

As Edward handed her the glass, their fingers touched. Jessica felt a spark jump between them. Her eyes met his, and for the first time she thought she recognized a portion of her own feelings, mirrored back at her. Slowly, they put their glasses down, and moved closer.

"Edward, I . . ."

"Sshh," he whispered, pulling her to him. "God, you don't know how long I've wanted to do this."

His arms enfolded her, cradling her to him. They lingered over their first kiss, feeling their way against each other's lips as Jessica's heart pounded in her temples. This was what she had feared to even dream about for the past few months. She hoped she wasn't dreaming now.

Edward drew her in deeper with his kiss, exploring her mouth intimately. When they finally, breathlessly, pulled apart, and gazed into each other's eyes, an aura of love surrounded them. Dizzily, she leaned her head against his chest, and remained that way for a long time, basking in the afterglow of that kiss, overwhelmed by its power.

It was a night she would never forget, the night of that first kiss. He had awakened in her feelings she had not known existed.

A squeal of tires outside her window jolted her from her reverie. The local hooligans were racing in the darkened alley. The BBC weatherman was predicting more rain. She sighed and clicked the remote control, turning off the mindless drivel.

For a long while she watched the phosphor of the screen slowly fade, letting the darkness enfold her.

So many memories—memories she thought she'd long since banished. She was a fool to carry on with this.

But she was going to do it anyway.

CHAPTER 2

Winston Van Der Meer stood in the building that housed the separation plant at the edge of Pit 23. The years had taken their toll on the old man. Not physically, so much as mentally. At seventy-eight he had weathered many decades of disappointment and frustration.

Winston was tall and gaunt, with a white shock of carelessly cropped hair, which he periodically pushed back from his nervous forehead. His intense eyes anxiously watched the activity in the room around him as the technicians prepared the equipment.

The building was dark inside, even in the burning heat of the South African afternoon. The darkness helped the spotlights that shone from the ceiling to reveal their sought-after prize. Or so he hoped.

The dimness of the room matched the old man's mood—maybe even matched the bleakness of his soul. Winston was a desperate man, and was watching the end result of perhaps his last gamble. Win or lose, he would know by nightfall.

Nervously he watched the falling gravel as the vibrating plates of the separating machine processed it, searching it for the tiny treasures that made up less than one part in 10,000 of the already heavily processed ore. It was neither the newest nor the oldest machine at the many separation plants owned by the Van Der Meer Diamond Company, but it was a type that Winston felt comfortable with. It was easy to understand—not like the vagaries of the ore pits themselves, which sometimes yielded hundred-carat gems that took one's breath away, but more often gave up nothing more than a fine grit of oyster shells, ironstone, agate, beryl chips and titanium dust.

It was up to the geologists to find the diamonds. He could only crush them out of their hiding places. At times he'd said he wished he could crush the geologists as easily as the ore.

His hand tightened involuntarily on the edge of the machine.

How many times during the past fifty years had he stood next to a machine such as this?

It had been easier back in the old days. Even in the sixties, when the troubles had started, it hadn't been so hard. He shook his head. The past thirty years had been cruel to him.

He eyed the end result of the thousands of man hours of labor expended by the Van Der Meer Diamond Company: a stream of fine gravel, pulverized, sifted and sorted from the thin layer of marine terrace buried deep beneath the hills of Namaqualand in South Africa.

The vibrating plates of the machine sent up a cacophony in the old building, shaking every loose object on the laboratory benches. The noise didn't bother Winston Van Der Meer. It was the sound of money being made—or found. He glanced at one of the white-coated technicians who stood nearby, monitoring the machine's progress. Winston smiled to himself at the ungainly hearing protectors the man wore. The man didn't appreciate that the vibrations of the machine were the sound of the lifeblood of the Van Der Meer Diamond Company, pulsing through the separation plant.

Winston watched the cascade of fine gravel as the wet slurry slid across the vibrating plates of the machine, spilling from one level to the next, sliding across the water-slickened layer of olive oil that coated each plate. The water and oil refused to mix, and their incompatibility carried the torrent over the edge of the last plate and into the reject hopper. But the diamonds were not wetable. Any of the precious gems mixed in with the slurry would stick to the olive oil coating the plates, suspended there like boulders in a swiftly flowing stream.

Winston's old hands moved nervously on the edge of the machine, feeling its vibrations, trying to gather some sense of the value of the impending flow. The machine had been operating for only about ten minutes. That was when the last load of ore had been crushed in the processing cylinder outside.

The large fragments had been run up the conveyor from the collection building next door, then dumped into the huge cylinder. Inside it, giant steel bearings reduced all but the hardest pieces to gravel. Only the diamonds passed through that merciless tube unharmed.

Beneath the crushing cylinder, the fragments had been puddled through a tank of silicon mud to float off material with a specific gravity of less than 2.5. Now, the remaining gravel had begun to arrive on the final conveyor.

Ten minutes was not enough time to assess the value of the load. And inconsistencies in the quality of the source material could cause wildly varying results, minute by minute.

Winston knew these things well.

And yet he had hoped by now to see the first diamonds begin to appear.

The Van Der Meer Diamond Company was not in a position to easily withstand another dry hole. In fact, if this new operation in Pit 23 yielded nothing more than the previous excavation, the company might well lack the capital needed for a fresh start.

Winston's father had told him stories about the early years of the century, and the founding of the company. It had sounded easier then. Many of the gems lay scant yards below the surface, and an established layer of diamond bearing strata might stretch for hundreds of yards before the lode played out. Winston's father and his partner had founded the company as young men, in the wake of the discovery of diamonds on old farmer DeBeers' land. That famous strike had led to the formation of the DeBeers Diamond Company, known locally as The Big Company. While DeBeers dominated the diamond business worldwide, through their sufferance smaller companies could exist and prosper, provided they didn't grow too large. For then they would be taken over by The Big Company.

And so the Van Der Meer Diamond Company had existed for the better part of the century, first under the leadership of Winston's father and his partner, then under that of their sons, Winston Van Der Meer and Charles Drummond.

Winston had grown up with Charles, and considered him his best friend. But when they reached manhood, Charles had begun to change. At first Winston attributed it to Charles' schooling in England. Winston had remained behind with his father in South Africa to learn the operation of the mine, while Charles had returned to England for his formal education as a geologist. Winston's father had been proud of his young son, and had turned over the management of the company to him at an early age. During school breaks, when Charles returned from England, Winston found him interfering in the operation of the mine, championing the causes of the kaffirs—blacks, mostly Ovambo tribesmen from Namibia—who worked the treacherous machinery, deep in the pits. Charles socialized with the Coloureds, the half-black, half-white machinery and office workers who also had no social status in apartheid South Africa. Charles protested their long work hours, the dangerous nature of some of the tasks they were asked to perform, the low wages that they were paid. Winston, involved in the operation of the mine full-time since before he was a teenager, understood how to manage the kaffirs and the Coloureds. He resented Charles' influence, which invariably reduced the efficiency of the operations.

By the time that Charles had returned to work at the mine full-time, the initial strata, the oysterline discovered by Winston's and Charles' fathers had been scraped down to bedrock, and the Van Der Meer Diamond Company was in desperate need of new leases and new operations. Charles, with his formal education as a geologist, seemed to have a sixth sense for where diamonds might be found. Time and time again he successfully located promising fields and succeeded in leasing or purchasing them from the simple farmers who owned them. And so Charles garnered the respect of both of their fathers.

And the resentment of Winston. Having invested far more time in the operation of the mine than newcomer Charles, Winston was incensed that their fathers placed the future hope of the company's success upon Charles' abilities, and not his own.

That was when Winston had caught Charles with the Mogamo woman.

He'd followed Charles on one of his field surveys, curious and suspicious about the long absences of his erstwhile friend. Keeping his own Land Rover at a discreet distance, he'd pursued the young man for hours through the barren South African terrain. Often they'd been more than a mile apart, but Charles was never difficult to spot, as he churned up a cloud of dust from the primitive cross-country roads. Sighting him from the top of a bush-covered hill, Winston watched him taking meticulous soil samples and making careful notes in his field book. But it was when Charles finally turned his Land Rover off the road altogether and headed cross-country in the direction of the Coloured township that Winston's pulse quickened. Following carefully over the unmarked terrain, he stopped outside the village, parking his Land Rover at the top of a rise, behind an overgrown thorn tree and advancing on foot.

Charles entered a simple yellow house surrounded by a ramshackle picket fence. Its unglazed single window was curtained with a white cotton material that served as mosquito netting. For a long time Winston stood outside that window, eavesdropping on the two within. As the sun set and the evening sounds took over around the perimeter of the village, he even dared to peer into the dimly lit room.

A Petromax lamp hung from one of the exposed rafters. Bathed in its warm glow, two lovers lay tangled on the small bed. Charles' youthful, muscular body pressed against the lustrous brown flesh of the young woman as they moved together, lost in each other's passion. He couldn't understand how Charles could sleep with a dirty Coloured. His opinion of the man went from bad to worse.

Later, smiling in satisfaction, Winston rolled the Land Rover downhill outside the village before quietly starting it and making his way back to the Van Der Meer compound.

It was one thing to champion the cause of the kaffirs and Coloureds, but quite another to have a romantic relationship with one. In apartheid-dominated South Africa it was anathema. Now Winston had the ammunition he needed to get Charles out of the way.

The next day Winston smiled as he stood outside the white clapboard house belonging to Charles' father and listened to the ferocious ranting of the old man. It was hours later when the elder Drummond finally emerged, climbed into his Land Rover and tore out of the compound in an angry shower of gravel. Winston watched until nightfall, but Charles remained inside. With quiet satisfaction Winston slunk back to his own quarters.

The following day Charles had been unceremoniously packed onto the train to Cape Town for the long journey back to England. The elder Drummond made it clear that Charles would not be returning.

Winston continued to operate the mine for their fathers, even during World War II. As a South African citizen he was largely uninvolved in the conflict, which never much impacted the North Cape area. Even those few who chose to fight never made it out of Africa. But Winston had never been a joiner. Or an idealist.

Shortly after the war his father had died. Winston was so immersed in his work with the mine that he barely seemed to notice. Nearly a decade later the passing of Charles' father also went unnoticed. Or it would have, had it not brought the return of Charles.

Older and wiser, Charles reentered the scene with a new wife, Margaret, and a daughter, Lilly, upon whom he doted.

Winston might have resented the return of his old rival, but the truth was that the last of Charles' geologic finds had been nearly fully exploited, and the Van Der Meer Diamond Company was in desperate need of a new source of diamonds. Charles drew upon his natural aptitude at geology, devoting himself wholeheartedly to the task, exploring previously untouched regions of the company's leases and the surrounding terrain.

After a few months Winston could tell that Charles was onto something big. One day Charles had even shown him some of his samples, which contained a nearly three carat blue white diamond, albeit slightly flawed. Still, it was VVSI, very very slight imperfection. It was unusual for a sample, which had to be obtained near the surface, to bear such a valuable stone.

Charles wouldn't reveal the location of his explorations. He said he wanted to be sure, and to assess the size of the field before getting Winston too excited. But clearly Charles was excited.

The kaffirs were excited too. But not about the right things. With Charles' return the problems had begun almost immediately. Within months Winston found himself in the midst of a full-fledged worker revolt. Hours at the mine had been cut back, and many of the most productive work techniques had been curtailed. Worse yet, Winston heard his own managers extolling Charles' virtues and, by implication, denigrating his own.

Winston had spoken with Charles more than once about the difficulties. Several of their conversations had escalated into screaming matches. As last Charles had demanded that if Winston would not improve conditions among the workers, there would be no new "find". Winston and Charles both well knew that without a fresh revenue source, the Van Der Meer Diamond Company would soon run out of operating capital.

So Winston had hired some men from Kimberley to come up to the company's property and scare Charles into submission.

That was when things had begun to go wrong . . .

A glint of light caught Winston's eye, and his attention snapped back to the separating machine in the building next to Pit 23. A single, small stone clung to the center of the second vibrating plate. The old man reached down and plucked it from the olive oil, turning it over in the palm of his hand. It was a small, Champagne-colored stone, called Second Cape. An obvious flaw ran through it, a girdle.

At barely more than a carat it was hardly the kind of stone that would pay for the Herculean effort required to extract the enormous amount of gravel that had been removed from Pit 23.

Of course, stones weighing less than a carat wouldn't even be visible while the separator was shaking. But it was the large stones that he was looking for. Those were the ones that he needed to make the operation pay.

It was still too soon to tell, but it was not a good sign.

Winston cursed silently under his breath. The geologist had warned him that without newer, more expensive separating techniques, Pit 23 had reached the end of its useful life. But he'd found new geologists, many of them, and eventually one of them had encouraged him to proceed with a further excavation on the Northeast face.

In a few hours he would know whether that gamble had paid off.

If it didn't, it wouldn't be the first gamble that hadn't paid off since Charles had returned to England, a broken man. Charles had even given Winston the other half of the company when his wife and daughter had died. But he hadn't given him his secret.

In the more than 30 years that had elapsed, the Van Der Meer Diamond Company had gone through some two dozen geologists, and opened six major pits. Some had paid their way. Others had been dry. Twenty-seven kaffirs had died in a cave-in at a pit that yielded less than 10,000 Rand worth of diamonds.

But always the company had made just enough to persevere. Always Winston had continued searching for the find that Charles had taken with him to the grave.

But now Winston was running on empty.

A few years after Charles had returned to England, Winston married Chassie, a professional woman he had met on a supply trip to Upington. Winston had hoped that the relationship would result in a son, a new generation to carry on the traditions of the family company.

But Chassie had stayed in the white clapboard house at the mine for barely two years. The life of a miner's wife was not what she'd been raised for. And, Winston reflected, he had not been the warmest of husbands.

After Chassie's departure, Winston had tried to lose himself in his work. But he found himself haunted by Charles' successes. He grew hard, and distant. He was neither trusted nor liked by the other employees, who viewed him as devious and dangerous.

When the letter had come, Winston knew it was in Charles' handwriting. He didn't know how, but he knew it was real. So he'd conceived the idea of going to England, to find out just how much Charles had taken with him.

It had troubled Winston all these years that Charles would walk away from a major diamond find without revealing its location. Had he left no papers or records of his greatest find? If so, why? Had Charles suspected Winston's complicity in the Mogamo affair . . . or in . . . the accident.

Winston shuddered, and returned his attention to the separating machine. Two even smaller diamonds clung to the edges of the first plate. He motioned toward one of the technicians, who swept them into a collecting dish. The man caught Winston's eye for a moment, and Winston saw disillusionment there.

There was a tap on his shoulder and Winston turned to see one of the other technicians standing behind him.

"Sir," the man spoke in Afrikaans, straining to be heard over the buzz of the separating machine, "Your car is here. The plane is ready." Winston nodded and turned towards the door.

Perhaps now there was a chance to find out what Charles had been up to.

With a final backward glance at the barren machine, Winston stepped out into the hot South African evening.

* * *

He was jarred awake by the wheels of the Leer jet squealing on the pavement at Heathrow. It had been a long flight from Cape Town, but he'd slept most of the way, and he felt fresh and ready to go. Too bad it was so late in London. Oh well. He had a couple of ladies he could look up.

Winston watched the lights of the charter hanger roll into view as the plane cleared the taxiway. It was raining. He shrugged. It always was, here.

It had been blisteringly hot when they took off from Cape Town. Winston liked the heat, the dryness, even the austerity of South Africa. He was a native, and felt completely comfortable wherever he went in the country. Even when those idiots had let the country slip into black rule, it hadn't affected him much. The Coloureds who worked the mine might be able to vote, now, but they still needed the Van Der Meer Diamond Company to make a living.

The plane rolled to a stop, and he watched the ground crew working the tie-downs.

London. He'd had some good times here. There were things—and people—he could get in London that were hard to come by in South Africa. Winston found himself grinning. He'd have some fun on this trip.

It still bothered him, though. Getting a letter from a dead man. Especially that dead man. Guilt?

No. But it was spooky.

He hadn't intended to have them killed. It wasn't as if he'd held a gun to their heads. But once he'd called the men from Kimberley, he could no longer control things.

Maybe he should have foreseen that.

It wasn't that he cared about Margaret and Lilly. But it was a foolish mistake. How could he have been so stupid? There was Charles, on the verge of a major discovery, and he'd destroyed the man's life.

Before Charles had told him where the diamonds were coming from.

Winston shook his head. Maybe it was time he stepped aside and let someone else take over the operation. It had been a long time. He'd spent thirty years struggling for a few pitiful pieces of rock. And the Van Der Meer Diamond Company had struggled through all thirty. Maybe that was enough.

But who was there that he could trust? Certainly none of the plant foremen. There wasn't a man in the lot that was really loyal to him.

Maybe if he cracked down on them, tightened up the operation, he could improve things. If nothing else, trim some costs and get a little extra work out of the kaffirs. Improving the margin would be a good first step in turning the company around.

He flipped through the small black book that he always carried on his travels, watching the names of women, tough guys and other connections flash past. He smiled again. He could have some fun in London, and get this job done. Perhaps Freddie could handle most of the dirty work, while he had some fun. He'd call Freddie as soon as he got to his hotel.

Winston closed the book and slipped it into his pocket. His pilot, Kip, would be just about finished with his post-flight check. Winston stood and collected his bag, waiting by the passenger door.

This nonsense about "rings" might take a while to puzzle out. His inquiries while still in South Africa had revealed that both Charles and his brother were dead. But the brother had a son, Edward, and a daughter too. They would be his leads.

Kip emerged from the cockpit and nodded at Winston, then opened the door and lowered the steps. The two men descended onto the wet pavement. Setting down their bags, they closed the steps and secured the plane.

"If you need me, leave a message with Ace Charter and I'll get back to you within the hour," Kip said.

"Where are you going to be?" asked Winston.

"Oh, making the rounds with my resume. There are a lot of charter outfits here at Heathrow, and I need to get to know some of them."

"You're leaving Van Der Meer?"

"Not necessarily. But I hear Van Der Meer may be leaving me."

"What do you mean?"

"Winston, it's no secret that the company's in trouble. I heard the latest recovery reports—fourteen carats in that whole last load? Not exactly the kind of yield you're looking for. And I know for a fact that the Leer is on the market. I've even had a couple of calls from prospective buyers asking me about features." Kip put his hand on Winston's shoulder. "You know I love buzzing about for Van Der Meer, Winston. But no plane means no Kip. And probably no Winston, soon, too. You might want to make some contacts while you're here, too . . ."

Winston pulled away from the man, and his eyes flashed with anger, but he kept his voice level. "Bladdy hell," he said, his South Africa accent thickening. "You're mistaken, Kip. The Van Der Meer Company will never founder. Not while I'm alive. I don't care what it takes; I'll find a way to keep it alive. And to keep Van Der Meer Mining profitable, you hear? Never forget that."

Kip shrugged, and picked up his flight bag. "Maybe, Winston. That's not what some of the others at the company think. We'll just have to wait and see, hey? Anyway, you know where to find me."

The pilot turned and strode through opening in the chain link fence at the edge of the tie-down lot and disappeared into the shadows of the building. Angrily, Winston grabbed his suitcase and stepped into the blackness.

Chapter 3

Jessica sat in the back of the taxi, nervously waiting for the lights to change. The green arrow came on, and the cab lurched around the corner, bringing her closer and closer to the man she had once loved.

She'd put him off for a full week since their meeting at his flat. First she'd told him that she'd lost her safe deposit key. Then it was a rush job at work. But at last she'd run out of excuses. Finally, she'd had to agree to meet with him again.

Gingerly she felt the lump in her purse. She shook her head in amazement at her own audacity. I'm a criminal, she thought.

She'd bought the pistol not long before, on a trip to Morocco, as a gift for Jack. He liked unusual objects—the more Bohemian the better—and contraband items were the best. As she'd smuggled it back on the ferry across Gibraltar she'd never imagined it might actually be used. But somehow, the smuggling didn't seem like the crime. Just a game, really. No, it was carrying it that made her feel, well, evil.

She'd been saving it, as a surprise for Jack. But when it came time to meet Edward again . . . was she afraid of him? No. She found herself shaking her head. What? In denial? Yet he had acted so strangely the other night . . .

In any event, something had made her slip it into her purse. Then, realizing that an unloaded pistol wouldn't do her much good, she'd rummaged for the handkerchief full of bullets that she'd insisted the dealer remove for her. Eventually she had figured out how to open the chamber and fill each spot. Finally, treating it like some poisonous snake, she had gingerly set it back into her purse and hidden it under her billfold.

She looked around guiltily, half expecting the cab driver to have read her thoughts. But his eyes were peering through the wet windshield at the darkened street, filled with anonymous automobiles slicing their way through the night.

She wondered what Edward would say if he knew that she was carrying an illegal firearm.

Edward. The closer she got to his flat the more nervous she became. All the old insecurities came rushing back. It had begun as a trickle: the smirks on the faces of his well-to-do friends; the condescending remarks when she joined them for dinner; the snide subtle comments about her clothes, which never seemed quite right among his friends' finery.

She could have coped with all that. But then the people she had regarded as *her* friends—the maids, butlers and gardeners that populated Drummond House—began to talk behind her back. Conversation stopped when she entered a room. The lively, boisterous camaraderie of the back rooms grew chilly whenever she was about. Jessica tried to talk to Edward about it—told him she felt caught between the two worlds—but he told her that she was being overly sensitive. He honestly seemed not to see it. And if he couldn't see it, he couldn't empathize. That was what hurt the most.

When he gave her the ring and asked her to marry him it had been overwhelming. The thought of being trapped in a household where she was regarded as a tramp was unbearable.

Yes, she had loved Edward—and Sarah—with all her heart. But there was one thing she couldn't give up for even him: her self-respect.

Tears were falling down her cheeks as the cab pulled up outside of Edward's flat. She brushed them away quickly and paid the driver, who gave her a questioning look as she turned and climbed the steps to the front door.

Edward opened the door grim-faced, and ushered her in without a word. His behavior struck her as odd from the very first. After their agreement to work together, she would have expected cordiality, even if it was plain that both of them wanted to avoid the subject of their previous relationship.

But Edward was cold and distant, almost harsh. Almost as soon as she'd seated herself he demanded the ring. It was as if he wasn't even the same person she'd spoken to earlier that week . . . or almost as if someone were listening . . .

"But Edward, I thought we'd agreed to work together, and that if I could help you find the treasure, we would come to some fair settlement between ourselves and Emma."

He stood before her, his back stiff with tension.

"That is all beside the point now," he said. "I have to have the ring back. It's . . . for Sarah. You remember her don't you? You did profess to love her. At one time."

Jessica looked down at the handbag resting in her lap. "You're not like the Edward I remember," she said softly, "I feel sorry for that child if this is how you act towards her, now."

His gaze slowly softened, his expression changing to one of dismay. The hurt in his eyes made her regret her words the moment she had uttered them.

"I . . . I just want the ring, and then you can go," he said hesitantly.

Jessica watched Edward carefully as he waited for her reply. Puzzled, she watched his eyes flitting from hers to the door on her right. She fetched a tissue from her purse, glancing back in that direction as she set it down on the floor. The door was definitely ajar. She made eye contact with Edward, then nodded her head toward the doorway, lifting her eyebrows.

Subtly, he nodded.

She sighed quietly in relief. Edward's demeanor had been so unlike him. Now at least she hoped there was a reason for it, whatever it might be.

Was there danger here? Why this strange role-playing?

Slowly she retrieved her purse, and set it on her lap. Opening it, she rummaged through the contents, carefully setting the pearl-handled pistol on top of the pile, then sitting back and allowing the purse to tip forward so that Edward could see what she had done.

Edward glanced down and took a step toward her. Then, in a somewhat too loud voice, he said, "Surely, Jessica, we can sort this out—"

Jessica turned at the sound of a crash behind her. Edward snatched the pistol from her purse. In three long strides he was at the door, flinging it open, raising the pistol.

A man staggered to his feet as the door was flung open. The bright light blinded him and he stumbled. Scattered around him on the floor were pieces of a ceramic vase. Edward stepped back out of the way of the falling man, slamming the pistol against the top of his head as he went down. The man slumped to the floor, unconscious.

Quickly Jessica ran to the doorway. The unconscious man lay amid the remains of the shattered vase. His face pressed into the seedy carpet, and she could see a lump already rising on his head.

"Quickly, help me tie him up," whispered Edward. Jessica looked about for a moment, then hurried to the curtains and removed the tie.

Crouching by Edward's side she whispered, trembling. "What is going on?"

As he hurriedly tied up the man, Edward spoke, his voice hushed. "There is no time for explanations now. This guy has an accomplice, upstairs, with Sarah. We have to get her out of here."

"*Sarah!* You must call the police."

"No, we can't. It's too dangerous."

Jessica started to protest, but Edward continued. "My sister, Emma, is missing. She may be dead, for all I know." His voice caught in his throat. He and Emma had been close. "She disappeared a few days ago. Apparently this fellow had something to do with it."

Jessica's head reeled, and she clutched at her stomach to control her rising nausea. When she'd recovered enough to straighten up, she stared at Edward blankly.

He shook his head as he finished tying up the man. "We have to do this ourselves. Did you bring the ring?"

"Yes, but—"

"It's what they're after. We may be able to tempt the guy upstairs with it."

Jessica nodded, her mind searching for answers. Why was everyone suddenly after the ring? What was so important about it? Dazed, she followed Edward back into the front room, and the stairs leading up.

Light spilled down the tattered carpeting of the narrow steps as they crept their way to the top. Jessica's breath caught as the risers of the flat's tired stairs creaked beneath her feet, but there was no response from above, and they gradually made their way into the short upstairs hallway.

The fussy décor of the downstairs continued, with ceramic knick-knacks littering a small table at the top of the stairs. Thrift shop artwork adorned the walls, their gold-tone plastic frames tarnished to a dull brown. Ribbons of peeling paint hung from the ceiling like forgotten party streamers.

A television's muted jumble leaked from behind the closed door of the room at the end of the hall. Pistol upraised, Edward slipped down the passageway, with Jessica following cautiously.

Edward approached the door, hand outstretched toward the knob when Jessica's muted hiss drew him back.

"Edward," she whispered, "we need a plan, or someone's going to get killed."

He paused, brows scrunched together in thought, then nodded. Turning, he slipped past her and carefully opened a door halfway down the hall. Slipping inside, he motioned for her to follow.

The room they entered was decorated in a similar style to the downstairs of the flat. It was comfortable enough, but all the furnishings were old and tatty. Not at all like anything she expected from Edward.

On the dresser was an old photo frame. She walked over to it and picked it up. In the dim light of the room she recognized Sarah. A soft smile formed on her lips as she remembered the sweet little girl, now looking all grown up in the photograph.

Headlights, reflected in the wet pavement of the alley one story below, traced a path across the darkened ceiling as a car passed. It was raining harder now. She put the picture down and turned to face the man she once loved; still loved.

Edward sat on the bed, the pistol cradled in his hands.

"Now, what did you have in mind?" he asked in a soft voice.

He looked thinner than she remembered him. His suit coat hung on his shoulders, giving an impression of a desperate, defeated man. She sat beside him, her fingers aching to touch his sagging shoulder. She breathed in the aftershave to which she'd grown accustomed so long ago, and clenched her fist, in an effort to control her emotions.

Edward turned toward her, searching her eyes for answers, the desperation etched into the lines of his face.

She smiled, trying to look encouraging. Her mind was racing, but her body was aching with long-forgotten desire.

Abruptly she stood and crossed to the window. Carefully, noiselessly, she slid it open and leaned out. Cold damp air rushed past her into the room, cooling her flushed face. The smell of rain and exhaust lodged in her nostrils.

Outside, a steel fire escape extended across the length of the rear of the flat. A ladder at one end could be lowered to ground level. The window of the room at the end of the hall glowed with the blue flicker of a television. It was not pulled all the way down. An idea began to form.

Pulling her head back through the window she turned to Edward and spoke quickly. "Here's what we'll do. You go back downstairs, and pretend to be the guy you knocked out. Call his accomplice—you'll have to shout—tell him you need help down there. I'll slip out onto the fire escape, and when I see him leave the room, I'll get Sarah outside through the window and down the fire escape. You make a break out the front. We'll meet you back at my flat—"

Edward had been nodding, but now he was shaking his head. "No, they know where you live. They've been watching you. When I found out they were going to break in while you were sleeping and . . ." Edward swallowed, then continued, "That's when I agreed to bring you here, instead. That and Sarah . . ." His voice trailed off.

"All right, then," she continued, undaunted, "we'll meet you tomorrow, at . . . The Rosetta Stone," she finished, naming the first public place that popped into her mind.

There was a noise from the next room, and Edward jumped up, then strode to the hall doorway and peered into the dimness. Seeing nothing, after a moment he turned and crossed to her.

"Alright," he said, "It's a good plan." He turned to the door, then back to her. "Jessie, if anything happens to me . . . Sarah . . . will you . . . ?" He stopped, seeming ready to say more.

She nodded.

"Take care," he whispered, caressing her cheek with his hand.

Quietly he slipped through the doorway and disappeared.

Jessica quickly crossed to the window and stepped out onto the rain-slick fire escape. Cold rivulets ran down her forehead and she blinked them from her eyes as she crept to the blue glow of the next window. Swallowing, she peered inside.

The accomplice was sitting rigidly in an easy chair, watching the television. He was dressed in faded jeans and a rumpled T-shirt.

Sarah sat huddled on the bed. She had grown a lot since Jessica last saw her. She must be what—nine, now?

Faintly, she heard a voice downstairs. The man leapt to his feet and glared warningly at the child.

"You move a muscle and you cop it, understood?"

Sarah nodded fearfully.

He barged out of the room.

Jessica counted silently to five, then made her move. She slid the window up further and slipped into the room, holding her finger to her lips to keep the child quiet.

"Sarah, it's Jessica. Remember me?"

Sarah shook her head, her pigtails bouncing on her shoulders.

"We have to get you out of here, away from that bad man. Your father will meet up with us. We must be very quiet."

"That man said he would hurt me if I moved," whispered Sarah.

"He will, if you don't come now. Quickly," she urged.

Hesitantly, the child slid off the bed and came over to where she stood by the window. Keeping an eye on the door, Jessica helped her over the sill. As Jessica started to follow she heard a yell from downstairs. She pushed herself through the open window and hurried the girl down the fire escape, then out onto the darkened street. A roar of frustration came from above. She glanced up. The accomplice was climbing through the window.

She urged Sarah into a run, down the shadowy alley and out onto the main thoroughfare.

A bus was just beginning to pull away from the curb on the far side. Jessica put two fingers in her mouth and gave a shrill whistle, then yelled at the driver. Startled, he stopped the bus. She hurried Sarah on board.

As the bus pulled away, she could see the man running out into the street behind them. She fished some change from her coat pocket and dumped it into the collection box.

With a sigh of relief, she guided Sarah down the aisle to an empty bench. They squeezed in and she put her arm around her, comforting her. The girl was weeping.

That was close, she thought. She hoped that Edward had made his getaway.

The whole affair was so confusing. First the sudden interest in the ring, then this . . .

She shook her head. There's not nearly enough information to sort this mess out right now.

She turned her thoughts toward a more pressing problem.

Where to go now?

Not home obviously. And her purse was still at Edward's flat, so that ruled out a cab ride to a nice, warm hotel.

Her thoughts were interrupted by Sarah. "Jessica, did you used to look after me?"

She nodded and smiled, hugging her.

"You were only four. We used to play checkers in the nursery. And we took walks in the park down the street. Remember?"

Sarah offered a tremulous smile, and Jessica hugged her even more tightly. It was nice being with her again. She could only hope that Edward had made out as well.

As she sat watching the streetlights slip past, an idea formed. She dug into her coat pocket, and came up another handful of change. Now all she needed was a telephone.

At the next stop she spied a telephone box on a well-lit street corner. She hurried the girl off of the bus and they dashed through the rain. As she dialed Jack's number she silently prayed that he would be home.

The phone rang twice, three times. Finally, with relief, she heard Jack's voice saying, "Hello?"

"Jack? It's Jessica. I need your help."

Now there was an understatement.

Still breathless from the desperate dash they had made to the telephone booth, Jessica listened to the sleepy voice at the other end of the line.

"I'll explain later," she said. Dear sweet Jack. "Right now, could you bring your car 'round and pick us up." She knew she could depend on Jack. "Yes, 'us.' Me and a little girl."

She thought she had once explained to Jack about the child. Oh well, that could wait.

As she spoke, Sarah pressed herself more tightly into her side. Jessica circled her arm around the girl protectively. She nervously kept looking in the direction they had come.

"We're in Westminster. Near that fish and chips place that we ate at last week, you know the one? We're in the phone booth on the corner, but I think for safety's sake, we'll step back into the shadows until you get here."

She was trying not to alarm him—or Sarah. At the same time she needed to impress upon him how important it was that he get there as soon as possible. Their lives might depend upon it.

The whole situation seemed ludicrous, even to her. But Jack didn't ask the obvious questions, and he quickly agreed to rush right over and pick them up.

Jessica set the receiver back in its cradle and gathered Sarah closer to her. *How had she gotten herself involved in this mess?*

The events of the past week swirled in her mind, and for a moment she reached for the door of the booth to steady herself. When her vertigo passed, she herded Sarah into the darkest spot she could find, the doorway of a nearby notions shop. It was far past midnight, and the street was completely deserted.

"Why can't Dad come and get us?" asked Sarah.

"He just can't right now, Sarah. Hopefully he'll meet us tomorrow."

"Tomorrow? Is he all right, then? That man was pretty nasty to us. Did he do something to Dad?"

'Your Dad can look after himself. And I'm going to look after you for a bit. Jack will be here soon."

"Who's Jack?"

"He's a very good friend."

It seemed a long while before she saw headlights slicing past her into the shadows. She prayed that it was Jack, for if it was not—if it was *them*—there was no place for her and Sarah to hide. She may have managed to escape once, but she could not hope to do so again.

* * *

Every part of him hurt, but he had to buy her more time. Only Sarah mattered. And Jessica. How could he have been so stupid as to get her into this? Now it might cost both of them their lives. He'd been selfish. And stupid. He'd wanted to see her again. Needed to see her again.

He slammed his fist into the man's gut, and the two of them lurched backwards into a side table. A lamp crashed to the floor, and suddenly the only light was what leaked though the tattered curtains at the front of the flat.

He'd been a decent boxer when he'd been in the service. It was a sport his father disapproved of, which was probably why he'd taken it up. But he was out of practice, now, and this massive hunk of a thug outweighed him by a good forty pounds.

He ducked a right cross and tried to back towards the door, but his foot caught on the carpet and he stumbled backwards, wincing at the pain from what he assumed were cracked ribs.

He had to get out of here fast or—

The fist caught him hard in the side of the face and he felt himself spitting blood as he went down. Then something crashed onto the back of his head, and the carpet was coming up to meet him.

Jessie, he thought as the world turned gray. He barely even felt the kick that crashed into his side.

* * *

A car moved slowly down the street, the way a hunting dog moves in on its target. She didn't recognize it. It definitely wasn't Jack's car. She clutched Sarah to her as tightly as she could.

When the car stopped near the phone booth, she surveyed her options and wondered which way she should have Sarah run.

A man got out of the car and looked around. It was too dark to make out his face.

"Jessica?"

"Oh, thank God, Jack, it's you!"

Jessica quickly ushered Sarah into the back seat and climbed into the front.

"Wouldn't you know it?" Jack said. "My car wouldn't start up. I had to wake up my neighbor Roger and borrow his. And he was none too pleased, if you know what I mean."

He glanced from her to the girl, and she caught his questioning look. "This is Sarah," she said. "I'll explain everything later, Jack. Right now, can we just get this poor child out of the cold night air?"

He nodded, and they were soon at the door of his apartment. He stood aside as they entered.

Sarah clung to Jessica's coat. Jessica sat down on the couch and pulled Sarah onto her lap. "Well, as I said on the phone, we need a bed for the night, if that's OK. Sarah is cold and tired, as am I, for that matter."

"Sure Jess." He looked at her questioningly. "Uh, maybe she would like something to eat first? She looks kind of hungry."

Sarah nodded shyly.

Jack knelt in front of Sarah, cocking his head to one side and asked, "Bacon and eggs, and I think I have some crumpets as well? What do you think of that?"

The small girl grinned and nodded again.

Jack ruffled the child's hair, and headed into the kitchen of the small flat. As he rummaged through the refrigerator he called out to Jessica, "If you want to get her into some clothes for sleeping, I have some of my niece's clothes in the cupboard in my room. They'll be a bit big, but they'll do, I'm sure."

"Thanks, Jack," said Jessica. She searched through the clothes and pulled out a pair of pajamas. Taking Sarah by the hand, she led her into the bathroom and helped her clean her face, hands and feet. In a short time, looking clean and cozy, she was seated at the kitchen table.

Jack dished out the meal onto two plates.

"What about you?" inquired Jessica.

"I'm still working off dinner. Sit down. Enjoy. It's not often that someone cooks up such a fine midnight snack for you, now, is it?"

"No, it's not," she smiled, as she sat down next to Sarah and helped the girl with her napkin.

Once their initial hunger had been satisfied, the child grew quiet, and Jessica worried that she was becoming distraught again. But Sarah's drooping lids reminded her of the late hour, and she ushered her off to Jack's spare bedroom, where he had made up a bed for her. As she snuggled into bed, Jessica pulled up her comforter. "How about a bedtime story?" she asked.

"Yes please," Sarah said sleepily, as she rolled over to face the wall.

With Jack watching from the door, Jessica began to recite what had been Sarah's favorite story all those years ago.

"Once upon a time, there was a princess named Sarah, who lived with her father, King Edward, in a great castle on the moors in Scotland. Sarah was a very smart little girl, who was constantly helping her father, the King, out of difficult jams, whenever trouble came their way. And trouble came their way a lot. One day . . ." She paused. Sarah had turned back to face her.

"Do you remember this story, Sarah?"

The girl nodded, and Jessica continued.

Sarah and Jack both listened, enthralled, as she told the tale. When it was over, Sarah asked for more, but Jessica shook her head.

"Tomorrow is another day," she smiled, "In the meantime, you need your sleep. Come on now, snuggle down."

She carefully tucked the blankets around her and tiptoed out of the room. Jack closed the door behind her.

"You're great with her," he said softly.

"I love her, it's that simple."

He looked at her with questioning eyes. "I take it she's Edward's kid?" he asked.

Jessica nodded.

"Ah, I see."

After a moment he looked back at her and added, "No, I don't see. Maybe you can explain while we have a coffee."

"A glass of sherry would go down much better right now."

While Jack fetched the sherry, Jessica reviewed the muddle of events from the past few days. How had she have been drawn into all of this? Less than a week ago she had been comfortably living in London, her memories safely walled off, focused on her architectural work, with no complications, no turmoil.

In a moment Jack returned with a glass of sherry and handed it to her, then settled next to her by the fire.

"You know," said Jack, looking at Jessica over his glass, "I thought you were over this Edward fellow. You seemed to have finally put it all behind you. I was hoping . . ." He looked away.

Jessica placed her hand over his. She *had* begun to get over Edward. And Jack was a great friend—perhaps more than a friend. She'd had to admit to herself, recently, a strong attraction to him. Although she had done nothing overt to express that feeling, she knew he sensed it in her. Now she was confused. The last thing she wanted to do was to hurt Jack.

Shrugging off her reawakened feelings for Edward, she took a sip of her sherry, and began to relate the events leading up to her phone call to him.

* * *

An hour later, sitting by the fire, Jessica finished telling Jack the events of the past week, leading up to when she'd called him from the phone booth.

"So do you know if Edward got away alright?" he asked.

She shook her head. "No, I don't. And I'm worried sick."

"Should we call the police?"

"I don't know, Jack. I just don't know. Edward said not to, before. And I don't know enough about all of this to make a decision. Sarah is safe. I think for now we'll just have to hope for the best."

She looked at Jack. He's such a dear, to be here for *me* when I need him, she thought. Then again, he always was, wasn't he?

"I should be angry at this Edward you know," said Jack, in mock irritation. "If it weren't for him, we two may have stood a chance."

"I know. I'm sorry. He was always between us wasn't he? But we are still the very best of friends, aren't we?"

"Yes, we are," he replied, brushing the hair from her eyes.

"And don't worry about Sarah tomorrow," he added. "I'm owed a day off, so I'll stay here and look after her while you go and meet with Edward."

"You are a dear," she smiled, kissing him on the forehead.

She yawned.

She sighed. "I don't know how I'll sleep. You know for five years I have tried to put that man behind me, tried to get him out of my thoughts, but he's still there, looming up when I least expect it. Now, after seeing him again, and knowing the danger he could be in, I just don't know how I feel."

Jack frowned, watching her yawn yet again.

"Don't worry, Jess, I'm sure he's alright. You need some sleep if you're going to meet him tomorrow."

She sighed. The sherry had relaxed her, and she was losing the battle to stay awake, despite her fear for Edward's safety.

Jack left her sitting by the fire as he rose and made up the couch for her. It was the foldout variety, and would make a comfortable enough bed, at least for one night. She knew that he had been hoping for different sleeping arrangements, and was grateful to him for not pressing the issue.

Gratefully she flopped down onto the bed.

"See you tomorrow then," he smiled, but Jessica was already drifting off.

* * *

It had taken only a minute for Winston to untangle himself from the bedding and slip on some trousers, then make his way into the other room. He knocked over a lamp in his hurry. If Freddie was calling at this hour, he must be finished. The woman stood next to one of the dinette stools in the kitchen. She held a towel under her arms to cover her breasts. He leered at her and swatted her ass as he took the phone from her. He'd enjoyed the week he'd spent with her, but he had to admit he was tiring of her tricks. Perhaps it was time to go back to his hotel.

"Winston here. Talk to me," he said into the phone.

From Freddie's tone he could tell immediately that something was wrong. He interrupted the excuses after only a few sentences. Winston had assumed that the man was bringing news about Jessica or Edward.

"What do you mean you can't find her? Did you try her apartment?"

More blather.

"What about Edward?" Winston demanded.

Out cold, Freddie said.

He should never have hired the stupid thug in the first place. Winston intended to make the man squirm. "I don't care if he did knock you out, if you kill him we'll never find that ring. This isn't rocket science, man. Those diamonds are mine. Now call an ambulance, you moron. Then find the damn girl."

He listened to Freddie stammer for a moment, shaking his head in disgust. The man simply had no balls.

Cutting him off, Winston yelled, "Listen, I don't care what they tell the police. You'll be long gone. Now just do it." He slammed the receiver back into its cradle and sat staring angrily at the telephone.

When his temper had cooled, he turned back to the woman. He snatched the papers from her hand and tossed them back onto the counter next to his briefcase.

"Those are personal, baby," he said. He reaching out and savagely yanked the towel from her torso. She flinched, but didn't back up. Good. He liked a woman with spunk. He smiled at her and pushed her back towards the bedroom.

"Now . . . where were we, Liz?"

Chapter 4

Jessica awoke with a heavy head. She found Jack preparing breakfast for Sarah, who was quietly drawing at the kitchen table.

"Sorry," he said, "Did I wake you?"

She shook her head and winced. "No, it's time I got up. Good morning Sarah."

"Hello," she replied, smiling weakly and then returning to her drawing.

"Would you have something for a headache, Jack?" Jessica asked.

"And a cup of tea to go with it?" Jack grinned.

She nodded and wandered into the bathroom. Maybe a shower would help. By the time she returned to the kitchen breakfast was ready.

"We don't get food like this anymore," said Sarah, taking a bite of eggs.

"No?" asked Jessica.

Sarah shook her head. "Daddy can't cook. We just have cornflakes."

"Nice to be appreciated," smiled Jack, handing Jessica her coffee and aspirin. "Are you OK?" he asked.

She shook her head, and indicated for him to follow her into the other room.

"I'm still worried Jack. Edward was all alone with those two, and I don't know what could have happened to him. I mean, he said he would get away out the front door, but what if he didn't? What if . . ."

"You can't live your life on what ifs Jess. I'm sure he'll be fine. He can handle himself can't he?"

"Oh yes, of course he can. He isn't a wimp by any means. He did do a stint in the army, and he once told me he was boxing champ of his school."

"There you go then."

"But I'm still concerned. What if he doesn't turn up?"

"Well, you won't know if you don't get a move on and turn up yourself now, will you?"

He maneuvered her gently back into the kitchen and sat her at the table. Putting a plate in front of her he told her to eat.

"I don't think I can," she protested. "I'm not that hungry."

"Eat it anyway. Humor me." said Jack.

She sighed, and began to eat, her mind going back to Edward, and the haunted look in his eyes when they had parted the night before.

Her train of thought was interrupted by Sarah. "Are we going to see Daddy today?" she asked.

Jessica looked at the girl over her coffee cup. "Well, I hope so, Sarah. I'm going to see him this morning, and then we'll work something out. Daddy is very busy today."

"Why can't I see him with you then?"

Jessica picked up a napkin, and gently wiped egg off the child's chin.

"Because Daddy is doing some grownup business. And he asked me to help him. Don't worry, you'll see him soon enough."

She seemed happy with that explanation, and carried on with their breakfast.

"Are you sure you'll be all right looking after her today?" asked Jessica, when they had all finished eating.

Jack was placing the empty plates into the sink. "No problem. In fact, we have a very special day planned, don't we?"

Sarah nodded happily. "Jack is going to show me his collection of dolls."

Jessica cocked her head.

"My curios," Jack explained, laughing. "Stuff from Tahiti, and such."

Jessica nodded. She pushed her chair out from the table with more enthusiasm than she felt. "I'd best be off then," she said, giving Sarah a kiss.

She found herself trembling as she slipped her arm into her coat sleeve. What am I afraid of? She wondered. Is it fear that Edward won't be there to meet me? That something's happened to him? Or am I afraid of what it will lead to if I do meet him?

Jack saw her to the door. "Be careful Jess. You don't really know what the story is here."

"I know. Don't worry. I'll call when I can."

Jack nodded.

"Bye Sarah," she called, but the girl was investigating the large cabinet opposite the front door, and was totally engrossed in the knick-knacks that Jack had accumulated over the years.

She smiled and shrugged, gave Jack a quick kiss on the cheek and hurried out the door, growing more concerned with each step she took about the fate of the man she had once professed to love.

* * *

The stone glistened black under the harsh lights of the museum. Its surface was covered with chalky scratches that looked more like the aimless wanderings of a hundred pecking pigeons than the key to an ancient language.

Jessica reflected on the surreal adventures of the previous night, and glanced at her watch for the tenth time. Where was he?

She thought of Jack back in the flat with Sarah and smiled. Jack had always led a bit of a Bohemian existence, and the collection of curios he called "furniture" had, at first, frightened Sarah. But curiosity had obviously overcome her fears. Jessica wondered what treasures they had found to amuse themselves with.

Now, standing by the massive monolith, she quietly cursed herself for not naming a time. She had expected he'd be here when the museum opened, or that she might even meet him at the entrance. Now it was nearly noon. Had something happened to him? Had the accomplice killed him? She hadn't really seriously entertained the possibility at first, but as the hours passed she was filled with an increasing sense of dread.

She fingered the money in her pocket. Jack had loaned her enough for several cab fares. Should she go back to his apartment and call the police?

A hand caught her wrist and she turned smiling. But her smile evaporated as she looked into the cold eyes of a woman she'd never seen before.

"Scream, and Edward is as good as dead," the woman said.

Jessica quickly looked her over. She wore a black leather jumpsuit with a silver zipper down the front. It glinted under the harsh museum lights.

Clutching Jessica's elbow, the woman steered her down the main steps into the foyer, past the information desk, and out into the courtyard. As they descended the broad steps in clear view of the entire plaza, Jessica yanked her arm away savagely and said, "Where *is* Edward?"

For a moment the woman seemed taken aback. "How should I know?"

"Don't give me that," Jessica said, "You just finished threatening him if I didn't come with you."

"It got you out here, didn't it?"

"Well it won't keep me here," said Jessica. She turned to go back up the steps, but the woman caught her arm and spun her back. In her right hand Jessica glimpsed the pearl-handled pistol she'd given to Edward the night before. "Over there," said the woman, nodding toward a bench that sat in a secluded corner of the courtyard. They crossed to it and sat beneath the leafless branches of a large tree. The woman kept her at arms length, but made sure she could see the pistol resting in her hand.

"Who are you?" asked Jessica.

"Liz."

"How do you know who I am?"

"A little bird told me."

"How did you know where to find me?"

"It told me that, too." Liz tossed her dark hair over her shoulder. "Now I'll ask a question. Where is the ring?"

"What ring?"

Liz's eyes flashed, and she raised her hand as if she was going to slap Jessica, but then she scratched her cheek, and smiled. Her eyes fitted across the plaza, and Jessica's followed.

Families skittered across the stone paving, youngsters towing their elders toward the grand edifice of the museum. A young couple strolled by the fountain, their hands slipped into each other's back pockets, sides brushing as they parted the doves begging for handouts. Jessica tried to imagine herself with Edward, carefree and happy again, strolling by the fountain. Or with Sarah urging them up the stairs into the museum. What was happening to her life? Everything had been so calm, so compartmentalized. A week before she'd been bored and restless, contemplating a trip to Nice, or perhaps Lausanne, just to break the monotony. Now her past seemed to be rising up around her like an angry swarm of locusts, trying to strip her existence to its roots.

Her thoughts were interrupted by Liz's voice, gentler this time. "There are dangerous people about. I'm not the worst of them. You have something they want. It would be easier for everyone if you simply gave it to me." She cocked her head. "Now, where is your ring?"

"I don't have it on me. I put it in a safe place. You won't get anything out of me until you tell me what's happened to Edward and Emma."

"Enough of this," snarled Liz, waving the pistol. "Get up."

With the muzzle pressed into her back, Jessica was forced into a car parked in the next block. Liz pushed her head down, and pointed the pistol at her. They traveled for about fifteen minutes.

When the car stopped Jessica looked up and caught site of a rundown inn. A row of efficiency apartments lined the parking lot, their battered fronts dripping tears of peeling paint. Liz pushed her out of the car and forced her into the nearest apartment.

There was no one around.

Liz fumbled with some keys, unlocked the door and shoved her inside, relocking it behind her. Lying on a bed, bound and gagged, was Emma, Edward's sister. She looked up at Jessica and, as recognition came into her eyes, she began to weep.

Liz motioned Jessica over to a straight-backed chair and began to tie her hands. When Liz lowered the pistol Jessica breathed a sigh of relief, feeling very slightly safer. She looked at Emma, trying to reassure her with her eyes.

The room was dirty. The furniture was a good indication of the type of person living there. A few springs sprouted from the sofa. A black and white television silently glowed in the corner. A soiled, makeshift curtain half-covered the opening into the small kitchen. The kitchen table was cluttered with week old dishes.

Where was Edward?

Once her arms were secured to the chair, Liz pressed her back against the broken cane weave and looped the rope around her middle, cinching it tight.

Next to her, Emma lay on the bed, bound at wrists and ankles, curled up on her side. Jessica could feel Emma's breath against her bare arm. Her eyes met Emma's. She tried to give the woman an encouraging look, but she didn't dare speak to her.

Jessica shifted her gaze to Liz. Her long black hair disappeared against her black leather jumpsuit, which was stretched taut across her wiry frame. There was something sinister about the woman's catlike smirk. When she caught her eye she felt herself transfixed, like a mouse invited to a banquet, only to discover that the other guests fancy it as the main course.

"Well?" Liz demanded. She raised the pistol and pointed it at Jessica's head. "Where is the ring?"

Jessica swallowed nervously. Summoning courage she hadn't known she possessed, she said levelly, "If that thing goes off we'll never get the ring, and the neighbors will have the constable up here in no time."

Liz glared at her, but she set the gun down. Crossing to the nightstand, she opened a leather satchel. Slowly, almost dramatically, she extracted a slim, silver oblong. Extending it beneath Jessica's nose, she pressed the edge. A long, thin blade nearly the length of the shaft sprang forth. Jessica flinched, and her eyes widened.

"Where is the ring, Jessica?" purred Liz, moving her mouth near her ear. The cold steel of the flat of the knife rested against her cheek, then traced an icy arc downwards leaving a pink scratch down the side of her neck, but not quite breaking the surface. Jessica swallowed, but didn't answer. How could this be happening? She knew the ring was valuable, but was it really worth all of this? For that matter was it worth it to her, either?

If she told Liz where it was, would she let her go? She glanced at the darkly clad woman just in time to see her licking her lower lip. Liz was flushed, and her pulse pounded in her throat. The barest trace of a smile curled the corners of her lips, and her eyes were fixed on Jessica's..

Her reverie was interrupted as Liz shifted position, withdrawing the knife. "You know," she said, "This is clearly the wrong approach. You may be stubborn, Jessie, but I feel sure you're not . . . callous." She drew out the last word, almost like the hissing of some deranged snake.

Apprehensively, Jessica watched her slowly move the knife toward the captive Emma, until it came to rest against her cheek. Emma's eyes widened in terror.

"Where is the ring, Jessie?" Liz hissed.

"Stop!" Jessica gasped. "I won't tell you . . . but I'll take you there."

Liz eyed her for a moment. Almost regretfully, she withdrew the knife and used it to saw through Jessica's bonds. "Fine," she snapped. "You show me." She picked up the gun and led Jessica to the door.

As she stepped from the room, Jessica caught a glimpse of Emma, tears still running down her cheeks.

At the foot of the steps they turned and skirted the building, winding their way down a narrow alley that squeezed between two buildings. Another turn brought them to a wider alley, where several cars were parked sticking halfway out into the thoroughfare.

Liz pushed Jessica toward a battered green Japanese import, motioning her into the driver's seat. Jessica fastened her seat belt, glancing at the woman warily as she took the passenger's seat. Jessica was extremely grateful that she had had the forethought to post the ring to her own private mailbox at the post office early that morning. The last thing she wanted to do was to get Liz anywhere near Jack and Sarah.

Putting the car into drive, Jessica moved smoothly into the traffic, noting their location.

"Where is Edward?" Jessica asked softly.

Liz shrugged. "How should I know?"

"He must have told you where to meet me."

Liz shook her head.

"I heard it from a guy I met. A rich bastard named Winston. He's even got his own Leer jet that he flies in from South Africa. I owed him some money. He said he'd take the rings instead."

Jessica's eyes had widened at the mention of South Africa. She wondered how this Winston fellow might have known about the rings.

"What's happened to Edward?" she asked again.

"Why do you keep asking that?" demanded Liz.

Jessica looked at her coolly. "Because you're holding the pistol I gave him last night."

Liz looked down at the gun in her hand, and a smile slowly spread across her face. "That bastard! Winston said he'd bought it for me as a gift." She shook her head. "He's a nasty piece, that."

Jessica drove in silence, trying to sort things out. She wondered if Liz really knew what was going on, any more than she did. "Why does everyone suddenly want my ring?" she asked.

"Apparently Edward's Uncle had several of them made. Edward has one. Together with Emma's ring—which she's hidden somewhere—and the one that you have . . . well, Winston says they lead to a . . . treasure."

"What kind of treasure?"

"We don't know, for sure. We think Edward knows, but we haven't gotten it out of him. Winston says that it's diamonds—maybe millions of dollars worth of them—since that was the business that Edward and Emma's uncle was in when he had the rings made."

"How are you involved in all this?"

Liz laughed humorlessly. "In ways you couldn't imagine."

"Try me."

Liz cradled the pistol in her lap. When she spoke her voice was steel hard. "I'm involved because I thought that being wealthy would make me happy. I got involved with a rich British family, mixing with the upper crust. They did this."

"Did what?" asked Jessica.

"Invited me into the clubs, the gaming houses. They encouraged me to gamble away all I had, and more. I couldn't control it. I stole so that I could carry on, and then I borrowed, and borrowed some more, and lost it all."

Jessica shook her head.

Liz saw the motion and turned angrily to face her. "You can give me all the dirty looks you like, but it's people like you, and Edward and Emma, that have brought me to this."

"I hardly think I run in the same circles as Edward and Emma," she said.

"I know you did once. Certainly Edward thinks of you that way. You were important to him—at least at one time you were."

"How do you know that?" asked Jessica.

Liz glared at her, but didn't answer. Instead she asked, "Do you know what the most important thing in this world is to me now?"

Jessica shook her head.

"My life," said Liz. "If I don't pay off what I owe, they'll kill me." She pointed the pistol back in Jessica's direction. "Nothing is more important than getting those diamonds."

Jessica gulped nervously, as she turned the car into the car park opposite the post office. She sincerely doubted that the ring would have arrived by now, but it was all she could think of to do. At least here, she thought that maybe she could do something to get out of the situation.

"I posted the ring to my mailbox. It's in this post office," she said evenly, her voice not betraying her feelings of fear.

"Out. And don't try anything. Don't forget that I have Emma. If you get away, she will suffer for it."

Jessica climbed out of the car slowly, and made her way into the mailbox area of the post office. She took her key from her pocket and walked to her box. As she opened it, Liz pushed her aside. It was empty.

"Why did you do this, why post it?" she hissed, pressing the pistol into her side.

"I didn't know what to believe, I thought this was the safest thing to do, in case something happened." she replied.

Liz glanced around nervously, and shoved her toward the car park. "Get back into the car, I need to think."

They sat quietly in the car as the seconds ticked by.

Finally Liz smashed both fists against the steering wheel. "Drive us to your flat," she snarled. "We'll wait there until the next delivery." She looked up and down the street, worriedly. "It's safer."

Ten minutes later they sat at the kitchen table in her flat, watching the rain drizzle into the flowerpots in the garden. Jessica fixed tea while Liz watched, her dark eyes glowering at her.

"Why didn't you just bring the ring with you to meet Edward? Everything would have been so simple, then."

"After last night, I didn't know what to think. I decided that I needed to put it someplace where I didn't have it, but could get it. I posted it on the way to the museum, this morning."

Liz grunted.

"I don't even know if Edward is still alive," Jessica continued. "That's why I didn't bring Sarah."

Liz stared into her teacup, swirling the leaves at the bottom. "Where is the kid, anyway?"

Jessica hesitated, looking for a way to change the subject. "What's so special about this ring, anyway? How could it possibly be worth all this trouble . . . this danger?" she asked.

"It's not the ring. It's what's in the ring," said Liz.

"*In* the ring? How can something be in the ring? It's barely more than a band."

Liz sighed disgustedly. "There is writing engraved inside the band. Haven't you ever noticed?" she asked incredulously. "According to the letter, the writing leads to a treasure."

Jessica's eyebrows lifted in dawning comprehension. "I've seen . . . something. I thought they were . . . jeweler's marks, or . . . something."

Liz snorted, jingling the mailbox key in her palm. "When does the mail usually come?" she asked.

"Umm . . . about now, I think. What letter?"

"A letter that Winston showed me."

"Where did he get the letter?" she persisted.

Liz rearranged the sugar bowl and the salt and pepper shakers idly. "How should I know? Some old broad gave it to him in South Africa, a couple of months ago. Said it was important."

"South Africa?"

"Yeah. Winston's South African. Come on. Let's get going."

Jessica rose. "Sure. Uh, just let me go to the bathroom first," she said, stepping into the hall. She slipped into her bedroom, then the bathroom beyond it and closed the door, locking it. She turned on the water in the sink and flushed the toilet. Carefully she lifted the window and squeezed through, dropping into the flowerbed below.

She was in the next block when she heard Liz's shouts, but the words were indistinguishable.

Two more blocks at a run brought her to a main thoroughfare where she hailed a passing cab, telling the driver to just drive while she sorted herself out.

Where to go? Obviously not to the mailbox, Liz would go there first, she was sure of that. And she had the key.

She could call the police and tell them where Emma was. But she didn't know the exact address. She'd have to show them. And the police would want to talk to her. She needed to check on Edward, first. He could be bleeding to death in his own flat.

Would Emma be all right if she waited to go to the police? Probably Liz would assume they'd go there first, and steer clear.. She'd have to chance it.

She gave the driver the address and sat back in the tattered seat, shivering inwardly.

Except for the significance she'd attached to it when Edward had given it to her, she'd never thought of the ring as anything very special. Certainly not something to risk one's life over. Was it really worth all of this?

She stepped out of the cab in front of 22 King's Cross, paid the driver, and turned to stare at the house. It looked different in daylight. Plain and somewhat dowdy. The garden was run down, and the hedge bordering this house and the neighbor's was overgrown.

With great trepidation, she made her way to the door, and rapped.

Her knocking echoed in the still morning air.

"You won't find anybody there dear," came a voice from over the hedge.

She jumped, caught unawares by the unexpected voice.

"Pardon?" she asked, peering over the hedge at the elderly lady who, broom in hand, was sweeping the path by the hedge.

"Right old kerfuffle last night there was. Ambulance an' all. The old Bill come along too."

"What happened?"

"Well," said the old woman, "There was yellin' and screamin', and me old man, 'e said to call the Bill, so's I did, see. They called the ambulance. Poor man in there was beat up real bad, he was. The constable questioned me, too," she added proudly.

"Where did they take him, in the ambulance?"

The old woman told her the name of the hospital nearest the house, and Jessica thanked her profusely. She ran to the phone box at the end of the road and called another taxicab.

On the way to the hospital, she wept silently. Edward could be dying, or crippled, or anything. All she could think of was getting to him.

At the emergency room reception desk, they gave her directions to his room. Quietly, she opened the door.

Edward lay in the hospital bed looking still and white. His eyes fluttered open as she took his hand in hers and sat beside him.

"Jessie," he whispered, "Is Sarah . . . ?"

"She's fine, safe with a friend of mine," she smiled at him. "Edward why did they do this to you?"

"I wouldn't tell them where my ring was. He wanted yours, too, and wanted to know where you had gone with Sarah."

"I know. But don't worry about the ring. It's Emma that I'm worried about. I must tell the police where she is."

His eyes widened in surprise and relief showed on his battered face.

"She's alive? You know where she is?"

Jessica told him about her attempt to meet him at the museum, how Liz had turned up, and how she had taken her to a room where Emma was being held. "The ring is in my post box at the post office," she finished. She didn't mention that Liz had the key.

Edward smiled weakly at her. "Good girl. Now go call the police and tell them about Emma. I didn't want to involve them before, but now that we know that she's alive, we have no choice. Oh. And Jessie . . ."

"Yes?"

"Better not mention the pistol. They'll want to know where you got it. And . . . I've lost it, I'm afraid."

"Don't you worry about it."

She smoothed the hair from his brow, and gently kissed him on the forehead, then saw that he'd already slipped back under the influence of the sedatives.

Just as well, she thought, regretting the impulsive kiss the moment she gave it.

Quietly she left the room, in search of a telephone to call the police. She sighed, relieved that Edward would be all right. Thinking of Emma, she hurried.

* * *

Detective Sergeant Wilbur Brightcastle sighed and put down his pencil. "You know, miss, this isn't a lot to go on. You saw as well as we did that the apartment you directed us to on Randolph Street has been completely cleaned out, and Data Division has no information on the tenant. Now the lab tells me the whole place was wiped for prints—and a real professional wipe down it was. And miss, I don't mind tellin' you, your story still doesn't quite add up. This business about mailing the ring to yourself—not to cast aspersions on your veracity, miss—but why would you do that?"

Jessica squirmed under the sergeant's gaze, trying to think of a suitable response. He was a large man, yet his jacket hung on his shoulders as if he were somehow deflated, perhaps by the boredom of the paperwork he'd been saddled with. Yet Jessica sensed he could be an imposing presence, and while her first reaction was to be evasive, she feared the consequences if he doubted her story. And she did need his help.

Sergeant Brightcastle narrowed his eyes and glared at her from beneath furrowed brows. He opened his mouth to speak, paused, then closed it again. Toying with his pencil he gazed at her steadily as she nervously fingered the arms of her chair.

"Look 'ere, Miss . . . Farrell . . . we'll run the description and composite sketch of this 'Liz' that you gave us through Research and see what they can come up with. But if you can't give us any better idea why there's all this fuss over what you've clearly described as a very modest ring, I don't see how we can—"

The sergeant was interrupted by the arrival of a constable, who burst through the door, then stopped short when he saw Jessica seated there. Standing at attention, he waited to be acknowledged.

"What is it, Pierce?"

"Sarge, it's about that post box you sent us to clear out. When we got there, my partner and I, we found that the door was, well, gone."

"Gone?"

"Yes. Ripped clean off the hinges, it was. Not a scrap in it, of course. The box, that is. Smith—my partner—he asked the postmaster if he recalled any deliveries to that box. The gent said he couldn't be sure, what with the volume of mail this time of year—but he thought there'd been a box delivered there this evening. Remembered it, he said, because the delivery and return addresses were the same, he said."

The sergeant glanced at Jessica, who had turned pale at the mention of the post box.

"Is the lab dusting for prints Pierce?"

"Nothin' to dust, Sarge. The door simply isn't there. But there's more . . ."

"Well, what is it?" he replied, his impatience evident.

"On the way back we swung by hospital to talk with that Edward Drummond chap you asked us to question. He's gone too."

Jessica's chair hit the floor as she jumped to her feet, but the sergeant held up a hand to silence her. "What do you mean 'gone', Pierce? That chap was pretty banged up, from what I heard from the ward mistress. How could he check himself out?"

"He didn't, sir. He wasn't even conscious at the time—in fact he was pretty doped up, according to the nurse. That's the queer thing. Some woman came and checked him out. Said she was moving him to hospital in the country so he could convalesce."

The sergeant glanced at Jessica, who shook her head, then turned back to the constable. "Did the woman who checked him out leave a name and address?"

"Hospital regulations," said the constable, fishing a notepad from his inside jacket pocket. He flipped it open and shuffled through several pages. "Here it is. Ms Liz Stark, 34 Randolph Street, Westminster. But that's the place that—"

"Yes, Pierce, that's the apartment that's already cleaned out. So obviously they aren't taking him there. Why did the hospital let a stranger check him out?"

"According to the head nurse, she wasn't a stranger, sergeant. Said she had the license to prove it, and everything."

"License to prove what?"

"She was his wife, Sarge."

It was the last thing Jessica heard before the room started to spin, and she saw the floor come rushing up to meet her.

Chapter 5

When Jessica awoke, she was staring straight into the eyes of a handsome young constable.

"You alright Miss?" he asked, concern etched in his face. "You gave us quite a fright there."

She sat up. Still on the floor, she noticed.

"The Sergeant said it was alright for you to go now, Miss. We have all the details we need for now."

She nodded dumbly, and with the help of the constable, got to her feet. Five minutes later she was in a taxicab, headed for Jack's home. When she arrived, they both greeted her enthusiastically.

"Where's Daddy?" asked Sarah.

Jessica looked at Jack, standing behind them, and shook her head.

"Sarah, let's sit down for a minute and talk"

They moved over to the comfy old sofa in the corner of the room and huddled close to her.

Poor little tyke, she thought. She's had a terrible time of it.

"Do you know anyone named Liz?" she asked.

She shook her head.

"Well, Daddy may be away for a little while, he has some . . . umm . . . business to attend to. Now why don't you go and watch some telly? The cartoons are probably on right now. I need to talk to our friend Jack, here."

But Sarah remained persistent. "Dad wouldn't have gone anywhere without saying goodbye to me," she said, suspicion in her voice.

"It's alright Sarah, really. He would have come to see you, but he was . . . delayed. Don't worry."

Reluctantly, the girl turned and shuffled over to the television. She switched it on and plopped down on the floor, obviously not satisfied with the answer she had been given.

Jack watched the girl for a moment, then turned to Jessica. "Smart girl, that," he murmured.

Jessica nodded, and brought him up to date.

"Married to her, well that's a turn up for the books. Do you believe it?"

"No," she shook her head emphatically. "She is a very abrasive type of person, he would not associate himself with a person like her, I'm sure of it."

Jack looked at her with a curious expression on his face.

"The only reason they would have taken Edward is to get his ring. I wish he'd just given it to them. Liz said they needed three rings. Edward has one tucked away somewhere, and so did Emma. Now Liz has them both. I'm not sure she's gotten the rings from them yet, though."

She pause a moment in thought. "I wonder if Edward's ring might lead us to Edward? Maybe if we asked Sarah, she might know something of the ring Edward has."

Jessica called her over.

"Sarah, can you tell me where your Dad might keep something very special. Like a ring," she asked.

Sarah nodded. "He has a special box in the bank," she whispered, aware of the seriousness of the situation.

"Can you show me where it is?"

She shook his head. "No, but it had a big park next to it, and after, we went to play in it. And we went and saw some wax people too. That was near it."

Jack looked at Jessica.

"Madame Tussaud's?" asked Jack.

The girl nodded her head vigorously, pleased to be able to help.

"There is a bank near there . . . with a park opposite, but what good will that do? We have no key to any safe deposit box."

"I know, but Edward does, and they have him. It wasn't all that long ago that Liz came and . . ." she looked at Sarah. "It's all right Sarah, you were very helpful. You can go back to your program, now."

Disappointed at being excluded again, the girl turned and went back to the television.

Jessica turned back to Jack.

"If we keep a watch on the bank, they're bound to come for it. Edward will have to tell them about it. They've already threatened his life, and Emma's. He doesn't have to worry about Sarah now."

Jack looked doubtful. "I don't know Edward, but are you sure that he would give away the location of the other ring?" he asked.

"He wouldn't risk his own life or Emma's for anything, not even a fortune in diamonds. He's all that Sarah has. If nothing else, Edward is a good father. He wouldn't want her to be alone in the world."

"OK, but you're not going out alone again. There's a lady downstairs that will look after Sarah. She adores children."

As he turned to go to the door, he stopped. Coming back to her, he placed his hand on her shoulder.

"I know that what we haven't gone very far in our relationship, Jess, but you know that I care for you very much. Aside from all that, well, you are my best friend. You always will be. So whatever happens, please be careful. I would hate to lose you."

She smiled up at him and gave him a hug. He was right. They were best friends, and she valued that friendship.

Half an hour later saw them in a bus on the way to the bank. Jessica had tried to disguise her appearance a little by putting on one of Jack's long coats, tying her hair up, and wearing a huge pair of sunglasses and a floppy hat.

Jack looked at her and laughed quietly.

"What?" she asked.

"Well, you do look rather ridiculous in that get up."

She grinned.

They arrived at the bank around three in the afternoon. It was due to close at five.

Jack went in first and asked if his 'brother', Edward, had been in as yet, and received a reply in the negative.

"No," he said, as he jogged back to her.

"Good, all we have to do is wait. Do you want a coffee?"

He nodded. They had come prepared, with a thermos full of hot coffee to drink and a blanket to sit on. To any bystanders, they would look like two young lovers out for an afternoon in the park.

After a few minutes of sipping coffee, Jack turned to her and asked, "Jess? Do you think they've got your ring?"

"I suppose. Why?"

"I was just thinking . . . If Liz had the post box key, why would she have wrenched the door off of its hinges?"

"Hmm . . ." she nodded. "Something was bothering me before, but I couldn't put my finger on it. You're right. She wouldn't. That means that someone must be following Liz around. The people she owes money to, I suppose." She looked around nervously. "I hope they're not following us around, too."

She shivered.

Half an hour passed, then another. Then at 4:15, a taxicab pulled up in front of the bank. Out of it stepped a tall, strikingly good-looking woman.

"It's Liz," Jessica whispered.

The woman turned back to the cab and reached toward the door. Out of the car, looking decidedly ill and weak, stepped Edward.

Jessica crossed the street, forced herself to wait until she had counted to thirty, and then slipped through the banks revolving doors, leaving Jack outside to intercept the pair when they exited. It took her a moment to find the pair, in one of the corners formed by a waist-high wooden partition. Liz was speaking to the woman who evidently governed access to the safe-deposit vault. In a moment Liz and Edward were ushered through the massive steel doorway.

Jessica surveyed the area and found a spot near the depositor's cubicles where she could pretend to be filling out a withdrawal slip. She pulled down the brim of her hat and waited. In a few minutes the pair emerged, carrying the deposit box. They entered a cubicle in the enclosed area on the other side of the rail, near the counter at which Jessica stood. Slowly Jessica edged her way closer, until she could peer through the crack in the corner of the frosted glass partition that enclosed the cubicle.

By tilting her head back and forth, Jessica could alternately see Edward and Liz. Edward looked gaunt, and tired. He immediately settled into the leather side chair against the far wall. Liz stood at the counter next to him.

It wasn't difficult to make out most of their conversation.

". . . what I ever saw in you," Edward was saying.

Jessica felt the blood drain from her face. *My God. He* is *involved with her.*

"Really?" said Liz. She slid her leather-covered leg against Edward's thigh.

"Apart from that." He pushed her away. "I have to admit, there was never a problem in the bedroom."

"Well, you know me, Eddie, dear. I'm a woman of many passions." She toyed with the zipper on her jumpsuit, tugging it several inches lower.

"Oh stop it. You're acting like a whore. There's more to marriage than sex and money."

Marriage? Was it true then?

"Like what? I can't think of anything else worth considering

"Like children. Remember? We had one."

What? It couldn't be . . .

"It was you who wanted children, remember?"

Edward stared at her. "You are without a doubt the most heartless woman I have ever had the misfortune to meet."

She smirked. "Like the moth, to the flame, Eddie. That's what you and I are."

He turned away.

Liz turned back to the deposit box and popped open its lid. She removed a single manila envelope. She opened it and extracted its contents, a folded document and a smaller envelope with a circular bulge. Dropping the papers to the counter, she tore the end from the smaller envelope and spilled the contents into her gloved hand. The delicate ring glinted up at her, even in the subdued light of the bank.

Edward sat watching her sullenly. Now that he knew that Sarah and Jessica were safe, he needed to focus on Emma. The rings were unimportant to him; he'd already learned what he could from them. Better to let Liz have them. If he played along, but remained uncooperative, she was almost certain to lead him back to Emma. Then he'd act. For now, he'd let Liz think that he was nearly incapacitated, to lull her into a false sense of security.

Liz extracted a second ring from her vest pocket and held it experimentally next to the first, rotating it to and fro, then finally moving it to the other side of the first. Peering into the circular bands she rotated them until the numbers lined up crossways, scowling at the two lines of digits.

"So, darling, what does this mean?" she purred, glaring at the man beside her. Edward stared at the floor, not acknowledging her question.

"Ah, well," she sighed, "Perhaps Emma will know. I'm sure I'll find out eventually." Edward remained impassive, staring.

He only looked up when the cubicle door banged open, and suddenly Liz was gone.

Caught by surprise, Jessica barely had time to round the corner before Liz had made her way across the bank's entryway and disappeared through the revolving door. She ran to follow, but a mother and daughter were coming in, and she had to wait for them to clear the door before she could step in. By the time she reached the street, the cab was halfway down the block. She looked wildly in both directions, but there was no sign of Jack. Where the hell had he gone?

She was still searching frantically for him when she heard Edward's voice behind her. "Jessie?! What the devil . . . ?"

Before she even realized what she was doing, her arms were wrapped around Edward, and she was breathing into his chest. "Oh, Edward," she said, "Thank God you're alright."

"Sarah . . . ?" Edward asked apprehensively.

"She's fine," she replied, "Safe at Jack's apartment." She looked up at him. His face was the color of writing paper. "Which is where we need to get you, for a good long rest."

Edward gently untangled himself and took a step back. "Jack?" he asked.

"A friend of mine. He's been helping me, but I don't know—"

There was a screech of tires, and a cab pulled up behind her. It looked like the same cab. And Jack was at the wheel. He climbed out at came around to the sidewalk.

"What . . . ?" said Jessica.

Jack smiled sheepishly. "Guess I don't pass for much of a cab driver, eh? I had her halfway to the police station when she caught on. But she got away. Dashed into the train station. I had to slow for pedestrians pulling luggage across the crosswalk and in a flash she was out of the cab and down the steps. I ran after, but there were too many people, milling all about. There was no sign of her."

"You stole the cab?" Jessica asked incredulously.

Jack gave her a hurt look. "Of course not. Cost me a hundred quid for an hour! And the cabbie's got my car keys. He wanted to make sure I'd bring it back."

Jessica touched Jack's cheek fondly. "That was a really stupid thing to do. You know that, don't you Jack?"

"You know," said Jack, smiling, "I told the cabbie that's what you'd say." He tousled her hair. "Now we'd better get to the police, and let them take care of this."

"And we've got to solve the puzzle of the rings," said Edward, "Before Liz does. I promised my uncle . . ." The thought floated, unfinished. It was nonsense, he knew, even as he said it. His real motivation was standing next to him. If only she weren't standing so damn close to Jack, too.

"But Liz took the rings with her, Edward," said Jessica.

"And she's probably on some train leaving Waterloo station by now," added Jack.

Edward reached into his coat pocket and pulled out the folded document that Liz had left on the counter. Carefully he opened it and held it out so that Jack and Jessica could see it. Across the top, printed in bold script, were the words "Jeweler's Appraisal Form". There was a paragraph of typing, a valuation of three thousand pounds, and a photograph of all three rings. Below the photo was a detailed sketch of the inside surface of each ring, showing a series of letters and numbers.

"Why, it covers all three rings!" exclaimed Jessica.

Edward nodded.

"Yes, and it shows all three inscriptions. You see, I never needed the rings. It was Liz I was trying to keep them from. This will lead us to the diamonds—if there are any. But I'll tell you all about it later. For now, we'd better go to the Police, and get them to Emma."

"What if we—" began Jack, but Edward interrupted.

"We can't go there ourselves. Liz is armed, and we're not."

They arrived at the police station a short time later, and asked to speak to Sergeant Brightcastle.

The Sergeant looked them over, shaking his head.

"No sign of your missing postal door, if that's what you're here about, miss," said the Sergeant. "You know there's a limit—"

"Look Sergeant," said Edward, "my sister is in grave danger." Edward sketchily explained the situation and gave him an address. "Please, hurry. They may still be there. Now that they have all three rings, they don't need Emma anymore. They've been doping her up somehow, and I'm worried about her."

"All right, I'll get someone there now." He stepped into the hall and issued instructions to one of the constables standing outside. The man quickly departed. Sticking his head back in the doorway he gestured at a second constable. "You three can wait here. Constable Litkey will make you a cuppa."

The three of them sat grim faced, sipping their hot tea. No one spoke, but Jessica's mind was full of questions. She did not want to ask Edward there and then about Liz being his wife, but soon, she would have to ask.

She wondered about her own ring, too. It was curious about the post box door. She had assumed that Liz had the ring. But she wouldn't have ripped the door off of the post box—she had the key. How much did the South Africans know?

Just over an hour later, the Sergeant came in, looking tired.

"Mr. Drummond, sorry to say you were right. A Mrs. Emma Bengarian was found at the flat. She has been taken to hospital."

Seeing the look of concern on their faces he put up his hands. "She'll be fine. I spoke to the doctor personally." He paused, then continued, "The place was cleaned out by the way. Probably nothing there to go on. There's a team there now, but it looks like another wipe down"

* * *

"It sounds like I should have this Liz working for me instead of you, Freddie, hey?" sneered Winston Van Der Meer. He switched the telephone receiver from one ear to the other and swiveled his hotel chair, drumming his fingers nervously on top of his desk. "I can't believe you had this guy in your custody, and didn't even end up with his bladdy ring." He sighed in exasperation. "So the one in the leather jumpsuit—Liz—she's got Edward's and his sister's rings?"

Winston listened to the man jabber at the other end of the line. Maybe he should send one of his managers to do this job. But whom could he trust?

"Well, at least you got one of them. What does it look like?"

The way that things were going, Freddie was going to get himself arrested for doing something stupid. Then Winston would have to send someone more competent.

"Hang on Freddie." He picked up the cell phone from his desk and dialed. When he heard his secretary answer he said simply, "Get me Hans." It had been a long time since Winston had bothered with politeness. They knew who he was.

He turned his attention back to the hotel telephone. "So, Freddie. Did he tell you what the numbers mean?"

Freddie responded, and Winston slammed his hand down the desk. "Well, damn it, you had Edward. He could've told you what they meant. Look, man. Edward's the key to this. You've got one of the rings, so you're nearly as well off as Liz. But if you lose Edward, you're dead." He hadn't wanted to get this involved, but there was no choice. "Look. Here's what we'll do. Come to the hotel and pick me up. I'll pack a bag and we'll dog Edward until we've got them."

Freddie interrupted him, and Winston snorted in disgust. "Of course he'll do what we tell him. He gave the girl the other ring. He obviously cares about her. We'll use that as leverage."

Winston listened once more, nodding. "Be here in an hour. I mean it." He dropped the receiver back on the telephone and drummed his fingers in irritation. The man was an idiot.

He'd forgotten the cell phone. He put it to his ear and said, "Hans?"

The man answered respectfully. "This is Hans, Winston."

"So, Hans, what's this I hear about four days to get the separator running?"

Hans sounded nervous. "Well, sir, it's the bearings in the crusher. She's seized up, and we're havin' a hell of a time freein' her."

"What do you suppose caused this?" demanded Winston.

"Age. Lack of maintenance. Improper lubrication. It's hard to say."

Winston sniffed. "Who's in charge of maintenance around here, Hans?"

Hans' voice tightened. "I am, sir." Winston could hear him swallow. The man continued, "And I do what I can. With the funds available. Such as they are."

Winston sat for a full minute, without speaking. If he fired him, it might improve responsiveness for a while. He'd been having a problem with some of the men showing him the proper respect, lately. It was money, he knew. They'd kick him when he was down, if he gave them half a chance. But Hans would be hard to replace. Not many men were anxious to work for the Van Der Meer Mining Company these days.

Winston sighed, and pushed himself away from the desk. "Very well, Hans. But see if you can do it faster than four days, eh?"

Hans let out his breath. "Yes, sir."

Winston turned off the phone and stood up. He needed to pack.

* * *

After giving a description of Liz to the police, Jessica, Edward and Jack left for the hospital.

The sergeant had called ahead, and the duty nurse was expecting them. Emma was sleeping peacefully. Aside from a couple of bruises, she appeared to be unharmed. They were just about to leave when Emma stirred. The first person she saw as she opened her eyes was Jack.

"Hi," he said, smiling down at her.

She attempted to smile back, but she still looked woozy.

"Emma, thank God you're all right," said Edward from the other side of the bed. Slowly she turned her head and looked at her brother.

"Eddie," she smiled, "Is Sarah all right? Are you all right?"

"We're fine. Thanks to Jessie, and Jack here. How do you feel?"

Emma moved to sit up a little. Jessica leaned forward to help, but Jack beat her to it. Gently, he raised her up, fluffed up the pillows, and settled her back down. She smiled gratefully at him.

Jessica looked over at Jack, raising her eyebrows. He shrugged.

"She really didn't harm me, Eddie." She interrupted Edward as he began to contradict her. "Yes, I know it looks bad. But she actually left me . . . yesterday, I think it was. I was still a little dippy, and I guess I must have slept the night through. When I awoke, there was a man there I didn't know. I don't think he was with them. He had a strange accent. I'm not sure where from . . ."

Edward nodded. He reached out and clasped Emma's hand in his. He blamed himself what had happened to Emma. But what could he have done? Stupid! He told himself. He should have sent her up to Edinburgh when this whole mess started. In a single week he'd managed to get nearly everyone he loved killed. He had to start thinking like he had when he'd been in the military—no not that. That meant minimizing losses. He had to do more than that. He had to see to it that they all remained safe, until he figure out what was going on.

"Anyway," Emma continued, "I couldn't tell him anything. I don't know where the rings are, now. Eventually, I think he believed me."

"I'm so sorry, Em. Don't you worry. You just get yourself better."

She sniffed and nodded. "Why are they so important, anyway?"

"I wish I knew, Em. I wish I knew."

Emma turned to look at Jack.

"It seems I have you to thank, and Jessica, too."

Jack smiled. "I didn't do anything, just helping out a friend. But I'm glad I did," he added, gazing into her tired eyes.

"I must look an awful sight," she said, smiling as she brushed her hair away from her forehead with one hand.

"On the contrary, you look lovely," replied Jack.

Edward cleared his throat. "Well," he said, "at least it's nice to see a smile on that face, for a change."

Emma turned to Jessica. "It's been a long time Jessica," she said. "I was terrified for you when they brought you in and tied you up. I'm so glad they didn't hurt you."

Jessica smiled down at the woman's bruised face. "I'm fine. Just you worry about getting yourself better." She looked up at Jack and Edward. "We really should let her get some rest now . . ."

"Of course," they said in unison.

"We'll come back and see you as soon as we can," added Edward. "Although it might be a few days . . ." he added thoughtfully.

"And if they can't make it, I certainly will," smiled Jack.

Leaving Jack's telephone number with the duty staff, they left the hospital and headed back to Jack's flat, where Sarah greeted him enthusiastically.

He sat on the couch with them, holding her close, reading her a story. It was long past her bedtime, and she was beginning to nod off.

Jessica settled into an easy chair in the far corner, watching. Her face was hidden in the shadows.

Edward hugged Sarah to him. The little girl wanted to know all about his adventures. Speaking softly to her, Edward gave her a somewhat edited version of the events of the past two days.

Jessica's heart swelled as she watched the two of them together. Memories came flooding back again: the happy times they'd had together; the sadness she'd felt when she could no longer be a part of their little family.

She had not just lost Edward five years ago, she realized. She had lost Sarah, as well. Seeing them together made her realize just how great that loss had been. She found herself trembling.

As she watched the scene on the couch, a thought from earlier in the day kept nagging at her, interfering with her enjoyment of the happy reunion. Why had the police said that Liz was Edward's wife. She scrutinized the man opposite her. It seemed impossible. He was so warm and caring, a devoted father, a considerate lover. Liz seemed cold, even cruel.

Yet surely the police had checked the records. Could it be?

She found herself sitting rigidly in the easy chair, her heart pounding.

If it was true—

She felt her happy mood dissipating, as the hopes playing in the back of her mind—hopes she'd not even dared admit—slowly died.

Jessica shook her head. This self-torment was pointless. If Edward had married that woman, there was nothing she could do about it. It was time for her to collect herself and get on with her own life.

She found Edward contemplating her, his warm dark eyes peering over the tousled head of his daughter. She returned his gaze coolly. He turned his attention back to Sarah, who was in mid-yawn.

"Time for little pumpkins to be in the patch," he said, lifting the girl with him as he stood up. Sarah giggled as he carried her to the guestroom.

Jessica, stood, stretched, and headed for the kitchen, where Jack was making coffee. In a few minutes Edward returned, and joined them at the kitchen table.

"Sarah wants you to come in and say goodnight, Jessie."

She smiled at him, pleased that the little girl had asked for her. She tucked her in and kissed her goodnight, and was about to leave when the child spoke.

"Jessie, is Jack your boyfriend?"

Taken aback, Jessie smiled a little awkwardly.

"No honey, he's just a very good friend."

"Oh, that's good then. Goodnight Jessie."

Sarah rolled over on to her side and snuggled into the blankets, a satisfied smile on her face.

A puzzled Jessica turned off the light and softly closed the door. As she was returning to the kitchen, she heard a coffee cup clatter noisily on the table. The men were speaking softly. She paused before stepping from the hallway.

". . . just so you know, *old man*," Jack was saying. "Jess was hurt very badly when the two of you split up. I care for her deeply."

Edward's voice was tense as he replied. "As it happens, so do I."

Jessica walked back into the room. "What's going on?" she asked.

"Nothing," said Jack, but his smile was strained. He handed her a hot steaming cup.

There was an awkward silence in the room as they each sipped at their tea. Damn. He wished that Jack would go into the other room, or something, so that he and Jessie could talk. But it *was* the man's apartment, after all. And he knew that he'd have to explain himself sooner or later. And Jack did deserve an explanation, too, he supposed, after all the help he'd provided. It would be better to get it out in the open with both of them now. That way, at least, Jessica would have no reason to go over it again with Jack—on their own.

He turned to Jessica and cleared his throat. "You have some questions for me, don't you?"

She nodded. "The police, they told me Liz was your wife, that she had documented proof of that fact."

"She is, or was."

A little of Jessica died inside, as she turned her head away, brushing at the tears forming.

"No Jessie, you don't understand. You see, Liz is really Sarah's mother."

"What? You said her name was Elizabeth. And she looks nothing like the photos I saw of her. And you said she was dead!"

He nodded. "Actually, I always said that she'd passed on, which was true, but misleading. It was easier to tell Sarah that. Liz left me a few years after Sarah was born. She said that she was too young to be tied down to a fuddy-duddy husband and a kid. Said she was destined for better things. She went back to her maiden name—Elizabeth Stark. Liz is her nickname."

Jessica grimaced in annoyance.

"Anyway," Edward continued, "she left the country. I didn't hear from her until you and I had been . . . after you left."

Jessica nodded, barely breathing.

"She came back when she ran out of money. Her gambling had gotten worse, and her taste for expensive thrills. She started threatening to take Sarah away from me. And she kept demanding more and more money, just to leave us alone," he added bitterly.

Jessica sat for a long while in silence, trying to sort out her feelings. At last, she asked him, "Why did you give me the ring?"

"You know why—I wanted you to marry me."

She eyed him skeptically. "But why did you let me take it when I . . . turned you down?"

He sighed and continued, "It had been my father's. He, Emma, and I inherited them from my Uncle Charles. When my father passed on, I ended up with two. I thought that if you had one of them it might somehow . . . bind us together." He smiled. "Little did I realize how true that would be!"

"Liz said something about diamonds . . ."

He nodded, pulling the jeweler's appraisal out of his pocket. "My father was the executor of my Uncle's will. He had this prepared before they were distributed to the beneficiaries."

He pointed at the inscriptions. "I never gave these much thought. I guess I thought they were jeweler's marks, or something."

Jessica smiled inwardly. She'd had the same thought. Edward continued. "But then that letter showed up. It started me thinking . . .

"I know very little about the history of the rings. The little I do know about them I learned from my father before his death. My Uncle Charles had them made, after he returned from South Africa the last time, in the early sixties. His wife and daughter had been killed in a tragic accident. The old man was devastated. On top of that, he lost the diamond mine he'd operated for over twenty years. So he retreated to his castle, but lived only a few more years. It was during that time that he had the rings made. So I assume that any treasure would be at Castle Drummond. In Scotland."

Jessica looked confused.

Edward continued. "Apparently, in his youth, my uncle's father was a partner in a diamond mine in South Africa My uncle worked there in his youth, although he had to return home during the war—that would have been about 1940. He returned after the war, traveling back and fourth between the mine and Scotland. When he married in the 1950s I think he planned to stay in Scotland, but the mine never seemed to run well without him. He finally moved his family over in the early sixties. Shortly thereafter, tragedy struck.

"For reasons I'm not clear on, he lost the mine about the same time. In the end he left South Africa and returned to Scotland for good.

"I'm puzzled why my uncle would hide a treasure—if, indeed, this isn't some horribly elaborate joke. My uncle never needed a treasure. The family's investments before the war amply funded trusts that supported him, and my father, and later Emma—until recently, anyway."

Edward looked up, and sighed. "I was four when my uncle died, so I barely remember him. He was the elder of the two brothers, and my father outlived him by over twenty-five years."

"And now you need the money?"

"Yes," he nodded grimly. "Liz has taken nearly everything. And I made a few very bad investments. I let the servants go long ago. I sold the house when I could no longer keep it up. Even auctioned the furniture. That's why I had to rent the flat.

"An investment banker's not much use without any money. Lately I'd even thought about going back into the service. I probably would have, if it weren't for Sarah . . ."

Jessica looked at him for a long while, studying the lines around his eyes, the rugged jaw, the searching look of his eyes. "So what now, once we know Emma is all right?" she asked.

"Now? Well, now we go to Scotland."

Jessica blinked. "*We?* What's this 'we' business?"

Edward looked at her in surprise. "I'm sorry, I just assumed that you were going to help me with this."

"Well, maybe you assume too much. Going to Scotland with you was not on my agenda. I was willing to help out with Sarah, and I still am, but going away with you . . . just the two of us . . . I don't know about that."

Jessica thought she could see Jack smiling out of the corner of her eye.

"I'm not asking you to resume where we left off Jessie, just come with me to help me. That's all. I promise. No strings."

Jessica looked over at Jack, who shrugged. She realized that he wasn't going to help her with this decision. But he was looking at Edward suspiciously.

She glanced at Edward.

Could she handle being alone with him again? Or would she fall into his arms like some tramp, her longing betraying her? If that was what he wanted, he wasn't going to get it. Maybe there was a chance for the two of them now that he was out of that stuffy old mansion, but she wasn't going to appear over eager.

On the other hand, if she didn't go with him, that would be the end of it, wouldn't it? She didn't want that either.

Well, she could help him solve the puzzle for Sarah's sake, she thought. After all, she was the one who'd always been the puzzle enthusiast. Edward had often commented on her patience for the Cryptics and Anacrostics in the daily news?

She sighed. She was fooling herself if she pretended that she was going for any reason other than to be with him again. Maybe he'd come to her on her terms, this time.

And she *was* going, wasn't she? She realized she'd already made up her mind, even before she began to argue with herself.

Her voice was wary when she spoke. "All right. I'll go. But as soon as it's finished, we come straight back."

Edward studied her expression before nodding. "OK, then. We go to Scotland."

Jacks shoulders slumped and he leaned back in his chair. I'm sorry to do this to Jack, Jessica thought, then wondered exactly what it was she was doing to him, after all. She'd made it clear that this was not a social trip. Evidently Jack didn't believe it. Did she believe it herself? For that matter, what did Edward think? She glanced over at him, half expecting a smirk, but he was contemplating the leaves in his teacup.

The three of them sat at the kitchen table, talking quietly, conjecturing about what the rings might mean. After a half hour Edward went into the living room and quietly folded out the couch, kicked off his shoes, stretched out on the far edge of the mattress, and dropped into an exhausted sleep.

Jessica and Jack remained where they were, half-shrouded in the shadows cast by the streetlight outside the kitchen window. They talked architecture, photography, and just enjoyed the quiet of the evening, in sharp contrast to the hectic days they'd been through. After another half hour, Jessica rose, stretched lazily, and reached for her coat.

"You'd best spend the night again, Jess," said Jack. "They know where you live. You can have my bed if you'd like. It wouldn't be the first time I'd slept on the floor."

Jessica looked startled. "I hadn't thought of that." She stood there, thinking. "I wonder if I'll ever feel really safe at my place, again?"

"I'm sure you will, eventually. But for now you'd best stay here. Go ahead. Take my bed."

She shook her head. "I'll be fine, here on the couch," she said. "From the looks of him, a bomb wouldn't disturb poor Edward."

Jack looked at her. His expression was hard to read. "All right. I guess I'll see you in the morning then. If the hospital rings . . ." He left the rest unsaid.

"Jack, I . . . I'm sorry . . . about everything . . . us."

He sighed. "Yeah. Me too." He brushed her cheek softly with the back of his hand, then turned and went into the bedroom.

After Jack left she sat up watching the telly, feigning fascination with the late news in order to avoid facing her discomfort over the sleeping arrangements. Actually, she was amazed that there had been no mention of their adventures on the television news. In retrospect she decided that even the most exciting day of her life could hardly match up with the level of mayhem reserved for the nightly summary of the world's catastrophes.

When she could no longer justify watching the drivel that the programming had devolved into, she reluctantly switched off the set, slid out of her shoes, and slipped onto her edge of the foldout bed.

Gingerly, careful not to wake Edward, Jessica slipped onto the edge of the mattress and lay staring at the ceiling for a long while.

What was she doing going to Scotland with this man? No good would come of this, she was sure.

She forced herself to close her eyes.

And how would you feel if you didn't go? She asked herself. Like you'd missed an opportunity, that's how.

An opportunity for what?

She listened to the ticking of the clock on the fireplace mantel, but resisted the urge to open her eyes and glance at the time. It couldn't have been more than a minute or two since she'd last checked.

Something had been bothering her since this whole thing started, but she couldn't quite capture the thought as it flirted in the corners of her memory. It was something Edward had said. Something about the appraisal.

"You see, I never needed the rings." That's what he'd said.

Of course! He had the appraisal. He didn't need Emma's ring, or his—or hers.

When Edward had asked her to meet him at his flat that first night, he already knew exactly what her ring looked like.

But if he didn't need her ring, what was he after? Her help?

Or . . . ?

She felt herself flush. Was it possible that Edward had used the rings as an excuse to try to rekindle their relationship? If so, should she be angry? Or flattered?

Well, she was angry. If he thought he could trick her into renewing their relationship, he was in for a surprise. In the morning she would tell him exactly how she felt.

Exactly? She was afraid of what she was feeling. And it definitely wasn't anger, no matter how much she tried to convince herself otherwise.

She sighed.

What am I doing here, anyway? I should be at my apartment. Well, maybe not there, but . . . where then? A hotel?

Jessica checked the clock. It was past 2:30 in the morning, and still she hadn't drifted off to sleep. The excitement of the past two days had completely disrupted the safe, if sedate, life she'd constructed for herself during the past few years.

Edward's face, then Liz's alternated on the movie screen of her eyelids. She listened to Edward's steady breathing. She could feel the warmth of his body, even across the large space that separated them on the foldout bed.

Sleep did not come easily. The adrenaline of the day's activities had left her muscles tense, and she lay uneasily on the same mattress as her one-time lover. She'd thought she was over Edward. It had taken a long time for his face to stop appearing in her dreams. She had never purged her fantasies of the memory of his fingers playing over her body. Even last week, lying between the cool sheets of her own bed she had explored her yearnings for him, and in her moment of climax had found herself calling out his name.

Edward. There had never been any other. Not before, nor since. She had been naïve, a young girl seeking the comfort of a large house and the stability of an upper class family when she had taken the job as nanny. The attraction between them had been almost immediate, and their affair, while brief, had burned with a fire she had never imagined.

She'd been a virgin, and an inexperienced one, at that, when she'd gone to live with them. Sensing her reticence, Edward had spent a long time getting to know her, courting her, drawing her out without pressing her, until it had been she that had fallen into his arms.

He had always been the perfect gentleman toward her, but once they had kissed that first time she was more than ready to respond. Gently he coaxed her responses to ever-increasing heights. He discovered within her a passionate and sensuous lover. Quiet and unassuming around others, at night she became an adventurous, almost wanton lover, who reveled in each new delight he exposed her to. She found herself amazed at her own passions, and eagerly awaited his return from work each day.

Their candlelit dinners were her courtship. Long, romantic meals devoted to learning about each other, and his subtle instruction of her in the ways of the upper class.

And yet it seemed there was much about him that she hadn't known.

When she caught his eye as he watched her playing with Sarah, she pictured them as a family, together always. Certainly she felt like the girl's mother. And Sarah, in her youth, was drawn to the feminine comfort she offered.

But then came the overheard comments. She'd heard the maid and butler talking about the "tramp", and wondered at first who they'd meant. One day she'd been coming into the kitchen when she heard the delivery boy from the grocery commenting on the "hot tart" of a new mistress that Mr. Edward had found himself. She began to notice the looks the other servants gave her when they thought she wasn't watching. A quick glance in the mirror as she left a room, and she could see their disapproval.

Edward had taken her to Paris for the weekend. He'd signed the register at the hotel "Mr. and Mrs. Edward Drummond". They'd dined at some tres chic bistro, a block off of the Champs Elysee, dawdling over more courses than Jessica could count. Over brandies he'd brought out the small, silk covered box. His words were a blur to her, something about becoming the real Mrs. Drummond, and he'd slipped the ring on her finger. She'd expected it, yet somehow been caught by surprise. He'd been surprised at her reaction, and a bit disappointed when she didn't give him an immediate answer.

Inside, she was in turmoil. It was everything she'd thought she wanted. And yet . . .

There was no getting around it. She felt cheap. She pictured the household servants chattering over the tawdry details in the back rooms as she and Edward dined in strained silence, growing old with no friends or outside acquaintances, ostracized by his upper class peers.

She tried to return the ring the next morning, telling him of her concerns. He discounted her worries, told her she shouldn't let such a small thing upset her so. She had reacted badly to his insensitivity. Was it possible that he really didn't see the class difference between them?

She told him she wasn't ready, wasn't sure, anything to postpone the decision.

He asked her if she loved him, and she lied, desperate to avoid a lifetime of disrespect, deceit and disgrace.

She told him that she was too young, confused, that maybe the attraction was to his money.

It pained her, even now, to remember the hurt look in his eyes. He wouldn't accept the ring back, urging her to think about it.

That afternoon she'd packed, and called a cab to take her to the train station.

Edward had insisted on riding to the station with her. He'd seemed almost crumpled in on himself as the cab jostled through the evening traffic. A hundred times she'd almost thrown her arms around him and tearfully recanted her rejection. But at the station she'd kissed him reservedly on the cheek and stepped from the cab.

He'd followed her stiffly into the station, and watched in silence as she bought her ticket. She'd hardly even noted the destination. It was simply the next train. Her fingers brushed his as he handed her bag up to her where she stood on the steps of the coach.

It was the last time they'd touched.

She remembered seeing the tightness around the corners of his mouth as he waved to her. His face had been set in stony impassiveness, his feelings buried deep as he stood on the platform of the Gare de Lyon. She swayed in her seat as the train began to move, craned her neck to watch him recede to nothingness.

What if she'd lowered the window? Leaned out and called to him? Told him how confused she was, how she wanted to build a new life with him, far away from his upper crust neighbors and gossiping servants? Leaped from the train window toward his waiting arms. Falling, far, far down, toward the steely rails and the churning wheels—

She screamed.

Shaking, shaking, someone was shaking her.

"It's alright, Jessie, it's alright. You were dreaming." She opened her eyes. Edward was holding her, stroking her hair, gazing into her eyes. She pressed her face against his neck and clung to him, still shaking. Gently he stroked her cheek, pulling her warmth against his, pressing himself into her.

As her shaking calmed, her body awakened to the heat of him, the smell of his aftershave, the coarse stubble of his beard. She was dizzy with the scent of him, overwhelmed by the feel of him against her after all those years.

His eyes searched hers. Those deep dark eyes. Oh, God, she thought.

He leaned close and as the voice in her head screamed, "No! No!" she let the kiss happen.

His lips were covering hers, his mouth hungrily seeking hers, their breaths mingled as they pressed together. The tautness of her nipples pressed into his chest through their clothes as she squirmed to maneuver his hardness against her abdomen. His tongue greedily sought hers as he rolled on top of her, letting his weight press against her from head to toe. Her hands tore at his shirttails, and he pulled himself up long enough to work his hand down the row of buttons at the front of her blouse.

Separating the material, he bent to kiss the swell of her breasts, then slid her bra up to reveal the wrinkled peaks, slipping his mouth around one, then the other, teasing the sensitive points with his tongue.

His deft fingers found the button of her skirt, and in a moment, it and her underthings cascaded to the floor beside the bed. He pressed his face against her warm stomach, kissing her navel, slipping his face lower to catch her scent, then taste her sweet warmth as she arched into him.

Tangling her fingers into his hair she half-dragged his face back to hers, kissing him deeply as she forced his pants down over his slim hips and pressed herself desperately into him. His hardness found her hot center, and they slid together in a continuous wave of shuddering pleasure.

* * *

When she awoke the next morning she was instantly filled with regret. No gradual coming to her senses, no reverie as she recalled the passions of the night. Just a cold, hard ball of regret lodged firmly in her stomach. And she was mad, too.

At whom? Edward? Herself? At fate, for bringing her bad dreams?

Yes, yes, and yes.

Damn! After all her resolve, she'd ended up throwing herself at him like some—

What must he think of her? That she was easy? That it didn't matter that they weren't involved anymore?

She cursed herself under her breath. How could she have been so foolish? How could she have succumbed to her own desires like that? She'd never felt ruled by her passions before.

Damn, damn, damn.

She slid out of the bedclothes hurriedly, and quickly showered and dressed. She couldn't look Edward in the eye. When he approached her, she shied away.

What had come over her last night? In the heat of the moment, it had been impossible to resist him, but in the cold light of day, she knew she'd made a mistake. A terrible mistake.

If she didn't want him, she should have kept her distance. And if she did want him, she shouldn't have been so easy.

After numerous attempts to engage her in conversation, he eventually gave up.

Jack, too, seemed to sense that something had happened.

Jessica could feel both of them watching her. She felt like a deer, frozen indecisively in the middle of the road, caught in oncoming headlights from two different directions.

Chapter 6

The station was still shrouded in gloom as their carriage began to glide past commuters waiting for other trains. Jessica had wanted to visit Emma again before they left for Edinburgh, but Edward had pointed out that Liz probably knew that the rings led to the ancestral home of the Drummonds, a castle a short distance outside of Edinburgh. He was afraid that even if Liz had only two rings, she might be able to decipher their meaning and find the treasure.

He was also concerned about Mr. MacGregor, the caretaker of the castle, whom he'd known as a boy. The MacGregor family had worked for the Drummonds for many generations. Liz had no legitimate business at the castle, but that wouldn't stop her from trying to gain entry. Thinking of what had happened to Emma, he was concerned for Mr. MacGregor's welfare.

Jack had decided to take the week off from his free-lance photography business in order to entertain Sarah. He had offered to check in on Emma each day that they were gone, and Sarah looked forward to seeing her aunt again.

Jessica and Edward had taken a cab to the train station, stopping by both of their flats on the way to pick up clothes and other traveling necessities. At Edward's flat Jessica had reclaimed her purse, and was surprised to find her money and passport still in the pile of possessions that had spilled on the floor when Edward had attacked the man in his flat.

Now, each laden with an overnight bag, they made their way down the swaying aisle of the train. Peering at the numbers at each compartment, Edward nodded, and slid open the glass door, allowing Jessica to slip in ahead of him. He followed her, closing the door and stowing the bags in the overhead rack before taking a seat beside her.

Luckily they had managed to get a compartment to themselves. There were three front facing seats, and three facing the rear, with a window and lift-up table between them. Jessica and Edward sat facing forward, she next to the window, watching the patchwork of brick buildings flash past, a visual staccato of color and texture. Gradually the flash of passing buildings became more irregular, as the city sloughed into suburb, then village, and finally open country, dotted with an occasional farmhouse, fence, stone wall, or cattle.

Jessica sat in stony silence, her hands clasped in her lap. She was thinking of past travels together, when she just enjoyed being with him. Now it was awkward.

Edward seemed to be enjoying her company. She noticed him watching her, and felt somewhat guilty about her strange mood in the wake of their lovemaking the night before.

His thoughts turned to the last time he'd seen her. She'd been leaving him, on a train much like this one.

After a long while, he opened his mouth to speak, hesitated, then decided to plunge on. "Why did you leave me, Jessie?" he asked softly.

Jessica turned from the window and studied him. There was a bruise above his left eyebrow that was slowly fading, and he looked tired. But his eyes were the same deep pools she remembered from five years ago, and she felt herself drawn to him, lost in his steady gaze. Warmth flooded her, deep inside, and she felt almost embarrassed to realize the strength of her physical attraction to this man.

She'd never known another man who made her feel this way. Jack had tried to get close to her. In his way she supposed he loved her. They'd met when he was on assignment, doing a photo shoot at the architectural firm where she worked. He'd taken her out nearly every weekend for the better part of a year. They'd toured nearly every old manor house within a hundred miles of London, arguing architecture and history for hours, picnicking at the center of hedge mazes or sitting on the stone rim of old fountains. They'd been the best of friends. But never more than that.

Jack had wanted her, she knew; had even suggested she move in with him. But she could never let him get any closer than being her best friend. Now, looking into Edward's eyes, she realized why. It was because she'd never stopped loving Edward.

She loved everything about him. She loved his kindness, towards her, and towards his child. She loved the casual comfort with which he 'took on' the world. She loved the passionate, albeit sometimes headstrong, energy that he devoted to any new challenge. Most of all she loved the way he went out of his way to help people whenever he could. And then there were his humor, his grace, his sophistication. But it was that very sophistication that had driven her away—not his, because beneath it all he was like her, down to earth, but the trappings and accoutrements of the society that came with it.

But she'd left him, not the other way around. Why was she so angry? He had a right to be angry with her. If she wanted him back, under some new arrangement, she would have to be careful to show that she still cared, without throwing herself at him. Like she had last night.

"I left you out of . . . fear, I suppose," she said softly.

"Fear?" He looked at her quizzically.

She returned his gaze, surprised that he still did not understand.

Jessica clasped her hands together tighter. Looking down, she continued, "Fear of not measuring up—not fitting in. Fear of not being good enough for you—for your friends. I'm no society girl, no 'lady of the court'. I knew that no matter how much I played at being the grand society wife—no matter how much you could accept me for what I was—I'd never truly be accepted by your friends, your neighbors . . . or your . . . servants."

Edward was silent for a moment, studying the set of her jaw, the graceful curve of her neck, the tendrils of silky auburn hair that had escaped from behind her ear and floated in the currents of his breath, caressing her cheek. A cheek that he longed to touch.

"You knew about that?" he asked sheepishly.

Of course she'd known it. The servants had made it no small secret that they felt she was beneath him. Her eyes flashed. "Of course I knew it. We talked about this, remember? Or have you forgotten?"

He shook his head. "I haven't forgotten. Anything. I just wasn't sure how much you'd heard. It really didn't matter to me what people thought. And what could I do? Many of those servants were hired by my parents, and had been with me all my life. I guess I somehow hoped that they would come to know you as I had, and would come to appreciate you for what you are, not who you were born to." Edward sighed. "It was foolish. I know that now." I should have been more responsive to your fears and concerns."

Smiling wanly he continued in a flippant tone, "Well, all of those concerns are behind us now. I'm broke! There's no house, no servants, and no neighbors."

What did he mean? Was this an opportunity for a new start? She'd be cautious, and wait to see what developed.

Edward turned to face her. "When we get back to London—"

The compartment door slid open with a bang, and two men burst in.

The thinner of the two men eased himself down on the bench opposite them while the heavyset one descended upon it with a loud thud, sprawling his legs in front of himself and forcing Edward to move his feet.

Jessica felt Edward tense, and pressed closer to him.

The heavyset man leaned forward, glaring at first Edward, then Jessica. He looked like he'd been squeezed into his clothes. He wore a cream-colored golf shirt and black pants that clashed with his brown loafers. His curly black hair matched a bushy mustache that drew attention to his bulbous nose, which appeared to have once been broken. He looked like an ex-prizefighter.

The thinner man was dressed in an obviously expensive navy suit. His hair was gray, nearly silver, and he was clean-shaven. A mole on his forehead leant a certain complexity to his face. He would have been handsome, if not for his dour expression.

With a growing sense of dread, Jessica realized that she knew who they were. She clutched her armrest as memories of that night at Edward's flat came flooding back.

"Good afternoon, Mr. . . . Drummond," said the thinner man, contemplating Edward menacingly. "I must say, you are looking decidedly better than when I last saw you, hey?" His clipped accent placed his nationality immediately. He was South African.

"No thanks to you," said Edward. He leaned forward, and Jessica realized that he was shielding her. She detected a slight tremor in his voice that belied his steely tone.

"It's a shame we didn't part on a more friendly note," said the man, ignoring Edward's comment. "Perhaps if you'd made an attempt to be more accommodating . . . ?"

"I told you then, and I'm telling you now," said Edward, "I don't have any diamonds, or any money for that matter."

"Well," said the heavyset man, gruffly, "We got this sudden intuition that you might be coming into an inheritance soon. So we thought we'd make sure nothing untoward happened to you. Or it. Or your little lady friend either," he added, looking meaningfully at Jessica. "Can't have you ending up in hospital again—"

"Shut up, Freddie," snapped the thinner man opposite them.

"Who are you?" asked Jessica, quietly.

The man looked at her evenly, but didn't answer.

"He's Winston Van Der Meer," said Edward.

"You're correct, Mr. Drummond. Edward. Although I must admit, you look enough like Charles that if I hadn't been expecting you, you'd have given me quite a fright."

"And you look like the devil," replied Edward.

Winston glowered at Edward for a moment, but then seemed to make a decision to be civil, and turned to Jessica. "Yes, I'm Winston

Van Der Meer, miss. I think you've met Freddie. He's been instrumental in helping me collect from those who owe me." He turned to Edward. "Your Uncle Charles caused me no end of troubles many years ago."

"If so, I'm sure it was with good cause. Charles was an honorable man. A reputation he does not share with you, from all I've heard."

"I beg to differ." Again he turned to Jessica. "You see, years ago my father, was a partner with Charles' father in a diamond mine. When they died, Charles and I inherited it. Of course, I did most of the work, but Charles would visit from time to time. He had this incessant habit of slowing production in the name of what would these days be called 'employee relations' or some such nonsense. Every time I made an improvement, Charles would come back from Scotland and, using some trivial accident as an excuse, shut the mine down for days while he reorganized things. Whenever production restarted, it was invariably slow and inefficient again. Eventually I had had enough. I was finally forced to take over completely.

"There have always been rumors that Charles took a sizeable quantity of diamonds when he left—diamonds which would, rightfully, belong to the company, hey? I never pursued the matter. I suppose I assumed it was only a rumor.

"But recently I received a rather strange letter. A letter from Charles." Winston paused and studied Edward's reaction. "Particularly strange since Charles is dead, wouldn't you say?"

Edward sat impassively.

Winston continued. "This letter suggested that Charles' brother Robert might be able to shed some light on things. It even implied that there were some rings that would somehow lead to the diamonds."

"I've taken the liberty of keeping tabs on the family, over the years. Just in case any diamonds should turn up unexpectedly. So it was with great disappointment that I read the letter, since I knew that Robert was dead. But you and Emma weren't."

Winston smiled. It was an ugly expression that reminded Jessica of a hyena's grin.

"And I've also developed a certain relationship to another acquaintance of yours over the years," continued Winston. "She and I share certain interests."

Edward looked puzzled, but with a growing certainty, Jessica knew what was coming.

"I believe you know someone named Liz?"

Jessica felt Edward stiffen beside her, and she squeezed his arm supportively.

Sniffing, Winston went on. "In any event, I engaged Liz in a few games—some of them at the tables. She fancies herself a great gambler—brags that she has a poker face like a brick. Turned out to be more of a head like a brick. Fortunately her body is considerably more curvaceous." Winston laughed. "Anyway, she soon owed me a considerable sum; a sum which proved bladdy impossible to collect."

Winston waved his hand abstractly. "I didn't care. I can be magnanimous. But it turned out that Liz did know about some diamond rings I was looking for. So I offered her a deal. She gets me the rings. I don't send Freddie," he nodded at the stocky man, "to visit her."

Edward cleared his throat. "How did you know where to find us?"

"We didn't. We followed you when you ditched Liz. It wasn't difficult."

Winston sat up straighter. He glanced at Freddie meaningfully, then back at Edward. Straightening his tie, he continued in an icy voice, "Now how about you telling us something? We have one of the rings here . . ." He slipped Jessica's ring out of his pocket. "Sorry about your mail box, Miss," he grinned. "You should have seen the expression on Liz's face when she showed up at the post office with the key, and there was no door to put it in!"

Both men laughed, then his eyes turned hard again. "Now tell us: why Scotland, hey? And what's with the rings? What do they tell you?"

"I'm not telling you anything," snapped Edward. "You're so smart, figure it out for yourselves."

The two men looked at each other. Winston nodded at Freddie.

Freddie opened his mouth to speak when the conductor opened the door, asking for tickets.

Edward grabbed Jessica's hand and pushed his way to the door, bowling the ticket collector over in the process. The man fell heavily onto the two South Africans.

"Sorry, wrong carriage," blurted Edward, "Bye, now."

They ran down the aisle and into the next car, leaving the two men trying to push past the frustrated ticket collector.

Many of the compartments were empty, but they all had glass doors, and there was no place to hide. Crossing between carriages Edwards contemplated trying to climb outside the train, but quickly discarded the idea as something that only worked in the movies.

As they crossed into the third carriage, the configuration of the compartments changed, and they realized that they had passed into a sleeper. These compartments had heavier, locking doors, with curtains at the windows. The first two doors they tried were locked, but the third slid open to reveal a dimly lit interior with a small convertible bunk on one side, and a chair and table on the other. Most important, it was unoccupied. Edward pulled Jessica into the compartment, quickly slid the door shut, and locked it. Then he carefully checked the door's curtain to make sure there were no gaps or cracks.

Jessica plopped down on the bunk, breathing hard, more from excitement than exertion.

They heard a commotion outside, slowly moving down the aisle. Their door rattled and they held their breaths, waiting. Then the noise passed their compartment and continued on.

Jessica let out a sigh of relief and slumped back against the back of the bunk. "That was too close. How are we going to get off without them seeing us?" she asked quietly.

"We don't. We stay on until we reach Edinburgh. We just don't leave this compartment." He sat on the bunk beside her and put his arm around her shoulders, comforting her. "As soon as we hit Waverley Station, we bolt for a taxi. Then just get lost somewhere in Edinburgh.

Once we're sure we're not being followed, we head out into the countryside. OK?"

As Jessica caught her breath, she tried to collect herself. But how could she? Pursued by madmen, hiding with an ex-lover on a train somewhere in Scotland, searching for diamonds? It's a nightmare, she thought. I'm bound to wake up.

But somehow, she knew she wouldn't.

Edward filled the time by bringing Jessica up to date on Sarah, what they had been doing, how school was going, and so on.

"Last year, on sports day, they had a father and daughter three-legged race."

"You didn't!" she uttered in disbelief.

"You better believe it. And better yet, we won. Sarah was so thrilled. You'd think we had won the crown jewels the way she carried on."

He smiled, lost in the memory. Sarah had been a lifesaver for him, after Jessica left. He'd almost lost her, too, in his remorse. But the past several years had drawn them closer than ever, and he found himself thinking of her often whenever they were apart.

Jessica smiled. "Well, I can honestly say I didn't think you had it in you. I thought you were too . . ." She hesitated.

"Staid? Yes, well, I've loosened up quite a lot, since you knew me before. In a strange way, this downturn in my affairs seems to have strengthened our relationship. I suppose I decided that if I could no longer give Sarah everything she wanted financially, I'd have to make up for it by giving of myself." He was thoughtful for a moment. "It seems that that was what she really wanted, all along. Anyway, in an odd way it's been great."

Jessica was quiet, thinking that *she* was more at ease with him now, too. She frowned as thoughts of the last night came pushing into her mind. Perhaps she'd been *too* at ease.

Edward tried several times to get the conversation restarted, but eventually gave up in the face of her pensive silence.

They arrived at Waverley Station late in the afternoon.

The trip had seemed interminable to Jessica. Not because she didn't enjoy Edward's company, but because she did.

Being in the confines of the rail carriage with Edward so close was difficult. She was still angry with herself, and him for that matter, for making love the night before. She knew that given the opportunity, they would probably do it again, and she was determined not to let that to happen.

Waiting in the compartment they had commandeered, they peered out the window looking for their pursuers. Loudspeakers announced that the train they were on was doing a turn around back to London.

Waverley Station was smaller than Waterloo, with a more provincial feel to it. There was a lull in the early afternoon traffic, with only a few stragglers making their way back from a late lunch to their offices around the station.

Just outside their compartment, a large woman with two children dressed in school uniforms waited by a bench that was piled high with luggage. Farther down the platform a short, fat man in a white suit was trolling up and down nervously followed by a small terrier. Edward pressed the side of his face against the window and craned his neck to see as far down the length of the train as possible.

"There," said Edward, pointing to the two men, who were questioning a porter.

"What are they doing?" she whispered, peering from behind the curtain.

"Trying to figure out where we've got to, I imagine. They know we'll get dragged all the way back to London if we stay on this train.

The men walked quickly up to the next platform, and boarded a train headed for the next stop on the line, presumably to search it.

"Now's our chance. Come on." Edward led her to the outer door of the carriage, the one leading away from the platform. "Where are you going?" she asked, "We can't get out on that side."

"Want to bet on that?" he replied, pushing open the door. "Come on."

He hopped out and turned to help Jessica down onto the train tracks, then pointed to the other side of the rails. There was a small service road leading away from the station. At the far end of it was a gate, leading out onto a busy street.

A dozen sets of tracks separated them from the gate, some angling together, but most running parallel for the length of the station. They picked their way through the rails, watching for oncoming trains.

Far down the tracks, a large locomotive approached, dragging another commuter train in the opposite direction. A brilliant light glared at them from its headlight as it lumbered into the station; it was moving fairly slowly, so they shouldn't have any trouble getting out of its way.

The train from which they had alighted covered their escape fairly well, but as they crossed the last rail, they heard a yell, and looked over at the platform. Winston and Freddie were peering beneath one of the carriages. As Edward and Jessica caught sight of them, the men rose and headed for the gap between the carriages.

"Come on!" shouted Edward, grabbing her hand and pulling her across the last tracks. He urged Jessica onto the service road. Glancing back, he saw their pursuers pull up short; with a clatter and a loud blast of the air horn, the oncoming train swept in front of them, and they were forced to take a step backward. Jessica caught a glimpse of their angry glares before the massive locomotive cut them off.

They dashed towards the gate that sealed the service road off from the main thoroughfare. Of course, it was locked. Edward clambered up to the top and straddled the gate, then leaned down and grabbed Jessica's outstretched hands. He yanked her to the top, and they climbed down onto the footpath on the other side. Running down the street, Jessica spied a bus pulling away.

That's two 'Hail Marys' I owe the god of buses, she mused, marveling at their luck as she whistled the driver to stop. In a matter of moments, they were safely on board, looking out the rear window at their two pursuers, coming to a halt at the gate.

"Whew," she puffed, "we made it." Sitting back on the seat, she felt exhilarated, almost giddy. "Just think," she added, with a smile, "a week ago I was sitting by my fire, sipping sherry and reading a good book. Now I'm running for my life from diamond mobsters. At least life with you isn't boring, Edward."

Her relieved smile dissolved as she saw how pale Edward's skin was, and that his hands were shaking.

"You look awful, are you alright?" she asked him.

"I guess I wasn't ready for the secret agent bit, just yet," he grinned sheepishly. "Still a bit sore from my encounter with the Ex."

The bus turned onto Princes Street—a major thoroughfare lined with historic-looking buildings on both sides. The weathered stone facades bore the modern trappings of society, though: fluorescent advertisements, neon signs, and colorful pictures of merchandise dotted every surface. Soon enough the bus turned off of the main street, and began to wind its way through a less congested part of town.

The architect in Jessica was fascinated by the buildings of Edinburgh. They clustered together in crazy conglomerations of old and new. As the bus made its way through the tangled streets, several times she was sure they had turned around completely and were headed back in the direction from which they came. But finally the bus arrived at the central bus station. There, they transferred to a rural bus that would take them out of the city and to the small village that was near the Drummond ancestral home.

The second bus was less comfortable than the first. It trundled along the outskirts of the city for a time, then headed out across the moor. A man in the seat opposite them looked as if he had chicken feathers stuck to his coat. But he smiled at them amiably, and cursed the bumps in his thick Scottish brogue.

"How long?" asked Jessica, as she bounced alongside of Edward.

"About half an hour. I think this is the same bus I used to take when I was a child."

"Mmm, I don't doubt it," she muttered.

Edward laughed. "I meant the same line."

In a half hour they came upon a small village, its main street only a few blocks long. The bus dropped them off in the center of town, next to a bakery, a general store, and a small hotel.

In the store they bought two replacement suitcases and a few clothes and toiletries. Jessica was grateful that she'd hung onto her purse through their mad dash down the train, and during the ensuing chase.

Outside the hotel there was a lone taxicab waiting hopefully for fares. Edward bent and spoke to the driver through the open window for a few moments, then motioned for Jessica to join him. He opened the door for her and she climbed in, then slid across to make room for Edward.

As the driver pulled the cab away from the curb, they passed another cab that was slowly moving in the opposite direction. For a moment Jessica thought she recognized one of the men from the train sitting in the back seat, but after a second glance she decided that she was wrong. Nerves. Anyway, they were past them before she had a chance to point him out to Edward.

The cab passed under an old stone railway bridge and again they found themselves in open country.

Jessica marveled at the scenery. Dull green bushes lined the narrow road as they trundled over the small rises and dips of the moor. She caught occasional glimpses of a farmhouse in the distance. Tumbled down stone walls periodically separated the fields. Once they passed the ruins of a large stone castle, and Jessica commented, "That's not yours, I hope."

Edward smiled. "No. The Drummonds don't go back quite that far. Drummond Castle is really more of a manor house than a castle. True, most of it's stone, but it wasn't constructed until the mid-1800's, and hasn't a very colorful history, from all I've heard. It was build by my great-grandfather, as a sort of summer retreat, I'm told. He was a Londoner—Drummond's not a Scottish name, of course—and wanted a place to get away from the soot and bustle of the city. When the rail first came through, this was the end of the line—as far as he could get from the big city—expeditiously, anyway. He kept a stable in the village so they could take a horse and carriage the rest of the way, and also for his frequent trips to town. He was quite the pub-hopper, from the stories I've heard."

The cab driver had been fiddling with the radio almost continuously since they boarded, but as civilization receded behind them, the reception faded, and he finally gave it up and switched off. He'd only been half-listening to their conversation, but now chimed in. "Yer friends wi' Harry, then? Mr. MacGregor, I mean."

"In a way," called Edward. "I knew him when I was a lad."

"Harry an' oy, we do our drinkin' t'gether, most Fridays, down at the King's Crown. I don't recall him mentionin' any out-o'-town kin, though."

"Not kin, no," replied Edward. "My family used to spend the summers here, when I was a lad. I'm Edward Drummond."

"Aye?" the cab driver replied, questioningly, turning around in his seat, then turning back quickly to keep the cab on the narrow, rutted road. "I been cabbin' for 'most twenty years, an' never yet hearrd o' no Drrummond comin' to Drrummond Castle." he said, rolling his 'R's. "Why, just last month Harry was sayin' as what a shame it was, all that money spent keepin' the place up, an' not a sign of visitors, not even a wee one." He paused a moment, contemplating the stir the news would make in the village. "Ye be thinking of movin' back in then?"

"No," Edward grinned, glancing at Jessica. "Not moving, just visiting."

"My, my, won't ol' Harry be surprised," mused the cabbie.

"I hope not," said Edward. "Our friend was to call ahead and warn him of our arrival. We wanted to make sure things were . . . livable."

"Oh, no cause for alarum there," assured the cabbie. It may've been a long time since someone's been 'ere. But ye'll find that Mr. MacGregor has kept the wee place looking right grand inside. Takes pride in it, he does."

In another ten minutes the cab slowed, then turned onto an even smaller road, winding its way slowly between bushes that scraped first one side, then the other. Coming over a small rise, they passed a stone stable building and drove through an opening in an ancient looking stone wall, passing under wrought ironwork bearing a large, ornate letter "E". The next dip in the road took them across a narrow stone bridge that spanned a small creek. Then they climbed steeply up the hill, which was terraced and planted with rows of ornamental bushes, some of which had been sculpted into the shape of indeterminate animals, but most of which were twisted and gnarled by the harsh winds of the moor.

Cresting another rise, the main building came into view. It is more of a manor house than a castle, thought Jessica, admiring the handsome structure. A sturdy foundation of rough hewn stone delineated the boundaries of the building, which appeared to be largely rectangular, but probably had wings extending to the rear. The front face of the building was at least 100 feet wide, with several stone steps leading up to the central entrance. On either side of the door, lining all three floors of the structure from one end of the building to the other were thousands of panes of leaded glass, set into a hundred tall narrow windows. The sun was low in the western sky behind them, and as the cab pulled up in front of the manor, the sunlight was reflected in a thousand separate panes, casting a warm, golden glow across the forecourt.

Jessica smiled at the thought of this massive structure being a summer retreat. But with all that glass, she could see that the house would be nearly impossible to warm in the winter. Excitedly she twined her fingers in Edward's as the cab came to a stop. He paid the driver and then helped her out.

Standing beside Edward in the gathering twilight, they quietly admired the structure. Sounds of the cab receded in the distance as Jessica sighed, "It's beautiful, Edward."

"It is handsomer than I remembered," he acknowledged.

They started up the front steps just as the front door opened, and a smiling old man dressed in classic Scottish attire emerged.

"Eddie boy!" exclaimed Mr. MacGregor.

Edward reached out to take Mr. MacGregor's hand, but the old man stepped past his outstretched arm, and clasped him around the middle in a bear hug.

"It's grand to see you," enthused the Scotsman as he rocked Edward to and fro.

Jessica struggled to contain her giggles as she watched Edward's face turn a bright scarlet. "It's good to see you, too, Mac," smiled Edward.

Mr. MacGregor was short and wiry, barely coming to Edward's chest. His kilt was a colorful plaid, green predominating over blue, and he wore a white shirt with a ruffle at the neck and puffy sleeves. A cap perched jauntily atop his head, its plaid matching that of his kilt. Hand covering her mouth, Jessica watched Edward's face take on a mixture of amusement and sheepishness.

The old man took a step back, and held Edward by the shoulders at arms' length to examine him. "A right big lad, ye've grown into," marveled the Scotsman, giving Edward's cheek a pinch. His accent was thick, his R's rolled as if his tongue was reluctant to let go of them.

Seeming to notice Jessica for the first time, Mr. MacGregor released his hold on Edward and turned to her, smiling, still speaking to Edward. "And who's this right pretty young lass, Eddie boy?"

"Jessica, I'd like you to meet Mac. Mac, this is Jessica Farrell," said Edward formally.

"A pleasure, miss," said Mac, bowing to her. She offered her hand, but was surprised when Mr. MacGregor took it in his and raised it to his lips, giving her a wink at the same time. Jessica immediately felt affection for the kindly old man. His eyes hid nothing, and she felt the sincerity of his welcome.

Straightening himself, he took on an air of efficiency as he gathered up their suitcase with practiced ease and turned to march into the house. "Come, Eddie, Miss Jessica, let's get you settled. I'm sure you'll want to look around a bit before dinner, reacquaint yourself with the grounds, show the lass around."

"'Eddie boy?'" Jessica whispered in Edward's direction. She raised one eyebrow.

Edward grinned and motioned for Jessica to proceed.

She caught her breath as she stepped over the threshold behind Mr. MacGregor. If the castle had seemed as if it was all windows from the outside, the effect was even more pronounced on the inside. The last rays of the setting sun refracted through the leaded glass, scattering thousands of tiny rainbows across the wooden paneling of the entry hall. A massive oak staircase led up to a central landing, where it split into two smaller staircases on either side, backtracking on itself to what she assumed must be a second landing directly above their heads, across the front of the house. Indeed, as they ascended, she had a commanding view of the entire three-story space that was the front hall. The second floor landing was, in fact, the middle section of the second floor hall, which ran the length of the manor, with a dozen doors opening off of either side. Mr. MacGregor continued on up to the third floor landing, then paused to allow them to take in the magnificent view. This landing was the central part of the third floor hall. Like its downstairs cousin, it ran the length of the manor, but unlike the second floor hall, it ran along the front of the manor, making one side of it entirely glass panes, from floor to ceiling, and end to end. The three of them stood in silence, watching the last sliver of the orange globe of the sun slip behind the hills of the moor, turning the clouds above first red, then deep lavender.

"That is probably the most beautiful sight I have ever seen," whispered Jessica. Edward seemed somewhat awed, as well. He sighed, and turned to her, smiling. She felt a momentary urge to fall into Edward's arms, and Edward seemed to sense it too. Quickly she pulled back from him, and turned her attention back to Mr. MacGregor. She found him watching them with a twinkle in his eye. He grinned at them, then turned to the right and started down the hall. "Ordered that sunset up special, I did. Hope it was satisfactory?" he laughed.

Edward and Jessica followed Mr. MacGregor to the second door off of the hall. He opened it and stood back for them to enter.

"Mr. Montague wasn't specific about the sleeping arrangements. I've taken the liberty of preparing two guest rooms . . ." he let the sentence trail off.

"Well—" began Edward, but Jessica interrupted.

"Two rooms would be wonderful, if it's not too much trouble."

Mr. MacGregor smiled and continued in a breezy voice. "Of course not, miss. Drummond Castle has no shortage of space, these days!" He eyed Edward meaningfully. "'Tis been ages since we've had a visit from the family. Still, I do me best to keep her looking top notch."

He set down Edward's bag, then ushered Jessica back out into the hall. "If ye'll follow me, miss, I think you'll find the room next door to your liking."

She smiled at the man gratefully, and he beamed back. She liked Mr. MacGregor. He didn't seem to be judging her, like all of Edward's other servants had.

While Mr. MacGregor placed her things on the bench at the foot of the bed, Jessica surveyed the room. She'd expected the castle to be a dusty old relic, but this room was anything but. The walls were covered with delicate yellow wallpaper that gave it a cheerful aspect. Freshly polished wood gleamed from the surfaces of the nightstands and dresser. On either side of the bed, large leaded glass windows opened out onto the rear courtyard of the house, two stories below.

There was an overstuffed easy chair, and a tall maple armoire against one wall. On the opposite wall a side door led to a marble bathroom shared with the adjacent room. A floral spread covered the four-poster bed, which was so high Jessica suspected she'd have to jump into it.

Mac busied himself with the fireplace for a few minutes while Jessica drifted about the room, tracing her fingers along the edges of the ornate furniture, fingering the lace doilies covering their tops.

Mac's voice interrupted her reverie. "If there's nothing else, miss, I'll get the other fires started?"

"No, nothing else," said Jessica, absently. She smiled at the old caretaker. "Thank you . . . Mr. MacGregor."

The old man nodded. "Very good, miss," he said. "I'll be in the kitchen if you need anything."

She sat on the bed, surveying the room. It was impressive, to say the least. She got up and wandered over to the fireplace, basking in its cozy warmth. Peeking into the bathroom, she gave a low whistle. The gentry of Scotland knew how to live well. It was beautiful, with a deep green marble bath almost big enough for two.

Scolding herself at that thought, Jessica walked back into the bedroom. But her thoughts kept wandering back to Edward.

What would it be like to live here, with him? With no overbearing servants, no whispering neighbors? Listening to the sounds of family life echoing through the manor . . . Quiet walks over the moor in the evening, hand in hand with Edward . . . The enormous tub, overflowing with bubble bath, the two of them entwined . . .

You're doing it again, Farrell! Cut it out. Thinking along those lines is dangerous. You'll be in bed with him before the night is through at this rate.

She shook herself out of her reverie, picked up her bag, and sorted through the things she had bought. She'd have a bath, and a change of clothes before going back downstairs. It would give her a chance to get her thoughts straight. She needed to get her thoughts straight.

Chapter 7

The teakettle was just beginning to whistle when she entered the kitchen. It was a large, cheerful room, centered along the rear wall of the manor. There was a black and white checkered floor that gleamed in the light from a large fireplace at one end of the room. Floor to ceiling cupboards, some with glass fronts, lined one entire wall. A wood burning stove and large double sink occupied the outside wall, next to an exterior door. Through the large window above the sink, Jessica could make out the two rear wings of the manor, which protected a small courtyard outside the kitchen door.

Edward was seated at the table, and smiled at her when she looked his way.

Mr. MacGregor rose from the kitchen table and moved the kettle onto the warmer. "You're just in time for a cup of tea," he smiled. "And I must be getting back to me cottage. I've cat's who'll be wanting their supper." He poured them each a cup of tea, and set them on the table, arranging milk and sugar nearby. "Speaking of supper, I'm sorry I've not had a chance to lay in more extensive supplies. Tomorrow I will go into town and properly provision things. In the meantime, I've brought over a few things from the cottage to tide ye over—milk and eggs, and such. I hope they'll suffice?"

"They will be just wonderful, Mr. MacGregor," smiled Jessica.

Mr. MacGregor nodded, and smiled back. "Ye'd best be calling me 'Mac'. Everyone does. We're not so formal in these parts," he added, donning his cap and opening the back door. "If ye need anything, there's a buzzer by the telephone."

"We'll be fine," assured Jessica. "And thank you. Thank you for everything. Mac."

Mr. MacGregor nodded, then turned and stepped out, quietly closing the door behind him.

"What a nice man," mused Jessica, and Edward smiled.

"Mac spent about as much time raising me as my own parents. I spent every summer here, when I was a lad."

"A 'lad', eh? I think this Scottish accent is infectious."

Edward grinned, as they began to search through the pantries for some supper. Jessica scrambled some eggs while he set about making some toast.

"Tell me," she said, as she stirred the eggs on the stove, "Why didn't you sell this place, being short on money and everything?"

"This place," he said, gesturing with his hand, "doesn't belong to just me. It's divided up between my sister and me, now. It was done that way so that it wouldn't leave the family. So none of us could sell it, even if we wanted to. A trust fund pays for the upkeep—such as it is. It's mostly just Mac who keeps it up. Far too much for one person to handle, but he's worked hard to make this visit special."

He was thoughtful for a minute. "I'd forgotten how happy I always was whenever I was here. It is nice, to have an old castle in the family. It goes back a long way. Not so long for some, I suppose, but it makes me feel—connected, somehow, with the past."

Jessica smiled at him. It seemed a happy place to her, as well.

After supper they sat sipping their tea, while Edward examined the jeweler's appraisal form, and the three rings.

Inside each ring, the band was engraved with a series of numbers and letters. They read:

3 L13 L15

1 L4 L18

2 R21 R13

Edward was thoughtful for a moment. "You know, I've been thinking in terms of the treasure being hidden inside the castle," he mused. "But now that I think about it, I wonder if it's not just as likely that it's outside—perhaps somewhere nearby. I wonder if these could be measurements of some kind?"

Jessica got up and went to his side, leaning over the paper.

"I suppose that it could mean to go left, or right. But in which order? And how far? Paces, feet, yards, what?"

"Yes, and whatever it is, where is the starting point?"

"Your uncle didn't leave any indication of where that would be?"

He shook his head.

"No, but we have to sort this out quickly. Liz must be on her way by now. If she's not already in Edinburgh, she soon will be. And let's not forget our South African friend and his *assistant*."

"They wouldn't be here somewhere would they?" she asked, glancing around fearfully.

He shook his head. "I doubt it. Those thugs didn't know where to go. And as for my ex-wife, well, hopefully she has tripped herself up. No, I doubt they could be here yet."

Jessica turned her attention back to the drawings of the engraving in the rings. She always loved puzzles. As a child she thrived on mazes, cryptograms, anything with a secret. This could be fun.

"Why don't we start at the front door?" she began enthusiastically. "Then—"

"Whoa," laughed Edward. "I think it's a bit late for treasure hunting tonight. If it's outside, we won't be able to see a thing. It's black out there on the moor," he added, glancing at the dark square of the window.

"Besides," he added, rising. "I had other plans for this evening . . ."

"Oh, me too," Jessica said, quickly pushing her chair back. "I've been looking forward to a good night's sleep." As she turned and headed for her room she could feel his gaze upon her, following her up the stairs.

Contrary to her expectations, she did sleep well. She awakened to the gentle warmth of the morning sun streaming through the windowpanes of her room. Jessica yawned and stretched, relishing the luxurious comfort of the huge four-poster bed, and lay for a moment watching the sunlight dancing along the walls. She stretched out her arm and for just a moment wondered what it would be like to wake up next to Edward.

She shook that thought from her head and quickly arose, shivering as her feet touched the cold floor. After a short shower, she dressed and made her way down stairs. Stopping outside the door of the kitchen she grinned, as she listened to Mac telling Edward about the benefits of a good breakfast, almost as if no time had gone by since he was a boy.

"Morning," she said cheerily, as she opened the door and stepped into the warmth of the kitchen.

"Morning Miss, you're looking lovely this mornin'."

She blushed and looked at Edward, who was sitting at the table, teacup in hand smiling blissfully.

"Thank you Mac, and how are you today?"

"Aye well, as good as you kin expect of an old gentleman like myself. Sit down here Miss, next to our Eddie, and have a nice cup of tea."

She did as she was told, as Mac bustled around making her tea.

Turning to Edward she murmured, "and how are you this morning?"

"I'll let you know in an hour or two, if we've found the diamonds." he replied quietly. Then, thoughtfully, he murmured, "I missed you last night, Jessie."

Ignoring the comment, she turned to Mr. MacGregor and asked, "What's for breakfast, Mac? I'm starving."

"There be porridge on the stove there miss, and the bacon and eggs are keeping warm in yonder oven. Eddie my boy, I'm havin' to go and do some errands in the village. Need a bit of food for the kitchen here, and some rat poison. Heard them yesterday I did, afore you came, scrabbling away in the basement. Which reminds me, if'n you need to go down there at all, be a mite careful. The cellar steps are rotted through in patches. I caution you to tread lightly."

"We will Mac, and thank you for the lovely breakfast," replied Edward.

"No need to be thanking me. It be a real pleasure to see you again, Eddie boy, and to meet you, Miss Jessie. It gets lonely here, and the visitors are few and far between. Now I will be back a little later."

Leaving the two of them to dish up their breakfast, Mac left to run errands in the village.

"Well," said Jessica. "I'll be mother, you sit there."

She got up from the table and dished out the porridge, then, placing a large plateful of bacon and eggs in the middle of the table, sat down opposite him and began to eat.

Edward took the appraisal form out of his pocket and laid it flat on the table in front of him.

"The way I see it," he said, gesturing with his spoon, "These numbers, at the beginning, I think they are the numbers of the rings."

"What do you mean?" she asked.

Taking another mouthful of breakfast, Edward then sat the spoon into the bowl and tried to explain his theory.

"I've been thinking about this. My ring had a number three on it, Emma's was number two and my father's was number one. What if . . . what if those numbers indicate the order in which the rings are to be used? See here?" He pointed to the form.

3 L13 L15

1 L4 L18

2 R21 R13

"You mean that perhaps we should not be looking at each ring individually?"

"That's just the sort of thing my Uncle Charles would do. Make things as difficult as possible. If that's true, then the first thing we should look for is. . . . L4, R21, L13."

"Oh I see. Well let's finish this off and get cracking then."

They hurriedly finished off their morning meal, and cleared everything away.

"Let's go," he said purposefully.

Standing at the front door a few moments later they again pondered over the engravings.

"If our theory is correct, then we should go left four paces."

They looked left, and found that the wall was only a short distance away.

"Come on, let's try this outside.

Grabbing their coats off the coat rack, they opened the large front door and stepped out into a sunny, but cold Scottish morning.

Their breath came out in puffs of white, and their feet crunched on a light layer of newly fallen snow.

Left four paces took them to nowhere in particular. They turned right and walked forward twenty-one paces.

"OK, now left thirteen," she shivered.

Thirteen paces later, through the small overgrown garden, across a cobblestone path and into a fishpond, they stopped. Bushes had concealed the fishpond, and they had both inadvertently stepped onto the thin ice covering it. It had, of course, broken, and now their shoes were sopping up the icy cold water.

"Somehow, I don't think he would have put anything here, but we had better check," Edward sighed.

Shivering, they both stepped out of the pond, and using sticks broke the remainder of the ice away.

After feeling around for a few minutes they gave up. Jessica straightened up and looked around. They were in a garden, which would, in spring be beautiful. The garden was arranged in rows, covering a semi circle around a gazebo in the center.

"You know, she said, "these gardens are really quite beautiful. That Gazebo over there would be perfect for summer picnics."

"It was—is," he corrected himself. "Every time we came here, Emma and I used to have our picnic lunch right there in the Gazebo. In the spring and summer it's covered with beautiful, sweet smelling ivy. And on the tree over there," he pointed across the lawn, "we used to have a tire swing on a rope. A bit lower class for my father, but my uncle put it up for us. We loved it." He smiled, reminiscing. It seemed so long ago, yet the smells of the garden brought it all back to him vividly, and he saw a woman pushing a young girl in the swing. But in his mind, the young girl was Sarah, and the woman behind the swing—

Well, no use pursuing that line of thought at present. He turned to Jessica and said, "Come on. We'd better go change our shoes and socks. Should have thought to put wellies on."

She nodded. Together they sloshed back to the front door of the mansion.

Later they sat by the fire in the great room, warming their toes, discussing their next option.

"Edward," she said quietly, staring into the fire.

"Mmm?"

"About the other night . . ."

"Yes, Jessie."

"I just want to say that I'm sorry I let you . . . Well, you know."

Edward looked at her for a long time. At last he swallowed, and said, "Of course." There was an air of resignation in his voice. He was quiet for a moment, then softly he said, "There is one thing I would like to know though."

"What's that?" she asked. Her voice caught, and she had to clear her throat.

"Is it Jack?"

Before she could reply, Edward held up his hand to stop her, and continued, almost apologetically, "He seems a very nice chap, and is obviously fond of you. He made that pretty obvious."

"I *thought* something was going on in the kitchen. Jack is . . . well, he and I are very good friends. In other circumstances it could be more."

"Other circumstances?"

Jessica ignored the question.

"We were never lovers . . . It was my fault. Jack is a good friend, that's all. And I hope that he finds happiness with someone."

Edward contemplated her for a moment, then nodded. "I have a feeling that he may already have his eye on someone . . ."

Jessica's eyes widened. "Emma?"

Edward nodded. "Did you see the way he looked at her in hospital?"

"You may be right," she said quickly. "But Jack is like that with everyone he meets, very caring." Why did she sound so defensive? Who was she trying to convince, anyway?

But Jessica felt as if a door had closed. Stop that, she thought. You should be happy for him. Besides, the man beside you is all you ever wanted, face it Farrell.

She sat quietly for a while, immersed in thought. She saw Edward rise from his chair, and as she stood to join him their eyes met. Why didn't he say something? Maybe it had all been said now. Maybe it was too late, after all.

Edward turned away from her. "Let's get on with the search then, shall we?"

Jessica nodded, then realized that he was no longer looking at her. "Where do we start this time?" she asked.

"The library. He spent a lot of time in there."

The library was impressive. A huge desk took center stage, its intricate carvings woven down the legs. The overstuffed chair looked worn and out of place, and was obviously well loved. The walls were lined with shelves, each one full of books. Jessica pulled one out, and exclaimed in pleasure.

"This book was published in 1843. All of these books look ancient."

"They are. My uncle prided himself on his book collection. He would spend literally hours in here, going over his books, cataloging them. We were not allowed in here. It was his domain when he was staying here. There is a book in here somewhere," he laughed, indicating the dusty shelves, "that has a list of all his books, their authors, and what he thought of them, as I am sure he read them all."

It was good to be getting on with things. The tension eased a little, and they were able to get on with the task at hand without too much awkwardness.

They began to search for a place to start. Upon choosing the desk, they checked the numbers.

"Let's see now, left four," they paced, "right twenty-one," they came up against the wall.

"It wouldn't be behind any of the books would it?" she asked.

"God, I hope not. It would take us years to sort through this lot."

"Mm, well try from the door, maybe leading out of the library," suggested Jessica.

This time their pacing took them to the stairs.

"Well," said Edward, standing in the hall, "that's no good. You know I have been thinking, maybe it's not paces, maybe it's something else. I mean, I can't think of any room in the house, or anywhere outside that would fit into these paces."

"Unless we are wrong about how the engravings work."

"No, I don't think so. You see he was adamant that all three were needed at the same time to find the diamonds. He made it quite clear before he died that we would need to combine them all to solve the puzzle."

They sat on the steps, stumped.

"Let's just explore the house, all those little nooks and crannies that may hold a clue. Let's try the attic first. Come on."

She raced up the stairs, Edward close behind her, laughing.

The attic was huge and dusty. Cobwebs hung down from the angled ceiling—the sun's rays shining through the skylight shimmered on the strands. It was still dim however, so Edward felt around for the cord to switch on the solitary bulb suspended from a beam. The artificial light cast an eerie glow in the room, bringing to light countless cardboard boxes and wooden crates, scattered around the dusty floor. First they checked the walls, hoping to find a hidden door, or something similar, but it was to no avail. They then turned their attention to the contents of the attic.

"Oh no," cried Jessica in mock horror. "Where do we start?"

"We can ignore these boxes, most of them are mine and Emma's. I had them moved here when I sold the estate. Over there in the corner is what we're after."

He pointed to several old chests in the corner.

"Marvelous, I love old things," Jessica exclaimed, as she quickly dodged her way through the boxes to the far corner of the attic.

One by one they sorted through the chests, looking for clues, checking every item.

"Hey, look at this," cried Edward, holding up a very old porcelain doll. "They don't make them like this, anymore. I should take it home to Sarah."

Jessica examined it. "It's still beautiful, just needs cleaning up a bit."

Edward looked at the doll and nodded. "It's perfect. She's just mad about dolls."

Carefully, they put the doll aside and opened the last chest. It was full of ladies dresses. Jessica pulled out the one on top. It was a light powder blue satin, with a lace bodice and dropped lace sleeves. A deep blue velvet ribbon was interwoven through the bodice, making a delightful contrast to the rest of the gown.

"This is gorgeous," she breathed.

Edward looked up from the chest. Jessica was holding the blue satin dress against her chest. The lace bodice lay against the creamy skin of her neck, and the blue satin ribbons followed the curve of her breasts. Edward felt his heart skip as he watched her. In the warm glow of sunlight from the dormer windows she looked like the woman in the picture downstairs. His voice caught as he softly said, "Take it, Jessie."

"No." she looked up at him. "I couldn't." The last time she had accepted a gift from him, it had all turned out so horribly. She thought of the ring, and that day on the train, as she left Paris.

"Go on. It was Margaret's—Charles' wife. It's just gathering dust up here. You may as well take it. If it doesn't fit, perhaps you can have it altered."

She didn't need any more encouragement. Carefully she folded the dress and set it near the doll.

They spent several more hours wandering the large mansion. The master bedroom seemed to hold some possibilities. The dressing room off to one side was full of hidden cupboards. The shelves were lined with red velvet and embossed with gold braid. Nothing of importance was found however, and they moved on. In the nursery, Jessica exclaimed over the rocking horse, and the dolls' house resting in the corner of the room.

As they were leaving the nursery Jessica asked, "Why are there bars on the windows?"

"Just a precaution," smiled Edward. "You didn't know Emma and me when we were little. They put them up after they caught us trying to climb down the trellis one afternoon while Nanny wasn't watching."

Jessica walked to the window and contemplated the two-story drop to the courtyard, then looked at Edward and cocked one eyebrow. "A bit reckless in your youth, were you?" she teased.

Edward burst out laughing. "The worst of it was, we were trying to carry the rocking horse down, at the time!"

After another hour of futile searching, the two went back downstairs and sat together on a beautifully carved divan, resting in the great room.

"Well, what now?" she asked, as she gazed at a painting on the opposite wall.

"God knows. I don't."

"Who is that in the painting? The child looks a little like Sarah."

"She does, now that you mention it. The woman was Charles' wife, Margaret. The little girl was their daughter. My uncle painted the picture himself, from memory, after they died in an automobile accident. She was wearing that dress when she died, I was told. He always said that the green in the dress matched her eyes, and made them sparkle all the more. The brooch she is wearing was made from the first diamond he ever found. Gone now, of course, to pay Liz's debts."

Jessica shook her head sadly. "What was the child's name?"

"Lilly. She was only eight."

The child in the painting was holding a children's book. The characters on the page seemed to leap out at the viewer.

In fact, thought Jessica, the whole book seems to leap out of the painting.

She got up from the seat and walked over to the painting. Reaching up, she lightly ran her fingers over the book.

The cover moved.

"Edward, come here, look at this." she cried excitedly.

He came over, and watched as she again touched the book in the painting. The cover moved again.

"Try lifting it."

The front cover of the book did indeed lift up completely, as a real book would.

"Would you look at that. It's a poem of some kind."

They both stared at the poem. It seemed to have nothing to do with the painting or the book the child was holding, and everything to do with what they were looking for.

To find what's hidden, a path to make,
As black as coal, the trail to take.
Daughter and wife, rings' secret keep,
'Neath diamond's mother, safe and deep.

"It's about the rings!" exclaimed Jessica. "What could it mean though? A keep . . . that's some part of a castle, isn't it?"

Edward nodded. "Yes. But this house certainly doesn't have one. I don't think that's it, though. It sounds like it's buried somewhere . . . or underneath something. Diamond's mother?" He raised his eyebrows and looked querulously at Jessica.

There was a pause. Then, simultaneously, a flash of insight lit up both their faces.

"Coal!" they said together.

"Diamond's mother is coal," continued Jessica. "Carbon before it's heated under pressure. Does this house have a coal cellar?"

Edward snapped his fingers. "The cellar. It must be in the cellar."

"What are we waiting for?" asked Jessica, closing the book. When she turned around, Edward was already halfway down the hall.

The door to the cellar was locked. Pausing a moment in thought,

Edward reached to the top of the door jam and ran his fingers along the edge of the wooden molding. Dust motes floated in the shafts of sunlight filtering in from the front hall and the detritus of many years cascaded off of the molding and over the two of them. Waving her hand in front of her face and coughing, Jessica watched as Edward triumphantly produced the key and held it up between them.

"It seems strange, knowing my way around a place I haven't been in 20 years," remarked Edward.

He inserted the key in the cellar door and turned it until he heard the latch drop out. Carefully turning the handle, he eased the door open. The cobwebs clinging to the edge stretched, then snapped and settled to the jam as he opened the door onto the blackness below.

The cellar seemed like a black hole, absorbing not only light but also sound, as they stood there peering down into the darkness.

"There's a light, I trust?" asked Jessica.

Edward reached in around the door jam and she heard a switch click. Nothing happened.

"Well, there was," said Edward.

He retreated into the kitchen and Jessica heard rummaging sounds from down the hall as he opened and closed several drawers, rearranging their contents.

A moment later he returned carrying a pocket torch, its bulb glowing dimly in the sunlight of the short hall.

Edward stepped experimentally onto the first step of the cellar stairs and heard it groan beneath his weight.

"Best stay to the edge of these, I think," warned Edward, "And try to put some weight on the railing."

Using the torch to light their descent and to clear away the remaining cobwebs, Edward gripped the railing with his other hand and carefully moved down along the left edge of the stairs, one step at a that time. Jessica followed, eyeing the dusty railing suspiciously. When they had both safely reached the floor of the cellar, Edward stopped and cast the light of the torch's beam about, trying to orient himself and to assess their next move.

The cellar stretched away in three directions into blackness. It appeared to extend all the way to the exterior walls of the house above them. The stairs they had descended were backed by the foundation beneath the rear wall of kitchen. Along that wall, the stone blocks of the foundation were piled almost to the floor above with a crazy-quilt assortment of wooden crates, cardboard boxes, old appliances, steamer trunks, furniture, tools, building materials and hundreds of other items that Jessica couldn't identify. The collection seemed relatively free of cobwebs, but everything was covered with a quarter inch layer of fine dust.

Ahead of them Jessica could make out several of the regularly spaced stone pillars which supported the first floor of the house. Each pillar sprouted from its own sea of crates, boxes and implements. The gaps between the debris formed crooked aisles that led off into the dark distance. Jessica could see some aisles meandering into the far reaches of the cellar, while others came to abrupt and unexpected ends.

The floor of the cellar was comprised of flagstones, about one foot square, neatly seamed together to form a flat, regular surface. Here and there the layer of dust on the flagstones had been disturbed by the passing of other feet. Near the foot of the steps a cardboard box had been overturned, and a collection of still-shiny wooden toys lay scattered across the aisle.

"It looks as of someone has been here before us," said Jessica.

"Mmmm . . . or it could be the rats that Mac was talking about," suggested Edward.

"Mmm hmm," said Jessica, dubiously.

Edward played the torch beam down several of the junk-strewn aisles, peering into the distance. "It seems to me that the coal bin was down this way," he said, pointing in the direction of the left rear corner of the cellar.

Slowly he made his way down the leftmost aisle, weaving between the obstacles that jutted out onto the flagstones here and there. He stopped once to flick a cobweb from his face and blow the dangling strands away from him with a puff through his pursed lips.

Jessica watched the debris pass by as she followed him carefully. It was like passing backwards in time, through implements so long unused that even their purpose had been forgotten. She noticed an old washing tub with side-mounted rollers, its crank so thoroughly rusted that it looked like a barnacle-encrusted pier fitting. She passed a garden rake with only two feet of handle left before the splintered wood ended abruptly, where it rested against a butter churn. Near the end of the aisle they detoured around a pile of paint cans stacked like vertical bowling pins, their paper labels long since eaten off by the resident population of rodents or insects.

At the end of the aisle Jessica saw that in places the outside walls of the cellar were interrupted by alcoves that extended out from beneath the body of the house above them. In one such alcove a large rusty boiler sat unused, a casualty to the electric heating she'd seen in the remodeled areas upstairs.

Turning right, Edward followed the outside wall of the cellar to the far corner. Along the way they passed a second alcove, which held a water heater and what appeared to be a full bookcase, its shelves lined with assorted jars, each filled with a variety of nuts, bolts, screws and nails. They also passed a number of intersecting aisles that led back into the middle of the debris field.

The rectangular square of light from the open cellar door couldn't penetrate this far into the cellar. Even the light from the torch barely penetrated these darkened aisles, and Jessica shuddered at the thought of how much more junk must be piled in each of the long winding passageways.

As Jessica's eyes became accustomed to the darkness of the far recesses of the cellar she began to notice other sources of light. Cracks in the hardwood planks of the first floor above let slivers of light penetrate into the blackness, where they glinted in the cellar dust like tattered gauze.

Periodically the foundation was pierced by small, grate-covered holes, designed to let in enough air to prevent mildew and mold. The light from these grates illuminated sections of the outside aisles, in tiny, glowing squares.

A little beyond the corner, Edward stopped in front of another alcove.

Here, a one-foot high metal fence extended from the alcove out into the aisle, allowing the coal to spill out into an area from which it could easily be shoveled. Looking up, Jessica could see metal doors above the alcove, which allowed the delivery wagon to dump its load directly into the cellar.

"Under all this?" cried Jessica in exasperation. "We'll never get through all of this."

"Maybe it's just under the easy part?" suggested Edward hopefully.

It wasn't.

An hour later, hot and sweaty, Edward set the coal shovel back against the wall and sat down on a wooden crate across the aisle from the coal scuttle. The section of the scuttle that extended out into the aisle had been almost completely cleared of coal. The black stuff was piled higher than ever towards the back of the alcove, where Edward had tossed shovel full after shovel full.

"Well, this isn't getting us anywhere," he sighed.

"Maybe we're on the wrong track?" asked Jessica.

"Hard to tell," Muttered Edward, "We haven't got much to go on."

"You don't suppose it's under the flagstones, do you?" asked Jessica.

"Could be, I suppose . . ." replied Edward absently.

"Let me borrow that torch for a moment," said Jessica. Edward handed her the torch, and sat in the gathering darkness listening to her receding into the far-reaches of the cellar. In a minute she returned, dragging a push broom with her. Its handle wobbled crazily on the broom head, but it was useable. Jessica handed the torch back to Edward and began to sweep the area that he'd shoveled, removing the black dust that remained scattered in irregular mounds.

In a few minutes the floor was nearly clear of the gritty black grime, but the air was filled with it, and Edward and Jessica were both coughing and waving their hands in front of their faces trying to find some clear air to breathe.

"Sorry about that," choked Jessica.

"You look like a coal miner!" exclaimed Edward, eyeing her blackened face and hands.

"So do you!" she grinned, then turned to inspect the floor. "I don't know. This floor looks pretty solid," she observed, carefully examining the surface that she'd cleared.

"That one stone in the center seems almost . . . red," suggested Edward.

Jessica stooped to look closer. "You're right!" she exclaimed.

Again using the push broom, Jessica carefully removed all traces of the coal dust from the red flagstone, then stepped over the metal fence and squatted next to the area of interest. Red paint covered the entire stone, and some of it had slopped over the seams onto the adjoining stones. But the intent clearly had been to paint one of the squares red.

"You think this is it?" Jessica asked excitedly.

"Only one way to find out," said Edward. Standing, he stepped over the fence, picked up the coal shovel, and began to pry at the edges of the stone.

After a few minutes, the paint around the edges of the stone had been chipped, and the end of the shovel had been worn to a shiny metallic gleam, but the red flagstone hadn't budged.

"I don't know. This thing seems like it's in here pretty solidly," observed Edward in a discouraged voice. "Nothing short of a jackhammer is getting this baby out."

"Maybe we need to use the numbers?" suggested Jessica.

"Hmmm. You may be right." Edward stopped his efforts to dislodge the flagstone and glanced absently around the darkness of the cellar, lost in thought. "I wonder . . . This might be . . . the starting point?"

"And the numbers are flagstones?" suggested Jessica, hopefully.

"Let's try!" said Edward, already counting flagstones to the left.

The fourth flagstone was just outside the metal fence of the coal scuttle. Sure enough, it was red.

"Jessie, I think we've got it!" shouted Edward, excitedly

Turning right they could see that they were now lined up with one of the aisles that led into the center of the cellar. Carefully counting flagstones they advanced down the aisle, passing several stacks of magazines, and a pile of woodworking tools.

The twenty-first flagstone was red.

"Edward!" exclaimed Jessica, "This is so exciting!"

They were standing at the intersection of two aisles that crossed in the midst of the cellar at right angles. Eagerly Edward turned left and wound his way between some boxes of books and a stack of cloth bundles. He stopped at the next intersection.

"This must be it!" cried Edward, standing over the thirteenth stone, which was also red.

With renewed vigor he attacked the flagstone with the coal shovel, prying at the edges and trying to lift the stone.

Ten minutes later the coal shovel was decidedly the worse for wear, and the flagstone relatively unscathed. Edward got down on his hands and knees and peered at the joints around the flagstone. They were sealed tight, and seemed identical to all of the other joints in the cellar.

"This stone sure seems like all the rest, except for the red paint," mused Edward. "I suppose we can try a sledgehammer, or something . . ."

"Maybe we should think about this a minute, before we get carried away," suggested Jessica, her earlier enthusiasm waning. "The count between the red flagstones has got to be more than a coincidence. They definitely indicate that we've got the order of the rings correct. Maybe we should use the second number on each ring now."

"It's worth a try," said Edward, standing. Turning left he counted off eighteen stones.

The flagstone in question wasn't red.

And it looked just like every other flagstone they had passed.

"Damn," said Jessica. "I wonder what we're missing?"

"Let's check the rest of this aisle, just to make sure," suggested Edward in disappointment. "Maybe I turned the wrong direction."

Jessica knew as well as he did that he hadn't, but she followed him as he retraced his steps, crossing the red flagstone and proceeding down the aisle in the other direction.

The fourteenth flagstone was red.

"What does this mean?" asked Jessica, looking querulously at Edward. She plopped herself down on a cardboard box next to the stone and sighed in exasperation. "And I thought we were so close," she moaned.

Edward sat opposite her, cautiously testing the strength of a steamer trunk before he put his full weight on it. Together they sat, staring dejectedly at the red flagstone between them.

After a minute Jessica sighed. "Edward," she asked, "Could there have been a fourth ring? Or are you sure there were only three?"

He considered for a moment. "I suppose it's possible," he said thoughtfully. "My father always mentioned three rings, but I never heard my uncle speak of them. And they weren't explicitly mentioned in the will . . ."

"So there could have been a ring that started: 4 14R . . ." she suggested.

"I can't say that there wasn't. But I have no idea who might have it. Or what the other number might be," he finished, dejectedly.

They sat for a long time staring at the red flagstone. Suddenly, Edward cocked his head and looked at the stone more carefully.

"You know, Jess, this stone looks a little different than those others . . ."

Jessica sat up straighter and stared at the stone. "You're right," she said. "It looks less . . . permanent, somehow."

Edward got down on his hands and knees again and ran his fingers around the edges of the stone. "This stone's not cemented in, Jessie!" he said excitedly.

With his fingernails he tried to dislodge the stone. It wouldn't budge. He tried to insert the shovel into the crack at the edge of the stone, but the blade was too curved.

"I need something . . ." he pondered.

They both cast about in the dim light for something that would help, then Jessica held up a metal strap that looked like it might have once held a battery in place in an automobile. "How about this?" she asked.

Taking it from her he nodded. "Let's give it a try," he said.

Edward ran the metal strip along one edge of the flagstone. It slipped easily into the crack, then snagged on the sand that held the stone wedged in place. He worked the strip back and fourth, digging sand from the groove until it slipped easily from one corner to the other. Then he repeated the procedure on the other three sides of the flagstone. Sitting back on his heels he eyed the stone. The red square was outlined by a ring of light-colored sand. A quarter inch gap separated it from its neighbors on all sides.

Edward set aside the metal strap and gingerly squeezed his fingertips into the gap nearest Jessica. Pressing his fingers into the stone with all his strength, he lifted up. The stone slowly tipped until it was standing on one edge. Beneath it was the black face and silver combination dial of a metal safe.

"That's more like it!" exclaimed Edward.

"I'll say," came a voice from down the aisle.

Edward and Jessica turned in startled apprehension to see Liz standing at the intersection of two aisles. Her face wore a self-satisfied smirk. And she was holding Jessica's pistol.

"Running true to form, I see, Liz," said Edward. "You always did manage to turn up when you were least expected . . . or wanted."

"Charming to the end, Edward," said Liz. "I haven't had a very comfortable night, but if we must trade barbs, I'll be happy to accommodate."

"I never engage in a battle of wits with an unarmed person, even if they are holding a gun," said Edward.

"That's an old one," said Liz. "Haven't you anything fresher?"

"From the smell in here, I'd say not." Edward's eyes narrowed. "How did you get here, anyway?"

"I was here two days ago. What kind of fool do you take me for? You're not the only one who knows about this castle."

Looking around, Liz said, "I always did hate the very idea of this place." She swiped her hand across a dust-covered cardboard box, then blew the dirt in their direction. "I got in through a window, upstairs. I made a pretty thorough search for anything with these numbers on it," she said, reaching into her jumpsuit pocket and extracting a pair of gold rings. "I'd be done by now if that caretaker hadn't shown up and started rummaging around—no doubt to get ready for your auspicious arrival. So I decided to wait you out down here in the cellar, and watch. But the door was locked. Then I found that," she added, nodding in the direction of the coal scuttle.

"So," she said, straightening, "you two have been busy little beavers this afternoon. Or should I say moles? What's all the digging about?" She stepped closer to Edward, then, unexpectedly, she snatched the appraisal from his hand and looked at it. A smile slowly spread across her face.

"So this is why you weren't interested in the rings. You knew what was in them all along." She looked at him with cold, deadly eyes. "What does it mean?"

Edward shrugged.

Liz eyed Jessica critically. "Personally I don't know what he sees in you. A little on the scrawny side aren't you?" She raised her arm, making sure that they could see the pearl handled pistol cradled in her palm. "What's the combination?"

"We don't know," Jessica replied, darkly. "We think there's something missing."

"Rubbish! How did you get this far, then?" said Liz, moving Jessica aside and clambering down on her knees to peer at the safe.

After examining the appraisal she eyed the dial of the safe. "What order do I put the numbers in?"

"That's not the problem," replied Edward. "The problem is, we think there's another ring."

"Another ring? Why on earth do you think that?"

"You wouldn't understand," said Edward.

"Try me."

Edward sighed. "There are two sets of numbers on each ring. The first set is the distance and direction between the flagstones, starting at the coal scuttle. But it's one number short."

"Then how did you find the safe?"

"Mostly luck. And the flagstones are marked . . . if you know what you're looking for."

Liz straightened up, and glared at Edward. "You found the safe without one of the numbers. You can open it without one of the numbers. How many possibilities can there be?"

Edward glanced at the combination dial. "One hundred, I'd say."

The cellar remained silent for a moment.

Jessica could feel her heart beating as her eyes darted from Edward to Liz and back, poised in their contest of wills.

"Try them," Liz snapped, and sat down on a box.

Edward glared at her a moment, then squatted next to the safe and began to spin the dial. "Read me the second set of numbers, starting with the ring numbered one."

Liz looked at the paper for a moment, orienting herself. "L18 . . . R13 . . . L15," she read.

Edward dialed in the first three numbers, paused to consider for a moment, then turned the dial right to the number ninety-nine and tried to turn the handle. Nothing happened.

He tried again, using ninety-eight as the final number. Again, nothing happened.

"There are one hundred numbers on this dial, you know . . ." he commented. "This could take a long time."

"The less you talk, the sooner you'll be done," sneered Liz.

Jessica watched Edward try the next two combinations in silence. Liz was acting extremely fidgety, and she wondered why. Did she know that Winston and Freddie had also taken the train to Edinburgh? Even though she was pointing a gun at them, she had a hard time believing she'd actually use it. Winston and Freddie seemed far more dangerous. Did they know about the castle? Liz could have told them, but that would have been stupid, if she expected to get the treasure for herself.

Edward had worked his way down to eighty-seven when Jessica decided that she really needed to sit down. It had been a long day, and she was beginning to feel the affects of skipping lunch. She settled herself back onto her box and continued to watch Edward's fruitless attempts with the safe. Liz eyed her, but made no comment.

Edward had just dialed in seventy-four when there was a loud creaking moan, as of rusty hinges complaining against movement, and bright light spilled into the coal scuttle. With a crash, the iron door was flung open.

All three of them squinted against the brightness of the light piercing the dark cellar. Liz took a step toward the coal scuttle, then a step back, holding the pistol in both hands nervously.

With a crunch, a large man dropped though the hole formed by the open door, and stumbled around on the loose coal. Jessica recognized him immediately as Freddie, from the confrontation on the train. Crushing bits and pieces of coal underfoot, he made his way over the fence surrounding the scuttle, then stood peering into the gloom.

Liz was nearly beside herself with anxiety. Her whole body was vibrating, and she looked from Edward to Freddie and back in panic.

"Well?" came a voice from outside the coal scuttle doorway. "Anything?"

At that moment, Freddie's eyes, adjusting to the darkness of the cellar, opened in recognition, and he took a step towards the group. "Yeah," he shouted, "they're here!"

It was too much for Liz. In terror she turned and fled down the cluttered aisle, knocking boxes and tools onto the floor in her panicked rush to escape. Her foot hit the bottom step at a run, and she bounded up the stairs two at a time. She was halfway up when, with an ear-shattering crash, the entire step cracked in two and she plunged downward. Her body struck the steps above as she fell, and they, too, buckled and shattered into sharp edged fragments, pulling the sides of the stair down on top of her with a crash.

There was the sound of stray bits of wood and dirt sifting their way down through the dust-shrouded rubble, then silence.

Jessica and Edward exchanged glances, and both began to rise, but Freddie was already pushing past them, roughly shoving the debris out of the aisle. He wrenched one side of the fallen stairs off of Liz's inert form, looking like he was ready to finish the job that the timbers had begun. For a moment he eyed the motionless form suspiciously, then shrugged his shoulders in frustration. Liz was either dead or out cold. Freddie turned away, then back. Stooping, he reached in and extracted the pistol. He fingered the weapon tentatively. The delicate antique fit entirely into his enormous palm.

Cautiously he eyed the two of them, where they stood motionless. Then he spotted the safe.

"Well, well, well, what have we here, eh?" asked Freddie.

"An excellent question, my friend," came a voice from behind them, its clipped tones echoing in the dusty cellar.

Edward and Jessica turned to find Winston smiling at them. His expensive suit was unwrinkled, seemingly impervious to the grime that covered everyone else. He was wiping his hand on a linen handkerchief.

"No response?" said Winston. "It seemed so obvious to me. It's a safe, Freddie. And I wouldn't be a bit surprised," he continued, fishing in his pocket and pulling out Jessica's ring, "If these held the combination."

"The other rings, if you please," he said.

"She has them," said Edward, nodding in the direction of Liz's prostrate form.

Winston made a gesture towards Freddie, and the heavyset man went over to where Liz lay and rummaged through her pockets. In a minute he returned with the two rings, which he handed to Winston.

The old man walked to the opening above the coal scuttle and examined the rings in the light, one by one, comparing them to Jessica's. Then, nodding to himself, he strolled back to the group and held them out to Edward, still crouched by the safe.

"Open it," he commanded

Edward sighed once again. "There's something missing. We can't open it."

Winston's look turned cold. Still holding the rings in his outstretched hand he lowered his voice until the threatening tone was nearly inaudible, even in the confined space.

"I just provided what's missing, you bladdy idiot. Here's the third ring. Now open it, you hear?"

Edward shook his head. "You don't understand—"

"No!" shouted Winston, and they all flinched. "It's YOU who doesn't understand. Now open the safe!"

Edward looked at Jessica, who sat next to him wide-eyed. She realized that she'd underestimated just how dangerous these two were. Would they even have the patience to wait for Edward to try all those numbers if they understood the situation?

Winston turned to Jessica. "Stand up!" he commanded. Quickly Jessica complied.

"Freddie," continued Winston, "If this safe isn't open in two minutes, shoot her, you hear?" He looked meaningfully at Edward, then considered a moment. Looking back at Jessica, he continued speaking to Freddie. "Freddie, don't kill her. Just wound her . . . at least for starters."

Turning back to Edward, Winston continued, "I would advise you, Mr. Drummond, to cooperate with me." He smiled. "I've had a bad week."

"I can't do this in two minutes," cried Edward in frustration. "This is going to take patience."

"Patience," mused Winston, "A commodity I seem to be a bit short on. Let's see what we can do about providing some incentive to speed things up." He turned to Freddie. "Freddie?"

Freddie raised the pistol and pointed it at Jessica's knee meaningfully. Jessica looked at Edward in panic as she heard Freddie cock the trigger.

An explosion rocked the cellar, and Jessica closed her eyes against the blinding flash, expecting to feel the pain of impact erupt from her knee, but nothing happened. When she opened her eyes, she thought at first that Freddy had disappeared. Then she saw him, lying face down a few feet from the bottom of the stairs, his head surrounded by a pool of blood.

She turned in confusion to look at Winston, but he was already halfway out the coal scuttle door, scrambling over the crumbling pile of rock. A few moments later there was the roar of an engine and the sound of spraying gravel as his car fish-tailed away from the castle.

Edward knelt over Freddie's body, his fingers pressed against the man's neck, feeling for a pulse. He looked up to the top of the ruined stairs, and for the first time Jessica noticed Mr. MacGregor standing there, a still-smoking shotgun in his hand.

"Good shooting, Mac," said Edward, "He's dead."

Jessica could see that Mr. MacGregor was white as a sheet, and visibly trembling. He gave no response.

Edward must have seen it, too, because he added, "Don't worry, Mac. He'll not be missed."

Mr. MacGregor nodded. "I'll call the police," he said in a subdued voice. "And an ambulance," he added, then disappeared from the doorway.

Edward advanced to the pile of wood that marked where the stairs had been, and gingerly moved several broken timbers off of Liz's prostrate form.

Jessica stood nearby, watching, then asked softly, "Edward, is she . . ."

Edward shook his head. "She's alive. I can see her breathing. But she's pretty banged up."

At the sound of Edward's voice, Liz opened her eyes. It took her a moment to focus, and when she did, it was on Jessica, not Edward.

"I wouldn't have hurt you," she whispered. "Please believe that. I'm sorry. I was bluffing all the time. I was . . . desperate . . ." Her eyes closed, and her head drifted to one side, but Jessica could see that she was still breathing.

Jessica was surprised to find herself crying. Perhaps it was the strain of everything that had happened, or the spark of humanity she'd seen in Liz. She felt Edward put his arm around her shoulders and pull her close. Putting her arms around him, she let her tears fall against his chest.

Chapter 8

Jessica watched Mr. MacGregor toss a second handful of chopped onions into the stew that simmered on the stove in the old man's cottage. The clock above the stove showed just past midnight, and Jessica's rumbling stomach confirmed the late hour.

"I hope that stew will be finished soon, Mac," said Jessica. "It seems like days since I've eaten!"

The Scotsman nodded and turned his head to look at Jessica over his shoulder. "Aye, lassie," he said, "Just a couple more ingredients and a few minutes to simmer, and you're in for a real treat."

Jessica looked around the small kitchen of the caretaker's cottage. It still bore the touches of the long departed Mrs. MacGregor: jars at the window sill brimming with herbs and flowers, lace curtains surrounding the window above the sink, and an assortment of faded pictures hanging on one wall. Some of the pictures showed the MacGregors in their youth, others contained people that Jessica presumed were Edward's relatives.

Her mother's kitchen had been similar to this one.

She rubbed her hands across the old wooden table. It was smooth, almost soft, like the table where she'd shared breakfast with her parents, long ago. Sugar, yeast, flour, butter—the aromas that lived within that room still lived in her memory. Fresh baked bread, and pies. Especially the custard pies. Dad had loved those as well, she thought. He had always kept the fire burning, never letting it go out, even when he was ill with the flu. He'd always joked that it was his duty to keep the home fires burning.

Unlike those of many of her high school friends, her parents had always been a happy couple. Their affection showed in the everyday consideration they extended to one another, and to their child. Their pride in her had been absolute.

When they died, as devastated as she was, she remembered thinking that it was better that they had gone together. For without one another, they would have been incomplete.

Still, she wished she could see them again, just once, to tell them how much she missed them.

"Jessie, are you OK?" asked Edward, seeing the look of sadness across her face.

"Fine, I'm fine. Just a little reminiscing."

He nodded and turned back to what he was doing.

She watched him pen the final sentence of the statement that he'd been working on for the past hour. He signed his name to the bottom. Setting the pen aside, he looked up. "That should take care of Constable MacGowan," he said. Then, turning to Mac, he added, "I don't think you'll have anything to worry about, Mac. The constable didn't seem to have many questions about the details of what happened . . . downstairs."

"Aye," replied Mac. "And it won't hurt that the constable's father and I are old drinking buddies, either." The old man grinned, then turned thoughtful for a moment, as if he couldn't quite believe he'd actually killed a man. He shook his head and murmured, "Well, I could'na let anything happen to you and the lass, now could I? After I heard the stairs collapse, I ran to see if you were all right. When I heard them other voices it was plain that you weren't. I thought I had better make my move. Fortunately my gun was nearby."

He paused with a twinkle in his eye, then added, "I told you there was rats down there, now didn't I?"

"You did at that, Mac," laughed Edward.

Jessica thoughts drifted back to the late afternoon and evening, and the bustle of people who had congregated in the cellar of the old castle. First came the ambulance personnel, who quickly ascertained that there was nothing they could do for Freddie. Liz revived somewhat as they loaded her onto the stretcher, and Jessica felt her eyes upon them as she was carried out to the ambulance.

Then the constable from the village had arrived. Soon after, an entire entourage of crime scene personnel, all the way from Edinburgh, had joined him, along with a Detective Sergeant. They had measured, examined, and taken statements from all involved. At first it seemed that it might go badly for Mac. The men from Edinburgh were more than a little skeptical. But by the time Constable MacGowan finished smoothing things over, Mac had an appointment to go to the village the following day to give a more detailed statement, and the Detective Sergeant from Edinburgh had a date to go grouse hunting with Constable MacGowan.

Finally Freddie's body had been carried off, and the crowd slowly dispersed. Jessica shuddered, thinking of the dead man lying in a pool of blood.

She still had to admit that she wasn't anxious to return to the castle where such violent events had occurred so recently. Sensing this, Mac had suggested that they have a late supper in his cottage, and she was once again grateful to the old caretaker for his thoughtfulness.

Her thoughts turned to the labyrinthine events of the previous week.

She thought of Winston, who now had three rings—although he was still unaware of the missing one. What would he do now? The police had his description. But she and Edward had had difficulty ascribing any particular crime to Winston, and she could tell that the police were not really taking his disappearance as seriously as she and Edward were.

Liz was another matter. The London police were already looking for her, although out of sympathy for her Edward hadn't mentioned that to the local authorities. Would they figure it out? If not, would they hear from Liz again, or had she had enough? She had the appraisal now, but she must know that she'd never get another crack at the safe. It would probably be best for everyone if she just disappeared.

Jessica looked at the folded notepaper on the table in front of her. Idly, she opened it and examined the writing. It contained the numbers from the insides of all three rings. The first thing that she and Edward had done when they got a spare moment was to combine their recollections from the past afternoon and jot down what they remembered of all three rings.

So the three separate parties, with three separate agendas, all stood with the same information, the same clues, and the same goal: to solve the puzzle of the rings and gain the treasure. The only advantage that she and Edward had was that they were, technically, in possession of the safe that contained the treasure. If worst came to worst, they could try all 100 possibilities until the puzzle was solved.

But what if Winston returned? The police inspector had assured them that he would post a guard at the only entrance road to the Drummond estate. And she felt fairly sure that Winston wouldn't have much stomach for trying to cross the moors to the castle on foot by some back route. Further, she doubted that he would want to expose himself to the possibility of arrest.

So the task at hand seemed clear. Get some rest. Open the safe. And see the jewels safely to the bank deposit box. Then she and Edward could get on with planning their lives, without having to worry about being waylaid by their adversaries.

But somehow she suspected that things were more complicated than they seemed.

Why had Edward's uncle gone to such lengths to hide the treasure? There had to be more at stake than just a handful of diamonds, or the old man could simply have left them in trust, to be drawn upon as needed by his heirs. Why the convoluted scheme? And what might Winston, and Liz, for that matter, do when they learned that Edward had retrieved the treasure?

The questions revolved in her head as she sat in the cozy kitchen, watching the old caretaker prepare his stew.

Mr. MacGregor turned when he heard Edward set down his pen. Glancing briefly at Jessica, he smiled, then said to Edward, "So, Eddie, what's this all about, then?"

Edward and Jessica looked at each other. Edward sighed. "It's a long story Mac."

"Well, ye nay goin' anywheres, are ye?"

Edward smiled and began to recount everything that had happened since the letter from Charles had arrived.

Mac had poured the stew, and they'd begun to sip it by the time Edward finished. "And so, in the last, we've ended up without any of the three rings that my Uncle Charles bequeathed to the family when he died."

"And what pray tell, do these rings look like?" asked Mac, with a curious twinkle in his eye.

Edward was in mid-sip, and nodded at Jessica, who answered, "Well, they're gold, with a very small diamond set in the center of the band. Each ring is basically the same, except for the inscriptions on the inside."

"It's funny," chimed in Edward, wiping his mouth. "I didn't give the inscriptions a second thought, until I received that letter. And then when I found out about the letter that Winston had . . ." He paused thoughtfully. "I wonder where he got it . . . ?" It was one thing to think that a letter had gotten lost at the post office and then been recently mailed by some well-meaning soul who'd found it behind a counter. But it was a stretch to imagine it happening with more than one letter. Whose game were they playing, anyway?

"So in the end," Edward continued, "We figured out that the inscriptions are basically map references. And a combination. And we're beginning to suspect there may be four of them."

Mac rose mysteriously from the table and disappeared through the door into the central hall of the small cottage.

Jessica looked at Edward quizzically, then her eyes opened wide. "It couldn't be. Could it?"

Edward was still shaking his head when Mac came back. A small, intricately carved box rested in the old man's hands.

"I keep all my wife's favorite things in here, and it seemed the best place to put it." He opened the box, and began to sift through its contents. "There we be, still shiny as ever."

He held the ring up for them both to see.

"That's it," breathed Edward, as he took the ring and examined it. Inside, the inscription read

4 R14 L4

"It would have been a long time before that safe opened if the last number is four," laughed Edward. "I started at ninety-nine!"

"It's a good thing you didn't start at one, or we'd probably all be dead now," said Jessica.

Edward's grin faded, and he soberly handed the ring back to Mac. "I'm afraid you may be right. If Winston had shown up after we already had the treasure, he'd have had no further need for us."

Jessica shivered, and Edward moved to put his arm around her shoulders. "Well, that should do it," he said. "Now we have the safe, and the combination."

Mac returned the ring to its box, and carefully closed the delicate lid. A far-away look came to his eyes.

"Yer Uncle was a fine man, he was. But he was a broken one, when he came back from that God-forsaken place. He loved his wife, Margaret, dearly, and the little lassie, Lilly, he doted on her. He'd traveled back and forth to South Africa for many years—nigh on to twenty, I'd say. But then he married, and then Lilly was born, I thought he'd settle here. 'Twas not to be, though. The mine never seemed to run itself when he wasn't around—accidents and such. I know it was a hard decision to take the family over. And he never forgave himself for what happened."

Mac sighed. "He came home that summer, his wife and daughter gone, his business gone. A shattered man. He only lived about five years, after that. Died a fairly young man. He said his days were empty. Spent a year painting the portrait of the two of 'em you've seen in the library.

Mac stood up with his plate. "I have lost my appetite, I'm afraid. Not that I have much of one these days, now my good lady has gone. Be ten years now since she passed."

He shook his head to clear away the sad memories. "You two finish up now, its good food there on your plates."

Silently Edward and Jessica finished their stew.

Later, clearing away the dishes, Jessica yawned. "Goodness, I'm exhausted. I think maybe we should get on with our treasure hunting tomorrow. Winston isn't likely to come back at this time of night, is he?"

"No, I shouldn't think so." Edward replied. "Besides, the marshes out there are quite treacherous. I think the threat of a police patrol will keep him away."

"Good," nodded Jessica. She turned to Mr. MacGregor. "Mac, thank you for your help, and your hospitality. I think we will head on over to the castle now, and get some sleep."

"It has been rather a big day, hasn't it? I'll pop over for a moment and get the fire burning in yer room."

"That's OK Mac, I'll do that," Edward assured the man. "You get some sleep now."

They left the old caretaker to settle down for the night, and carefully worked their way back to the manor, thankful for Mac's pocket torch. It was pitch black outside.

Inside the kitchen door, Edward flipped on the light switch and turned to her.

"Jessie, I realize that it's the middle of the night, but do you think Jack would mind awfully if we were to call and talk to Sarah? It's been such a terrible day, I just feel the need to talk to someone who loves me."

Jessica felt a momentary twinge that she wasn't included in that group, but she set it aside and said, "I'm sure Jack wouldn't mind. She must be missing you tremendously."

They went into the hall and she dialed Jack's number in London. After many rings, a groggy Jack answered.

At first he was alarmed, afraid that some harm had befallen her, but she assured him that everything was fine. She related the story of the cellar. Jack was relieved to hear that they were all right, and that Liz and Winston were far away from London. He told her that Sarah was doing fine. The two of them were visiting Emma every day, and she was doing much better, and was scheduled to be released soon. Edward, leaning over to listen, nodded and smiled.

She handed the receiver to him so that he could ask to speak to Sarah, but he simply asked Jack to tell her that he promised to call the next day.

Jessica looked at him questioningly.

"It's selfish to rouse her in the middle of the night, just to make myself feel better. I'll talk to her when she's awake."

When he hung up, the clock was striking two. He led Jessica into the great room and settled her on the sofa, then set about building a fire in the massive stone fireplace. After a couple of false starts, he got the tinder to catch, and soon the wood was crackling. Jessica slipped off her shoes, snuggled into the corner of the couch, and pulled a pillow into her lap for warmth. With the fire cheerfully blazing, Edward disappeared into the kitchen, and returned a few minutes later with two glasses of sherry. Holding one of them out to her, he raised an eyebrow.

"You're too good to me," she said. "Thank you."

"My pleasure," he said, sitting beside her on the couch.

Jessica sipped her sherry and watched the flames flickering over the gnarled logs as she thought back over the events of the very long day. She'd never seen anyone killed before. Even if he'd deserved it, she couldn't get the image out of her mind. She supposed Edward was used to this sort of thing, having been in the service. Or was he? She remembered that day of the picnic, and how upset he'd been over the fox. Surely it was worse with people?

"Another sherry?" asked Edward.

Jessica looked down at her glass and was surprised to see that it was empty. "Mmmm . . . Maybe just a small one," she said sleepily.

He rose and returned to the kitchen.

When he came back into the great room a few minutes later, Jessica was curled up on the couch, her eyes closed. The firelight was warm and soothing on her face, and the sherry had given her a warm glow, all over.

He watched her for a moment, his eyes taking in her delicate features, the line of her body, as it rose and fell as she breathed. God, she's beautiful, he thought. He felt an almost overwhelming yearning to take her in his arms, but he hesitated. *She's had an awful day,* he told himself. *And we still haven't gotten over whatever this is that's come between us. This isn't the time.*

And yet you can't let her sleep down here all night, man. It will get cold in this big old room. Unless you plan to stay up and tend the fire.

Jessica heard him set the sherry glasses on the end table and suddenly she was being lifted in his arms. Surprised, she pretended to be asleep. It was pleasant, nestling against him as he carried her up the stairs to her bedroom. He laid her on the comforter and gently brushed away a strand of hair from her face. When he pulled back the comforter on the other side of the bed Jessica wondered if he was going to slip in beside her. But he simply folded that half over her and tucked it in. Then he slipped quietly from the room.

*　*　*

Winston Van Der Meer put his elbow on his hotel desk and rested his head on his hand.

So I got the rings. What bladdy good do they do now, eh?

What I really need is leverage. The rings don't give me any leverage at this point. That safe is long since open. Either it was full of diamonds, or a deed. I'm betting on a deed. Or both.

Presumably Edward has the deed, map, whatever by now. If so, he's won. He's got the diamonds.

Winston sighed.

There's nothing for it but to do it. I've got to get something that Edward wants. Then make a trade.

Maybe the girl? Or . . .

He picked up the phone and dialed Kip's number. He'd need the plane ready, to pull off this stunt.

*   *   *

The morning sun dappling the bed woke Jessica. The bedside clock read 9:00 am. She smiled at the golden droplets of sunlight that played across the comforter, sighing contentedly.

But her smile faded as her mind wandered to the events of the day before. Freddie's death had shaken her. She thought of Uncle Charles, and wondered what had happened to make him so bitter, to weave such a crooked trail to his remaining fortune.

She shook her head lightly. Enough of that, she thought. She slipped out of bed, dressed, and made her way down to the kitchen to prepare breakfast.

Half an hour later Edward came in, looking refreshed.

"I don't suppose you know how I got up to bed last night, do you?" she asked him with a smile.

Edward grinned. "We're here to serve."

She placed the plates on the table and sat down.

They ate their scrambled eggs in comfortable silence. There was a bird in the tree outside the kitchen window. Its cheerful trilling filled the room with a peaceful ambiance.

"What will you do with the diamonds, Edward?"

"Do with them . . . ?" He thought for a moment. "I don't really know, I guess. Maybe fix this place up. It wouldn't make a bad home. There's a school in the village. And it's not that far from Edinburgh. Maybe we could all live here?"

She looked up, startled.

"Me, and Sarah, I mean," he quickly added.

Jessica nodded. "I think she'd like that."

"What I do know," Edward continued, "Is that the diamonds aren't that important to me. I'd give them up in a moment if only . . ." His gaze drifted to her.

She looked down, studying the pattern the eggs had left on her plate.

"Would you like to move here, to Scotland, live in the Castle?" He ventured.

"You know I can't. I have a job. In Battersea."

"You could find work here, too," he suggested. "I'm sure someone in Edinburgh could use an architect—it's not that far by car, you know."

In a way, it was tempting. And yet, there was something about the way he asked that made her angry.

"Edward, I have no interest in being kept by you, or offered favors, or having you be patronizing about my career. I came up here to help you find the treasure, so that you could provide for Sarah. I've no interest in being a mistress. The other night should not have happened, and I have said as much. Now let's get to it."

"But—"

Jessica pushed back her chair and stood up. "Seriously, Edward," she said, "We need to find that safe and look in it. We need to finish this and move on with our lives."

Edward closed his eyes tightly, and when he opened them, it was as if a curtain had been drawn, and she couldn't read him at all. "Yes," he said. "Finish it." He stood up. "Well, let's just clear this stuff away, and go to it."

The kitchen door banged open and Mr. MacGregor stepped in. "'Tis Long John Silver, come fer me treasure!" he exclaimed with a grin.

"Good timing, Mac," Jessica smiled. "We were just about to go treasure hunting. It seems like you should be a part of that, too."

Mr. MacGregor smiled at her, and nodded. "Aye. Well, let's git on with it then." He followed them into the hall.

The cellar was creepier than Jessica remembered it. She stepped off the bottom rung of the ladder that Mac had lowered to replace the ruined stairs. Skirting the pile of wooden debris, she gave the bloodstain where Freddie had laid a wide berth.

Seeing her shudder, Edward said, "We'll make this quick."

He stooped over the safe, spun the dial several rotations to clear it, and entered the numbers as they whispered them in unison, "Left 18 . . . Right 13 . . . Left 15 . . . Right 4 . . ."

Holding his breath, Edward clasped the lever on the door and twisted. At first it seemed to be stuck, but he increased the pressure and smiled with relief as the lever pivoted and he lifted the door open.

The safe was smaller inside than Jessica had expected, and much cleaner. Spotless, really, compared to the surrounding cellar. At first glance it seemed empty.

Alarmed, Edward flashed the pocket torch into the interior, revealing a single, dark rectangular object centered in the bottom. Gingerly he lifted it out and shone the torch over its exterior. It was a carved wooden box, about six inches on a side and several inches thick. Its surface gleamed with the luster of carved wood, shaped into the bodies of running animals, which covered it completely.

"It's beautiful," whispered Jessica, with delight.

Rising, Edward handed Jessica the pocket torch and inspected the lid in its slender beam. After some experimentation he determined that the top slid sideways. Carefully he opened it, and set the lid aside.

The top layer consisted of yellowed newspaper clippings. He lifted them out to reveal . . . more newspaper clippings. His pulse rising, he riffled through the papers until he reached the bottom. He lifted the stack out, and the box lay in his palm empty.

"Papers. Nothing but papers," he moaned in disappointment. "What a terrible joke."

Mac's shoulders slumped, too, and he turned and started up the ladder.

Jessica touched Edward lightly on the shoulder. "I'm so sorry," she whispered.

Edward smiled bravely at her. "It doesn't matter. Really."

Taking him by the hand, she led him to the stairs. "Come on," she said. "Let's see what your uncle thought was so valuable about those newspaper clippings.

Later, at the kitchen table, Edward worked his way through the papers from the box, as the others looked on.

The first was a newspaper clipping from 1961. It was about the opening of offices for the Transvaal Rural Utility Service. The article indicated that the company had been founded by a young man named Arthur Murcheson, with the charter to establish utility service to the outlying townships in Namaqualand. A second clipping also detailed the operation of the company, and a third indicated some local white opposition to the company's efforts to establish right-of-ways for their utility distribution. Other clippings also dealt with the company, which proved to be successful in several court cases, and had established as significant distribution grid within a couple of years of its founding.

Another newspaper clipping detailed the automobile accident that had killed Margaret and Lilly Drummond, with a picture of the crumpled vehicle at the bottom of a rocky ravine. Edward set it aside with a grimace. There were also newspaper clippings about a diamond mining company opening a new pit, and several pages of notes in Charles Drummond's handwriting.

Edward unfolded a long, narrow piece of linen stationery. It was a list of the graduating class of the University of the Orange Free State in Bloemfontein from 1960. He was still scanning the list for people that he recognized when Jessica pointed to the name Arthur Murcheson.

The last piece of paper in the box was a hand-written letter, inscribed in a shaky script on plain white notepaper.

"Dear Robert, Edward, Emma and Maureen," Edward began reading aloud.

"Robert?" asked Jessica.

"My father."

"Oh, yes. And Maureen?"

"That would be me dear, departed wife," Mac indicated. She looked at him and smiled. Edward continued.

"Dear Robert, Edward, Emma and Maureen,

"It seems strange to be speaking from beyond the grave, but the fact that you are reading this indicates that I am gone, as is my son Arthur."

Jessica looked quizzically at Edward, who shrugged his shoulders.

"The path that has lead you here has admittedly been convoluted, but I could not risk its accidental discovery until the time had come when my revelation could no longer hurt those that I loved.

"Perhaps some of you—surely not all of you?—have also passed on. In a way that does not sadden me, for it means that Arthur has had a long and happy life. And I have absolute confidence in the integrity of any descendents of Robert and Edward. They are good people."

Jessica put her hand on Edward's shoulder.

"There are evil men in this world. As a young man setting out to make something of myself in South Africa I would never have believed that there could be people with so little feeling for others. Especially others whom they viewed as so inferior.

"I always tried to do right by Margaret and Lilly. They were my life. But in the end, my politics destroyed them.

"Arthur was the result of an indiscretion, long before I met and married Margaret. I never told her. In a way, I'm sorry, although I suppose it would have hurt her. Her life ended with enough pain, as it was.

"But Arthur has made me very proud. He is a man of principle, and has risen above the secret of his heritage. I must remind myself that, as you read this, Arthur is dead. Hopefully you read this in some far-flung future, and he has lived out a long and happy life. I cannot know."

Edward turned the notepaper over, and continued reading aloud.

"But now the time has come for the denouement. With any luck, some of those who would have harmed Arthur, and who destroyed my life and my family, are still alive. If not them, their heirs. If you follow my instructions, justice will at last be served.

"I have also left an entitlement to you, my heirs. Perhaps I do this in the hope that out of gratitude, or perhaps even guilt, you will assist me in my search for justice. In any event, it is yours. In return, I ask that this castle, where Margaret and Lilly and I were once so happy, be kept in the family, so that others may perhaps cherish what we once had.

"The treasure lies behind the name in the rings, forged in that year when the combination of events so overwhelmed me that all that was left for me was revenge.

"A revenge that I now implore you to carry out. Find Mary Mogamo, or her heirs. She has the papers.

"Respectfully,

"Charles Drummond

"January, 1968"

Edward looked up from the notepaper and found Jessica staring at him.

"That's it?" asked Jessica. "'Find Mary Mogamo'? Where? In South Africa?"

Edward shrugged. "Perhaps there's something more in these clippings. We didn't read all of them . . ."

The telephone rang, and Mac went into the hall to answer it.

"What's this about an 'entitlement'?" Jessica asked, "Does he mean the rings?"

"I don't know. It seems that way . . . Anyway, there's no rush now. This has waited over thirty years, I doubt than it's very critical at this point." He smiled. "At any rate, first things first. We need to get you back to London."

Jessica was startled. She'd been so absorbed in the puzzle of the rings; it seemed hard to believe that it was over, just like that. In a day she'd be back in London, and she and Edward would go their separate ways. It might be years before she saw him again. Perhaps she'd never see him again.

She doubted that Edward was trying to get rid of her—not after his remarks about Edinburgh—nevertheless she *had* been pretty beastly to him, ever since they . . .

Well, any way, I have my job. And it will be nice to see Jack again.

But if Edward was right about Jack, maybe he and Emma would make a go of it. They might even move to Scotland, since Emma still had a right to the castle.

But would Jack want to move? Jessica knew the answer to that before she even asked it. Jack had been all over the world. He loved travel and adventure, loved trying out new things. As a freelancer, there was nothing tying him to London. And he loved collecting old things. He'd move to Drummond Castle in a heartbeat.

That would leave her completely alone in London.

Her thoughts were interrupted as the kitchen door burst open and Mac leaned in, the telephone receiver still in his hand, its cord stretched tight.

"Eddie!" he exclaimed, "Eddie! Miss Emma's on the phone. Come quick! It's Sarah—she's been kidnapped!"

CHAPTER 9

Jessica was subdued on the trip back to London. She fretted over Sarah, fretted over the box full of papers, fretted over her future. She felt guilty for even thinking about her future when the life of the little girl was at stake. But she couldn't help it.

Spending the past three days with Edward had reminded her of why she'd fallen in love with him all those years ago. He was so strong, yet so gentle, so caring. And life with Edward was never dull.

It certainly wasn't dull now, she thought fearfully. Emma had said that the London police were looking for the kidnapper, but after the call Jack had gotten they all knew it was useless. It had to have been Winston. No one else would have known about the safe. And Liz was still in hospital. Anyway, she certainly wouldn't have kidnapped her own child. She didn't even want her, according to Edward.

No, Winston had the girl. And Winston had a plane. Liz had said so. And Winston lived in South Africa.

Jessica shuddered.

Give me the mine and I'll give you the kid, the ransom note had said. What did it mean?

Even if Winston thought there were diamonds in the safe, that certainly wasn't a mine. Did he think there was a deed to a mine in the safe? There certainly wasn't anything of value among the papers that she and Edward had gone over yet again. Nothing worth kidnapping an innocent child over.

She shook her head, trying to clear her thoughts, but another sprang up just as quickly. Edward really *was* broke, now.

She refused to admit to herself the number of times she'd thought of him during the intervening years, imagining him seeking her out, carrying her off on his white horse, so to speak. But always she thought of the voices, the comments behind her back, the neighbors, the servants, anything to dispel the fantasy. She'd even imagined him coming to her as a pauper, ruined in some financial crash, begging her to take him in.

Now, that's exactly what had happened.

There were no neighbors, no servants—well, there was Mac, but he was different.

And how had she responded to her wildest dream coming true?

She'd been beastly to Edward. She knew she had. She'd slept with him, then shut him out, hardened her heart against him. When he'd suggested that she move in with him she'd essentially told him to shove off.

Well, he did have a nerve, expecting her to drop everything and come running to be his mistress. Because she'd slept with him, now he thought she was cheap.

Well she wasn't.

She glanced over at him. He looked tired, and worried.

Her heart softened as she realized how selfish she was being.

Of course he's worried about Sarah. She's all that matters to him right now. If that weren't so, he wouldn't be the man she loved.

Oh, God, there it was. She wasn't going to admit that to herself, and it just sort of came out. I do love him. And I've messed things up so much now, I doubt that I'll ever get him back.

Anyway, if there was any chance for her to have Edward without the baggage of the past, it would have to wait. She was happy to put off thinking about it. Even the thought frightened her. What if they got together and then things went right back to the way they'd been before? Could she really leave it all: her little flat, her friends, her architectural design job in London? She'd run away from commitment before. Would she again?

The thoughts swirled round and round in her head, chasing themselves endlessly, going nowhere. Finally, as the train neared London, she came to a decision. She'd do nothing to encourage Edward during this difficult time. She'd be a friend, provide him with all the support she could, stick with him through whatever it took to get the Sarah back, but she would say nothing of their relationship. And if he brought it up, she would demur. Until they got Sarah back, it was only right.

But Sarah might be dead, for all she knew. Jessica swallowed. She couldn't let herself think that, or it was hopeless. First they needed to find Sarah. She could think about the rest later.

She looked at Edward. He was staring out of the compartment at the countryside slipping past. She watched the way his soft brown hair flopped down over his dark eyes. The curve of his mouth as he frowned at some unknown thought. The rise and fall of his muscular chest.

Gently, she squeezed his arm, and he turned to her quizzically.

"What is it?" he asked.

"Nothing." She said, looking down. Was he feeling the same thing that she was? She toyed with the sleeve of her blouse. "Actually, I was wondering what you were thinking."

He sighed. "I was thinking that I shouldn't have left Sarah . . . about how selfish I've been, just thinking of myself, and how getting the diamonds would give you back to me . . . maybe. You know, the last time I left her was not long after you left me. I went on a binge of sorts, a pub crawl. Stayed away for a couple of days. No one knew where I was. The staff took care of Sarah, but not very well it seemed. She went out looking for me and got lost. By the time I got back, bloodshot eyes and hung over, a full-scale search was on. It took five hours to find her. It was dark and cold, and wet, as was usual for that time of year. She had a raging fever when they brought her in. I sat by her side in the hospital all night." Edward sighed again. "I vowed then that I would never leave her again." He was silent for a moment. "But I did."

"Edward, you can't have known that she would be kidnapped. No one could have known."

"Maybe not, but that's no excuse is it?" He looked at her.

Unsure of what to say to him, Jessica returned his gaze in silence.

Outside the window the sky was growing dark.

* * *

Emma opened the door of Jack's flat.

"Emma," Edward said, "It's good to see you out of hospital."

He set his bag down and stepped forward, gently hugging her. Jessica came alongside and put her arm over Emma's shoulder.

"Jack brought me home yesterday," Emma said. "He very kindly let me stay here with him."

Behind Emma, Jessica saw Jack actually blush. He cleared his throat.

Jessica had to admit that Emma was looking better. Jack, on the other hand, had a large white bandage on his head.

"Jack, did they do that to you?" asked Jessica, as she hugged her friend.

"It's nothing, just a bump," he answered, kissing her on the forehead. "Good to see you back"

Edward watched the two of them, frowning. "Emma, were you here when they snatched Sarah?"

"No. Just Jack. I discharged myself when Jack called to tell me about it. They were going to discharge me tomorrow, anyway," she added, anticipating Edward's protest.

"Edward," began Jack, "I can't tell you how sorry I am. I should never have answered the door . . . We'd been so careful, barely even going out, because I was afraid there might still be danger. Then, when you called the other night and said that they were all up in Scotland . . . well, I'm afraid I let my guard down."

Edward gripped Jack's shoulder and looked into his eyes. "There's no sense torturing yourself, man. None of us realized how dangerous this lot is. I don't think there's anything you could have done. I'm just glad you're not dead. Now let's see what the police have to say."

Jack nodded his head sadly, and collected his and Emma's coats for the trip to the police station.

A half hour later Detective Sergeant Brightcastle greeted them grimly as they walked into his office.

"I'll get straight to it Mr. Drummond. How much do you know?"

"Only that the girl was taken from Mr. Montague's flat, after the kidnappers knocked him out. And that there is a ransom note."

"Precisely right. This is the note," he said, handing Edward a piece of paper sealed in a plastic bag.

Printed in simple block letters was the message:

GIVE ME THE MINE AND I'LL GIVE YOU THE KID.

He looked up at the Detective as he passed the note on to Jessica.

"Do you know what this means?" asked the policeman.

"Yes. At least, I think I do."

Edward began relating the long story of Charles' life, the rings, and the treasure that turned out to be nothing more than papers. He finished by relaying their suspicions that the perpetrators were already in South Africa.

The Detective sat quietly during Edward's recitation, taking an occasional note on a lined yellow pad. When Edward had finished, the policeman spread his hands on his desk and pulled his chair in closer to the desk. "And have you these papers with you?" He asked.

Edward nodded, and placed the clippings on the desk. The five of them began to go through them, one by one, examining every word.

A half hour passed, then another. Aside from the occasional comment, the room was silent.

At last the detective rose and addressed Edward. "It would seem that you adversaries have been misled, Mr. Drummond. There is certainly nothing here that would suggest that Charles Drummond owned a diamond mine, nor any obvious indication that he had a stash of diamonds. That makes the situation even more dangerous, since you cannot even offer what is being sought.

"My advice is to remain near the phone in Mr. Montague's apartment. We will arrange for the line to be tapped, and at such time as the kidnappers contact you, we will dispatch all necessary police resources to apprehend them."

"But Sergeant," protested Edward, shaking his head, "We don't even know if the kidnappers are in this country. And even if they are, what you proposed could be very dangerous for the child."

Detective Brightcastle held up his hand. "Believe me, Mr. Drummond, we will exercise all due care in the apprehension of these criminals. I'm pretty sure that what we're dealing with here is nothing more than petty hoods. I seriously doubt that they've taken the child out of the country—it would make it far too difficult to negotiate a deal.

"As a precaution, though, I'll contact the Cape Town police, and alert them to the situation. And we'll make inquiries into this diamond mining company, and see if they have a company plane, and if so, where it is at present.

"Now if you'll bear with me a few minutes, I'll photocopy these documents for our records."

Edward, with a growing look of disgust on his face, handed him the papers.

The sergeant stepped into the hallway and Edward turned to the others. "This is ridiculous," He fumed. "There's got to be something more than this that we can do."

Jack and Emma nodded, and Jessica placed her hand on Edward's arm.

It was nearly a half hour before the detective returned. Edward was pacing the small confines of the office. He stopped abruptly when the door opened. Handing the papers to Edward, the sergeant reminded him, "Now just stay by the phone, Mr. Drummond, and let us take care of this."

"I can't just sit and wait around for my child to show up dead," Edward said angrily.

"Let me make something very clear, Mr. Drummond," cautioned Detective Brightcastle. "It would be better if you did not meet with these people. For the sake of the child, you should leave it to us. I can't make you stay here in England, but I strongly advise you not to go to Cape Town. South Africa is a dangerous place, and the London police can't protect you there."

Edward stood, dragging Jessica with him.

"Jack, Emma, let's go."

He made for the door, then turned and looked at the sergeant.

"Do you have children, Brightcastle?"

The man nodded.

"Then you know where I'm going, don't you?"

Edward turned and left the room, the others filing out behind him.

* * *

Winston pushed Sarah toward the steps leading down from the plane. "You see that truck over there?" He asked, nodding at the vehicle parked at the edge of the tarmac. The girl nodded fearfully. "Get in it. Then sit tight." He gave her a push, and she started down the steps.

Winston turned back into the passenger compartment, and began to collect his things. The door to the cockpit opened, and Kip stepped out. "What the hell are you doing?" demanded Kip.

"What's it look like?" replied Winston. "I'm getting my stuff."

"You know what I mean," said Kip. "The kid. If I'd seen her back here before we took off, you know I'd never have put this bird in the air. She doesn't belong here."

"Nevertheless, she's here. She won't be any trouble out at the old maintenance yard."

"Does her father know about this?"

"Yeah. Sort of."

"You're crazy."

"Maybe so. But I pay your salary, hey?"

"Hopefully, not for long. And you don't pay me to be a kidnapper."

"I just did, my man," said Winston, patting the pilot on the shoulder. Kip flinched away. "Now keep your bladdy trap shut," added Winston, "and maybe you won't go to jail for it, you hear?" He turned and descended the steps.

The bravado was a fine act for Kip, but Winston was having second thoughts himself.

Am I out of my mind? Committing a crime in England, and then getting out is one thing. Getting caught kidnapping here in South Africa is quite another.

Maybe I should just get rid of her somewhere . . . before their prints get all over everything.

But I need something that Edward has. He wants the kid. And he won't hesitate to give up the diamonds to get her back.

But maybe I should've kept her in England. No. Even I'm not that crazy. Every cop in England is looking for this kid. The South African police won't do anything. Not without letting me know, first.

Perhaps I assume too much. He sighed, leaning against the car door.

There's nothing to worry about. Edward will show up. He'll bring the diamonds, and I'll give him the kid. They won't be any trouble. And if things get too hot . . .

He reached into his coat pocket and fingered Jessica's pistol.

They wouldn't be the first to die for these diamonds. Not by thirty years.

*   *   *

It had seemed cold and lonely to Jessica, spending the night in her flat, and she'd slept only fitfully, dreaming of break-ins and kidnappings. She'd wasted no time catching a cab to Jack's flat for the strategy meeting that they planned.

The early morning sun was just slanting through the window of Jack's living room as the four of them gathered around the coffee table. Jack set a tray with four cups of steaming brew on the table and settled next to Emma on the couch.

The four of them sifted once more through the papers from the safe. There were numerous articles from various newspapers. Some were about the Van Der Meer Diamond Company, some praised the community spirit of the Van Der Meer family. Several mentioned contributions to the political community, schools, and local hospitals.

"Mmph," snorted Edward. "From what my father told me, all these good deeds were simply tax dodges. They had an ulterior motive for everything they did back then. And I assume they still work on the same agenda."

"There's nothing here that tells us if Uncle Charles' son is still alive," said Emma in disappointment. "Maybe Jack could check it out for us, on the 'net.'" She looked over to Jack, raising her eyebrows.

"Sure, I can access all sorts of things," said Jack. "Let me see what I can find." He sat down at his computer and began to type.

Jessica picked up a few of the remaining pieces of paper on the table. She looked at the top page. There were several columns of numbers scrawled across it. She turned the paper over.

"Hey, look at this."

She showed the page to Edward. It appeared to some sort of survey.

"This might be useful," said Edward, thoughtfully.

"Here's something," cried Jack.

"That was quick," said Emma, surprised.

They gathered around the computer and looked at the screen.

The screen showed at list of death notices. Jack had highlighted one in the middle.

Murcheson, Arthur Charles

Beloved son of Mary Mogamo, Klienzee, North Cape

"It says where she lives," breathed Emma.

"That's it, then," said Edward. "I'll leave immediately." He looked at his watch. "I might even be able to get a flight today, if I hurry. Em, can you check the flights while I repack my suitcase?"

Emma nodded and went into the kitchen to use the telephone.

Jessica had retreated to the far side of the room, and stood there now, feeling frightened. This was all happening too fast. She'd assumed that when Edward had mentioned going to South Africa, he'd meant the two of them.

That was rather presumptuous of you wasn't it? Why would he want to have anything to do with you, after the way you've been treating him?

Edward must have noticed that she was upset, for he said, "Of course, you don't have to go with me, Jessie. I understand your feelings perfectly."

No he doesn't, thought Jessica. He doesn't understand at all.

"If you will all excuse me," said Jessica. She walked stiffly from the room, her head down.

In the guest room, Jessica sat on the bed. She picked up a ribbon from the nightstand. Running it through her fingers, she smiled, remembering sitting on the bed and brushing Sarah's hair.

Was it really less than a week ago?

Her gaze drifted around the room.

Propped on the seat of a chair was the porcelain doll. Jessica leaned over and picked it up. Would Sarah ever see it?

She hugged the doll to her chest.

How could she stay here, knowing Sarah was in danger? She'd go mad waiting for news, she knew she would.

There was nothing for it really. She would ring her employer and ask for more time to complete the plans she was working on. She knew he wouldn't mind, not really.

Why was she worried about her boss? It was Edward she'd need to convince.

Jessica placed the doll gently back on the chair. Brushing away the tears that had fallen on her cheeks, she made her way back out into the kitchen.

"Edward," she said.

He looked up. She felt Jack and Emma looking at her as well. Did she have the courage to do this?

"Edward, I want to come with you."

Edward raised one eyebrow. "To the airport?"

"No, you idiot, to South Africa."

He shook his head. "It's too dangerous, Jessie. You heard what Sergeant Brightcastle said."

"Edward, Sarah is like my own," said Jessica. "I've nursed her when she was sick, comforted her when she was frightened, rocked her to sleep, and loved her unconditionally. I'll go mad if I have to stay here worrying about her. I'm going with you." She folded her arms and waited for his response.

Edward's mouth opened in astonishment, but no words came out. He crossed his arms and they stood like that, staring each other down.

"There's a flight from Heathrow in three hours," called Emma from the kitchen. "Shall I book it?"

Before Edward could answer, Jessica called, "Book two seats, Em."

She picked up her suitcase and walked over to Edward's side. "We'll need to stop by my flat for a second so I can pick up some fresh clothes. I won't be a moment."

Edward shook his head. "Alright," he said. "I need to go back to my flat too. We'll hit them both on the way."

On the ride over to her flat, Jessica mulled over the situation. She was frightened, yet elated. Frightened for Sarah, yet elated at having a fresh chance to prove her worth to Edward. She wouldn't mess it up, this time.

In the rush of grabbing some clothes at her flat, Jessica barely even noticed that someone had obviously been though her things. Drawers were pulled out, and the contents of several of them littered the floor. She shrugged. After the week she'd had, it seemed almost irrelevant. She found herself amazed at how easily she'd adapted to her new high-tension life.

As usual, the airport was crowded and bustling, and traffic was backed up in the London drizzle. A cab had knocked over a newspaper stand, and it took a long while for them to get to their terminal.

Waiting for the plane, they strolled past the airport shops. Edward paused outside a small jewelry store. In the window, a collection of diamond rings flashed under the bright display lights.

"Amazing, isn't it?" he said.

"What is?"

"Those little rocks are the source of all our troubles."

"Mmm," she agreed, watching a couple inside trying on rings.

Chapter 10

As the plane touched down in Cape Town, Jessica was jerked awake. She had dropped off to sleep, her head resting on Edward's shoulder.

"Sorry," she mumbled, embarrassed.

They disembarked from the plane and made their way through the chaos of reunited families and limo drivers holding menu boards with the names of businessmen.

Walking through the terminal at DF Malan Airport, Jessica found herself analyzing it in architect's mode, and decided that it was pretty hideous.—all plastic and steel, but no grace or even convenience.

They selected a promising looking hotel from the information stand next to baggage claim. When the cab dropped them off, they hardly recognized the place. The man at the front desk seemed surprised when they asked for two rooms.

They dumped their bags in their rooms, and then met up in the lobby so that Jessica could call Jack to see if there was any news from the London police.

The phone rang for a long time. When Jack finally answered, he was breathless.

"Jack, is everything all right?" asked Jessica.

"Oh, hi Jess. Yes, of course."

"Is Emma Okay?"

"Yes, she's fine. Just fine."

"Oh." She had the feeling she'd interrupted something. "I'm sorry if I caught you outside."

"Yes, just getting in actually. Been for a stroll in the park.."

Jessica glanced at her wristwatch. It was already dark. A bit late, but perhaps not for a romantic stroll, weather permitting. Edward might be right about those two.

"Have the police come up with anything?"

"No," said Jack, pausing. "Actually, Jess, I have some bad news, I'm afraid."

"Bad news? What could be worse than this?"

"I may have let the cat out of the bag, I'm afraid."

"How so?"

"Some woman rang. Said she worked in the Police department, and asked about your flight. You know, times and so on."

Jessica looked at Edward questioningly, but of course he couldn't hear Jack's end of the conversation. She didn't recall anyone calling the police to confirm that they were even going.

Jack continued. "I thought they were trying to contact you, you know about the break in. Then she wanted to know whom you were going to see. Said they'd lost the details."

"You didn't!"

"I did. Sorry. I blurted it out before I thought. It was only after she hung up abruptly that I got suspicious. I rang them back. They didn't know what I was talking about."

Jessica groaned. She quickly briefed Edward, while Jack listened.

"Liz?" suggested Edward.

"Probably," said Jessica, "Jack doesn't know her voice. It was most likely her that broke in too. I wonder if she found what she was after."

"Well, she sounds pretty resourceful. That must be where she got my number. I'm sorry, Jess," said Jack.

Jessica told him not to worry. She told him to give their best wishes to Emma, and said goodbye.

"Just what we need over here," said Edward, as she hung up.

"Well, no point in worrying about her now. She's the least of our problems. Come on, we better see the police."

They caught a cab to the station.

It was a good half hour before any one would see them. At last they were ushered into a small, gray cubicle by a man wearing a lightweight, gray suit that nearly matched the walls. His eyes were overlarge for his small, pinched face, and his drooping mustache was black, although his hair was silver.

"Good afternoon, Mr. Drummond, Miss Farrell. I'm Inspector Johannsen. I'm the one who's been in touch with Detective Sergeant Brightcastle. I'm afraid I have no news for you."

Edward stared at the man as if he were speaking a foreign language. "No news? Inspector, surely Brightcastle filled you in on who the perpetrators are? We know that the Van Der Meer Company owns a private plane, and that it was in London last week. Surely it can't be that difficult to trace them here."

"Yes, yes, Mr. Drummond. We know all that. But these are only suspected perpetrators. Detective Sergeant Brightcastle was unable to provide any relevant evidence—in fact, he provided no evidence whatsoever to implicate Winston Van Der Meer.

"Mr. Drummond, you must realize that Winston Van De Meer is an important man. Very important. His mine near Springbok employs a lot of people. Many people. He is respected, powerful. An important political contributor with many friends, both in and out of the North Cape."

Edward opened his mouth to speak, but the inspector continued, "Nevertheless, in spite of this lack of evidence, we have made certain inquiries. We have checked all of the commercial airlines and found no unaccounted persons matching the description of your child arriving within the past three days. The Van Der Meer plane is not at the Van Der Meer hanger here at DF Malan, and there are no air traffic control records of the plane requesting clearance to land anywhere in North Cape during the past three days."

Edward let out a sigh, and slumped back in his chair.

The inspector continued. "Of course, there are numerous small airstrips around the city and in the country, where it could have landed. But that would have been illegal, without clearance."

"Does this mean," asked Edward coolly, "That you're doing nothing?"

"Mr. Drummond," replied the inspector in exasperation, "With no evidence, I cannot simply march into Mr. Van Der Meer's office and place him under arrest. You may feel otherwise, but that is precisely what we've got: no evidence.

He leaned across the desk toward Edward. "I can assure you that we are taking every possible step to find the child. But the fact is, you can't even really prove that she is in South Africa, can you?"

"You know as well as I that she's here," replied Edward gruffly.

"Mr. Drummond," cautioned the inspector, "You are a stranger here. But you too, should tread lightly where Mr. Van Der Meer is concerned. It is also our role to protect our citizens. All of our citizens . . . Do you grasp my meaning?"

"I do, sir," said Edward standing. "Only too well."

As he ushered Jessica from the cubicle the inspector called after them, "Do let the front desk know where you are staying. We'll contact you if there is any news."

Edward brushed past the front desk and led the way out onto the street. The afternoon was hot, the sun glaring at them through the telephone wires.

"Where to now?" asked Jessica.

"I'm thinking that we're in the wrong place. The police here in Cape Town aren't going to do anything but put us off."

Jessica nodded. "And so . . . ?"

"We've got one lead the police wouldn't be interested in. But she may be able to shed some light on all of this."

Jessica raised her eyebrows, then a look of comprehension came over her face. "Mary Mogamo!"

Edward nodded. "Let's go back to the hotel. Tomorrow we'll check out and head for mining country. We'll need a car."

Jessica nodded. "At least they drive on the left here. I'm not sure I could handle everything being reversed."

Edward grinned. "We'll rent you something hot and snazzy. I remember how you like to tool about."

Jessica laughed. "After we've been back to the hotel and changed, let's get a bite. I don't know about you, but that airline food did nothing for me. I'm starving."

They had dinner that night in the restaurant across the road from the hotel. It was a quaint little place, lit by romantic candlelight, a fact not lost on Jessica. But their lighter mood of earlier in the day had given way to doubts, and uncertainty.

Dinner passed quietly, with not much spoken between them, but their eye contact was almost constant, and Jessica found it difficult to concentrate on her meal. She had little appetite. She eyed Edward in the dim light across the table, as she pushed her meal around the plate. His dark eyes caught and held the candlelight, like fireflies in a jar.

"Well," he said, startling her out of her reverie, "here's to finding Sarah, safe and sound." He raised his glass of wine, but his expression belied the lighthearted toast. Without drinking, he set down his glass. "God Jessie, what if we don't find her. What if . . ."

"Edward," she leaned across the small table and clasped his hand, "You can't think that way. You mustn't. We'll find her, and take her home with us."

He shook his head sadly and stared into his glass. Jessica summoned the waiter, paid their bill, and led him back to the elevator.

On the way to their floor Edward sighed deeply. Worry lines were etched across his forehead. Gently she slipped her hand into his, and leaned her head on his arm.

"Thanks Jessie," he said. "You're a good friend." As the elevator doors opened he kissed her on top of her head.

He walked her to her door, and left her for his own room, but she called him back, saying "Edward . . . I don't think either of us wants to be alone right now." He nodded appreciatively as she nervously fumbled with the keys.

It was a typical tourist room: African motif wallpaper, tribal statues, a zebra patterned bedspread. The only chair was loaded up with Jessica's suitcase, so Edward sat on the bed. Jessica set her bag on the bedside table and walked over to stand before him.

"Are you alright?" she asked, searching his face with concern.

"I'm fine, really. It's just that, I can't help wondering what is happening to Sarah. Is she warm enough? Getting enough to eat? Is she trying to be tough, and getting herself hurt? Are the kidnappers—"

"Sshh," Jessica whispered, putting her arms around him and pulling his head against her.

"Don't torture yourself darling. She's a good, strong child. I just know that she'll be all right until we get to her. You'll see."

The silence stretched between them.

"Darling? Did you say darling?" he asked seriously.

"Yes. Yes I did." Her voice was very quiet.

Edward rose from the bed. He cupped her face in his hands and whispered, "Jessie, I love you . . . and I need you."

Jessica turned her head and looked into his eyes. "Edward—," she began. What could she say? *Be honest,* she thought, *not manipulative.* But was it manipulative to want him always, as a wife, not just a lover? Was it unfair to him, and to Sarah, to take advantage of him when he was so worried about her? Yet she was worried, too. And she needed him right now as much as he needed her.

He sighed. "You know, I've spent five years convincing myself that you didn't love me—and that I didn't love you. Then, when I saw you again at my flat last week, I realized that I'd been lying to myself all this time." Edward looked up into her face. "At first I thought that it was hopeless, now that I've lost my inheritance. Then I began to hope that perhaps—because I've lost everything—I might have another chance at winning your love. But the way you acted . . . I didn't know what to think."

Jessica nodded.

"I felt that things were still hopeless," she said, "since we were looking for the diamonds that would turn your life back into what it has always been."

Edward gave her a wry smile. “Do you realize that when there were no diamonds in that box, I was actually relieved? It was as if the weight of the world had been lifted from my shoulders. I tried hard not to show my elation, because I knew that everyone else was disappointed when it turned out there was no treasure. But for me it was almost as if I’d been given a new start.”

Jessica laughed. “I felt the same way, but I was afraid to show it.”

Edward continued. “Do you know that I was on the verge of asking you to marry me when that blasted telephone rang, and we got the news? Since that time—before it really—I’ve been unable to think of anything but Sarah.”

Jessica’s eye opened wide. “Marry me? I thought you wanted me to be your mistress. I thought it was because I’d left you, and you couldn’t forgive me.”

Edward nodded. “I know. And then you were so angry, I didn’t know what to say, and then the news about Sarah came, and it’s all simply been a nightmare.” He pressed his face to her abdomen. His voice was muffled when he continued. “In fact, for months I’ve been worrying about her . . . how I could care for her now that lost my fortune. It took the kidnapping for me to realize that it was never my money, or the mansion in London, or household servants that she needed.” He shook his head. “What she needs is me.”

He stood, and pulled her to him. “And she needs a mother, Jessie. She needs you,” he whispered.

Jessica felt her eyes brimming with tears. When she tried to speak, she found she had no voice. At last, struggling, she croaked, “Oh, Edward, I’m so worried about her.”

“If you weren’t, I wouldn’t love you, Jessie. And I do love you. You know that, don’t you?”

Unable to answer, Jessica nodded, and squeezed her eyes shut. Then Edward’s lips were on hers, and her tears were spilling onto his face. Their lips merged, softly at first, then passionately.

Jessica felt overwhelmed by her emotions. She felt her confusion fading, overwhelmed by her love for him. Things were so different now from the way they'd been. They *could* make this work. She was sure of it.

Her hands roamed down his back, and moved around to his chest. She freed the buttons of his shirt as she kissed him. Fingers sliding down to his belt, she fumbled at the buckle. Following her lead, he released the buttons of her blouse, and pulled it open. The front catch of her bra was no impediment, and he cupped her delicate breasts in his hands, then pulling her to him, and then down onto the bed. He cradled her to him, nuzzling her neck, stroking her breasts, caressing her abdomen, pulling her thighs against his.

Edward traced his fingers along her cheek, looking deeply into her eyes. His fingers drifted lower, stroking the downy softness of her stomach, toying with her navel, drifting through the silky hairs of her mound. His hand had slipped between her legs, and she found it increasingly difficult to concentrate as his fingers slipped into her warm wetness. Jessica felt her body rising to meet his fingers. She moaned softly. Her fingers clutched the sheet, and her breath became ragged.

She felt his hardness against her, and desperately wanted him inside her. She clutched at his back and pulled him on top of her. She spread her legs and pulled him against her center, willing him to enter.

But he held back. His mouth played against her lips, and his tongue found hers. She was panting hard, clutching at him. When the kiss ended he pulled away, waiting for her to open her eyes. At last he said huskily, "Jessie. Will you marry me?"

Before she'd even finished nodding, he plunged into her, and their bodies merged as one, moving together passionately as they celebrated their new beginning.

* * *

The knocking roused her from sleep. Edward was already sitting on the edge of the bed, pulling his pants on. "Did you order room service?" asked Jessica.

He shook his head. "Maybe it's the police."

Jessica sat up and pulled the sheet tightly around her. Edward, naked to the waist, crossed to the door and opened it. Jessica saw the muscles in his back tighten, and then Liz brushed passed him into the room.

She eyed Jessica with amusement. "Well, isn't this cozy! Thought you might be in this tramp's room since you weren't in your own."

Edward's eyes were slits. "How did you find us?"

"It's amazing what men will tell a crying woman. A few tears and that hotel clerk was butter in my hands. I told him I was your wife, and that you were having an affair. Not too far from the truth, is it?"

"You know what I mean," said Edward.

"I followed you back to London. I was sure you were on to something. When you left, I looked up Jack Montague's phone number and called him. I pretended I was a secretary from the police department, and asked which flight you'd taken. I even asked him to remind me of the name of the person you were looking for—Van Der Meer. But then he got suspicious, so I hung up."

Edward ran his hand through his hair. "What do you want?"

"I think you already know the answer to that, Edward. I want my share of the diamonds."

"What diamonds?"

"Come on, Edward. Do you expect me to believe you've come all the way to South Africa on a vacation?" She looked at Jessica. "Or a honeymoon, perhaps? I know you're after your Uncle's diamonds, and I intend to get my share, or I'll make things very difficult for you."

Edward sighed. He settled onto the bench next to Jessica's open suitcase and studied Liz. "You really don't care about Sarah at all, do you?" he said.

"What has the child to do with this?" she snapped.

"It's Sarah we've come for. And if there were any diamonds, we'd need them to pay her ransom."

"She's your child, not mine. Not any more," muttered Liz. She ran her finger along the edge of the mirror by the door.

Jessica thought she detected the slightest hint of sadness beneath Liz's bravado. She addressed the woman softly. "Surely you see that Sarah's safety is all that we're concerned about, Liz?"

Liz made a show of eyeing her naked shoulders, but she didn't immediately respond. She wiped the dust from her fingertips and blew it in Edward's direction. "The child is dead," she said simply.

Jessica let out a little gasp, but Edward shook his head and held up his hand to forestall her outburst. "How could you possibly know that, Liz? Are you in this with Winston?"

Liz snorted. "Of course not. And I don't know it. Not for certain, anyway. But isn't it obvious? You saw what Winston did to me."

"You did it to yourself," said Edward.

"I was lucky," said Liz. "Winston could have done worse."

"If that was luck, I don't need any of it," replied Edward. "Now please. Go." He held the door open for her.

Liz stepped to the door, then glanced back at Jessica. "He's good at it isn't he?" she said with a smirk.

Edward pushed her out the door and pressed it closed behind her. He rested his forehead against the closed door and sighed heavily.

The room was quiet until Jessica said softly, "You don't think she's really dead, do you?" She was close to tears.

Edward returned to the bed, and sat next to her, with his arm around her shoulders. She was trembling.

"I don't know, Jess," he said. His voice was tired. "I just don't know. But we have to keep believing, and not give up."

Jessica nodded. She was quiet for a long while, thinking of Sarah, of the last time she'd seen her. She'd been so happy that the three of them were back together again. They'd promised her that they'd be back from Scotland soon. Now that seemed like an awful lie. Would she ever see her again?

"What are you thinking?" asked Edward.

She closed her eyes, and tried to think of something that wouldn't drag Edward into the same well of despair into which she felt herself falling. All she could think of was to sidetrack him with thoughts of

Liz. She could see that he had no feelings for the woman at all, but he'd believe her if she acted jealous. "What ever possessed you to marry such a woman?" she said. "*You're* not like that."

Edward sighed. He stood and walked over to the mini refrigerator, opened it, then closed it again. The sky outside was fading, and the room was cloaked in gloom, but neither of them moved to light a lamp.

With his back still toward her, he began to speak. "When I first met Liz—Elizabeth—she wasn't like that. She was different. A bit on the wild side, but after a whole life of living in the so-called upper class, she was like a breath of fresh air. She was exciting. Doing crazy things with her was an adventure." He turned and leaned against the refrigerator. "And my father couldn't stand her, which made her even more attractive. He preferred the socialites that I had been dating. Wealthy families and all"

Jessica nodded.

"Her family had little money," continued Edward. "They were on the lower side of middle class—don't get me wrong," he added, quickly, "that didn't bother me. But it bothered the rest of my family."

He paused. "That's not true, really. I don't think the money thing really bothered my father, either. Although he tried it as an argument. What really bothered him was her character . . . he said she had none. Said that she was frivolous."

Edward crossed to the bed and sat back down beside her. "He was right, in that, although I couldn't see it at the time. Among other flaws, she has a fondness for gambling . . . in all things. A fondness, but not a talent. It's cost me most of my fortune. And a good deal of my self-respect." He contemplated his clasped hands.

"Go on," said Jessica. It was fascinating to hear the story of Liz, at long last.

"Well, it's pretty simple really. I was in the service by then, about to go away on my first extended mission, when she got pregnant with Sarah. I did the right thing. In retrospect, I think she did it on purpose to get me to marry her. She wanted the money behind the name of Drummond." He shook his head. "She certainly got that."

He sighed again, and rubbed his cheek. "Anyway, after Sarah was born, she decided that she'd had enough. She had money, and figured she could get more from me, so she left, without a backward glance. Frankly, I was glad to see the back of her."

He shifted position and the bed creaked with his weight. "So when my term was up, I came home to an empty house. My father was dead, and Liz had flown the coup. It was just Sarah and me. And the servants. The only times I heard from Liz were when she needed money."

He rested his face in his hands. Jessica leaned forward and touched his shoulder. His bare skin was cold, and she realized that the evening air was chilling the room through the cracks around the window. It was nearly dark, now. "We all make mistakes Edward," said Jessica. "You chose the wrong relationship, and I chose no relationship at all." She turned his head toward her and looked into his eyes. "But there's nothing for it but to pick up the pieces of our lives and get on with it." She brushed his cheek with her lips and whispered softly, "She's given you a wonderful child, whether she knows it or not. And we *will* find her."

He pulled her close and held her in the gathering darkness.

Outside, the orange glow of sunset surrendered to the night. Far below the traffic sounded, harsh and foreign.

* * *

Mary Mogamo's house was near Klienzee, a coastal town owned by the DeBeers company, South Africa's dominant diamond mining company. It was outside of Springbok, most of a day's drive from Cape Town. Jessica drove the Land Rover they'd rented in Cape Town, handling the pitted, gravel strewn roads with ease.

As they entered diamond mining territory they first noticed the razor wire. It stretched endlessly, defining the security zones around the mines. In a country where a single gem was worth a year's wages, security was everything.

As they neared Klienzee, Jessica was overwhelmed by the sea of squatters' camps and townships that stretched to the horizon. The settlements were divided by waste tips—mountains of overgrown blue rock, the remains of diamond mines. Everywhere there was the fine dust of Kimberlite. It blew through the razor wire that lined the road; it sifted through the cracks of the Land Rover's windows; and it settled over everything. Excavators and bulldozers moved through the haze, reprocessing the diamond waste.

Near one waste plant they passed an enormous graveyard for the blacks who worked in the mines. Heaps of rock marked the graves, many of them freshly constructed. A few precious possessions adorned the piles of rock: an old basin, a cracked teapot, a few chipped cups.

The towns of the whites provided a stark contrast to the surrounding desolation. Neat white houses with spacious green lawns lined the streets. But each town had its sister settlement of hovels. A stream of black servants, many in uniform, paraded the dirt paths that connected them.

The squatters' camps were even worse: endless shacks of corrugated metal lining streets crowded with black workers returning from their shift at the mine.

The townships of the Coloureds—those who were neither black nor white—were somewhat better. Modest homes were neatly laid out along dusty streets. The owners took obvious pride in their meager accommodations. Many of the Coloured workers were out sweeping their front steps, trying to make headway against the ever-present dust. Here and there an attempt had been made to plant a garden. Some of the modest houses even had more rustic servant quarters—for blacks—in the rear.

It was in one of these townships that Mary Mogamo lived. A tired picket fence surrounded the small house. Its rusty-hinged gate opened onto a small garden, with neatly tended rows of young sprouts. As Jessica and Edward walked to the front door of the modest clapboard house, they could see the faces of curious neighbors watching them from either side. Jessica wasn't sure which was attracting more attention: the two of them, or the Land Rover.

They knocked, and waited expectantly. A small, brown-skinned woman with gray hair, neatly dressed, opened the door. "Yes?" she asked. Her voice was soft, with a South African lilt, but she spoke English, perhaps in response to the incongruity of such visitors. Jessica saw her studying Edward with an unreadable expression on her face, and was certain that the woman already had some idea of their reason for visiting.

"Good afternoon, Madam. My name is Edward Drummond. This is Jessica Farrell. We're looking for a Mary Mogamo."

The woman nodded and stepped aside, motioning for them to enter. "You've found her," she said softly.

She led them into a sitting room. It was sparsely but tastefully decorated. There were simple lace curtains at the windows. An assortment of small china ornaments adorned an oak coffee table. They sat together on a comfortable old sofa.

"I'll put on some tea, and then we can talk," she said. She spoke with a soothing lilt, a few words of Afrikaans mixed in. But it was easy to understand her, and her voice carried the firmness of a woman who has seen much.

Watching the woman move, it was hard to believe that she had to be in her seventies. As Jessica watched her fill the teakettle and place it on the stove, she observed that each movement that Mary made was carried out with a subdued grace.

"You would be Charles' nephew?" the woman called from the kitchen, as she arranged cups and saucers on a tray, then carried it into the sitting room.

Edward nodded. "Yes. I'm the son of his brother, Robert."

Mary nodded. "You bear more than a passing resemblance to my Charles," she said. Carefully, she set a cup, saucer, and spoon in front of each of them.

"Charles never talked very much about his brother," continued Mary. "I suppose it was because he had no interest in the mine." A far away look came across Mary's face, and Jessica saw the years melt away, as the woman thought back to her youth. "Charles lived and breathed diamonds. Sometimes it seemed to me he could almost smell them, where they lay buried. When, as a boy, his father sent him back to England, it must have been awful for him."

"Did you stay in touch with Charles after he returned to England?" asked Jessica.

Mary nodded. "He sent me a letter, explaining what happened." She paused, seeming to decide how much to say, then continued. "Shortly after he left I learned that I was pregnant. Given the circumstances, I felt it was better if Charles didn't know."

Jessica nodded. She could imagine how hard it would be on Charles, knowing that he would never see his own son.

The teakettle whistled in the kitchen, and Mary left to fetch it.

"Do you think she got a letter too?" Jessica asked Edward quietly.

"She doesn't seem very surprised to see us," he said.

Mary returned with the teakettle, and poured them each a cup. She settled herself opposite them and continued. "Charles and I fell out of touch, and many years passed. I never expected to see him again. Then, one day, there he was at my door. We were both nearly 20 years older, but I knew him in an instant. I'm ashamed to say that I would have taken up where we left off on the spot, if circumstances had permitted. But it was not to be. He had a wife and daughter, he told me, and I could see from his expression that he was deeply devoted to both. We talked for hours, though, and at last I told him about Arthur."

She took a sip from her cup, then set it back on the saucer. "At first he was angry that I hadn't told him before. Then he was sad that he'd missed seeing Arthur grow up. He wanted to know all about our son—his likes, dislikes, ambitions, and so on. Arthur was in his first year of college then, and living halfway across the country, in Bloemfontein. He was studying electrical engineering—it was the beginning of the 1960s, and people were talking about electrification of the outlying townships. Arthur was determined to make a difference in the lives of people like us. People that he said were being taken advantage of by the diamond mines."

"It must have been very difficult for a Coloured during that time," said Jessica.

"Oh, Arthur wasn't Coloured. At least not officially," said Mary.

Jessica looked at her quizzically.

"You see, I had the misfortune of being an unwed Coloured woman. But Arthur had the good fortune of being very light-skinned. Of course, here in South Africa, they're very careful about such things. Color is everything. But, in a way, we were both lucky."

She leaned forward to pour more tea into Edward's cup, then continued. "At the time, I worked as a servant in the house of a white couple who treated me with great kindness. Their name was Murcheson. They had always longed for children, but in twenty years of marriage they had never managed to have one. When they found out that I was pregnant, they were kind enough to allow me to stay on. They even offered to help me raise the child. Then, when the child was born, they discovered that he could easily pass for white. They offered to raise him as their own son—if I was willing to give him up. It was a very difficult decision."

Jessica nodded. How awful to have a child, and be unable to keep him.

Mary folded her hands in her lap and closed her eyes. "And so, my son became Arthur Murcheson." She smiled wistfully. "He never knew that I was his mother. The Murchesons moved away, because their neighbors would have known their secret." She sighed; her hands were restless in her lap. "They offered to take me with them, as their servant. I was tempted. But I knew that I would never be able to watch my boy grow up, living with him every day, seeing each little success or failure, without revealing their secret."

Mary sighed again, and sat quietly until Jessica leaned forward and placed her hand over those of the older woman. Mary opened her eyes and smiled at Jessica, then continued. "And so I watched his progress from afar, experiencing his childhood through the occasional letter from the Murchesons. They sent me the photos you see on the mantle. Even a few of his report cards from school. And, I think in deference to his true heritage, they raised him with values very different from those of most of the whites with whom he grew up."

Mary sat up straighter, and Jessica could see the pride that she felt in her son reflected in her eyes. "My Arthur was something of a crusader. Straight out of college he founded a company—the Transvaal Utility Company—which was dedicated to bringing utilities to the outlying townships."

"You must have been very proud," said Jessica.

Mary nodded. "Charles and I were both very proud of him."

"Did Charles ever meet Arthur?" asked Jessica.

"He did. But not as a father."

"How so?" asked Edward.

"After Arthur founded his company, he began purchasing right-of-way to run the utilities to the townships. In the early years, the company was always pressed for cash. But Arthur knew that it was important to obtain the right-of-ways before the white landowners realized that they could extort large sums of money from the utility companies. So Arthur used his own money and credit to purchase as much right-of-way as he could, then let the company lease the land back from him in order to conserve cash."

Mary picked up her teacup, then realized that it was empty, and set it back down. "As a geologist, Charles used some of the same surveyors that Arthur's company used. Eventually, he convinced one of them to introduce him to Arthur, and they formed a sort of friendship. Charles and Arthur both shared a love of this land, and a concern for the people living on it. In fact, Charles even helped Arthur with the acquisition of some of the right-of-way for his utilities."

An alarm bell was going off in Jessica's head, but she couldn't quite identify its source yet.

Mary continued. "Charles was always afraid that Arthur would be found out. The Murchesons had covered their tracks very well, but Charles worried that his friendship with Arthur was also endangering the boy. Apartheid was very strong in those days, and if Arthur were found out, the consequences would have been disastrous. He would not have even been allowed to own property."

Edward shook his head. "It seems hard to believe that this country could've been so inequitable."

Mary smiled wryly. "Perhaps things haven't changed as much as you might imagine, Mr. Drummond."

Edward looked thoughtful. "You may be right, Miss Mogamo. It is 'Miss'?"

Mary nodded. "Yes. I never married. You see, Charles and I really did love one another. I knew there could never be another love in my life like his. In another time and place . . ." Her eyes grew distant, seeing a past that might have been.

"Perhaps you could've gone to England?" suggested Edward.

"Mr. Drummond," said Mary, "Have you any idea how difficult it would be for someone from the lower classes to try to function in the kind of society in which Charles circulated?"

Edward winced. He glanced at Jessica, who returned his look sadly. She could tell that he was thinking of her, and the past they'd once shared.

Edward sighed. "I'm afraid I do."

Mary looked from one to the other, then continued. "At any rate, Charles feared very little, himself; but he feared for Arthur. And he feared Winston Van Der Meer."

"Winston Van Der Meer?" asked Edward.

"The head of the Van Der Meer Diamond Company. Winston and Charles grew up together, yet they were rivals. Their fathers started the Van Der Meer Diamond Company. Winston and Charles inherited the mine, and were to run it as an even partnership. But they had very different ideas about how to do so. Winston's goal was to squeeze every drop of effort possible from each of the mineworkers; Charles' goal was to create an environment in which the workers would want to perform their best. Charles and Winston fought bitterly."

Mary shook her head, sadly. "Charles always suspected that it was Winston who had found us out, and gotten him sent back to England. Later, after he returned with his wife and child, he was terrified that Winston would learn about Arthur, and try to destroy the boy."

Jessica set down her teacup and leaned toward Mary. "Do you really think that Mr. Van Der Meer would have done such a thing?"

"I don't know. But I know that he is ruthless. And I think that Charles may even have suspected him in the death of his wife and daughter."

"You mean the auto accident?" asked Jessica.

"Yes. Before he left, Charles told me that he didn't believe that it was an accident."

Jessica shivered. These people were even more dangerous than they'd imagined. A dreadful thought occurred to her. "Mary," she said, "I'm so sorry about Arthur's death. But . . . may I ask how he died? You don't think it was . . ." She found it difficult to continue.

Mary shook her head. "No. Arthur wasn't murdered. My Arthur had a kind heart . . . but not a strong one." She sighed. "His crusade to bring electricity to the outlying townships took him to some of the least hospitable parts of this country. It was on one of those trips that he contracted malaria. It troubled him for over thirty years, and in the end contributed to his death." She turned her teacup idly in its saucer, then sat back in her chair. "Well. Now you know my life's story. Tell me. What brings you two to this God-forsaken corner of the planet?"

Edward said simply, "We believe that Winston Van Der Meer may have kidnapped my daughter."

Mary grasped the arms of her chair and stiffened. "Oh my God . . ." she whispered.

"Mr. Van Der Meer wants to trade my child for some diamonds he believes that we have," added Edward. "Some diamonds that Charles found. But we haven't any such gems. So our only recourse is to try to find and rescue my daughter."

"Diamonds?" asked Mary, dazedly. "That Charles found?"

"Yes," continued Edward. "We recently received a curious letter. It was from Charles, and was addressed to my father, Robert. Both have been dead for years. And yet it was mailed recently. The letter indicated that some rings that Charles had left to the family contained clues that would lead to the diamonds. But they led only to a safe that was filled with papers, no diamonds. Although those papers are what enabled us to find you."

Mary had gone pale, and Jessica leaned forward and touched her arm. "What is it, Mary?" she asked.

The woman swallowed and looked at each of them in turn, then seemed to make a decision. "There is something I haven't told you," she said. "I, too, received a letter from Charles recently." She paused. "You can imagine what a shock that was."

Jessica nodded, encouraging the woman to continue.

"I subsequently learned that the letter was sent as part of the execution of Arthur's will. You see, Arthur and Charles knew each other somewhat better than I have indicated. The land that Charles helped Arthur to buy was more than utility right-of-way. It was land upon which Charles had made what he described as a tremendous diamond discovery—diamonds just lying about for the taking, he said."

Edward set his teacup down clumsily and leaned forward. "Go on," he said excitedly.

"Apparently the terrain was uncommon for that type of diamond field," Mary continued. "Charles said something about the natural geology being altered by an unusual runoff pattern. That's why no one had ever noticed it before. Things were going badly at the mine, then. Charles was furious with the way that Winston was treating the workers. He was trying to decide what he should do about the find, when he came home one evening to the news that Margaret and Lilly were dead." Mary shook her head, sadly. "As far as Charles was concerned, his life was over. He came to me that night, and sat on the couch right where you are, and cried into my shoulder for hours." She closed her eyes, and her voice grew distant. "When the sun came up, he told me he had decided what he was going to do. He would give his half of the mining company to Winston, and leave South Africa forever. I tried to convince him to rest, to think about it, to put off the decision until the pain began to fade, but there was no reasoning with him. He arranged for Arthur to buy the diamond field. No one suspected anything—Arthur was buying right-of-way all of the time. That night was the last time I ever saw Charles."

Mary drew a handkerchief from her pocket and wiped one eye, then the other. Edward stood up and walked to the mantel, then turned back to her. "So Arthur ended up with the diamonds," he said.

"No," Mary sniffed. She stood and went into an adjoining room, returning a moment later with a yellowed piece of paper. "When Arthur died, he left his holdings to a trust established by the Murchesons, who are long since dead. But unknown to Arthur, that trust stated that any inheritance from Arthur's side of the family should be passed on to the Mogamos."

Mary smiled wryly, and shook her head. "You see, Arthur never did know that I was his mother. But the Murchesons remembered me. Even from beyond the grave."

She handed Edward the paper. He glanced over it quickly.

"So now you know," Mary finished. "I own all of Arthur's land—including the diamond field."

She sat down, and sighed. "It's ironic, in a way. In the days of apartheid I would not have been allowed to own property. Charles could not have foreseen how much would change after his death. But by this odd chain of events, I am now probably the wealthiest Coloured person in North Cape."

Edward walked over to Jessica and handed her the paper, then sat down in his former seat. "That's quite a story," he said.

"The sad part of it is," she said, "that I'm an old woman. I have no use for such wealth. In the week since that paper arrived, I've been trying to decide what is the right thing to do. Finally, yesterday, I decided that I would sell the property to the DeBeers company, and use the proceeds to establish a University here for the mineworkers' children."

Edward and Jessica looked at her in admiration. She shrugged. "It's what Arthur would have wanted," she said, collecting the teacups and setting them back on the tray. "I'm afraid that all of this doesn't help much with your problem, however. Unless you think that the diamond field might help save your daughter . . ."

Edward shook his head. "If Winston Van Der Meer really had Margaret and Lilly killed, I'm not sure what can save my daughter." He looked at Jessica grimly.

"I can't say for certain that he had them killed," said Mary. "You can be the judge of that yourselves. If you go to the Van Der Meer mine, you'll pass Maggie's corner—as the locals call it. It's just past marker seventeen, a few kilometers before the mine entrance. There's an enormous turnout there. So enormous that it's hard to imagine how anyone could accidentally go off the edge. But the drop is sheer, and there'd be no surviving it."

Jessica shuddered at the thought of Charles' family, plunging off that corner to their deaths. She squeezed her eyes shut in a fruitless attempt to block out the image.

"Do you think the child might be at the Van Der Meer Mining Company?" asked Edward.

"Winston Van Der Meer may be a criminal, but he's not a fool," said Mary. "I doubt that he'd take them there. It's a real company, with real employees. That's the last thing they need, with all the other problems they're having."

"Problems?" asked Edward.

"There are rumors that the company is on the verge of bankruptcy," said Mary. "It seems that Charles was much better at finding diamonds than anyone whom Winston has hired since. They're only rumors, however."

Jessica sighed. "It all seems so hopeless," she said, holding back tears. "We have nothing to go on, nowhere to look."

Edward took her hand. "Jessie, we'll find them. If we have to turn this country upside down, we'll find them."

She looked into his eyes, and tried to feel hopeful. But the situation seemed overwhelming.

"I wish that I could be of some assistance to you," said Mary.

"You've been more than helpful, Mary," said Edward.

"If you should need anything else . . ." she offered.

Edward nodded. "Thank you. We'll be in touch."

Edward stepped out into the warm night. It had grown dark during their time with Mary, and they were both surprised by how much more charming the township looked in the amber glow of the lights from the windows up and down the street. In the doorway a thought occurred to Jessica, and she turned back to the woman. "Mary, one more thing. Would you have any idea where the Van Der Meer mines would keep a company plane? A jet?"

"There's only one place they could keep one, if it's around here. Springbok Airport. Everything else is a dirt strip. I don't think you could land a jet on one of them."

The duo went back to the car.

"What now?" inquired Jessica.

"The mine. I think we should start there."

"Don't you think we're better off tracking down the plane that brought her here? Follow the lead from there? As Mary said, the mine is full of employees, it would be too obvious a place to hide a child."

"But we're certain to be able to confront Mr. Van Der Meer if we go there. It's wasting time trying to find the plane."

The two stared at each other.

"OK then, let's split up. You go to the mine, I'll check out the airport," said Jessica.

Edward hesitated. "That's all very well for me. I'll be at the mine site, full of people. But you'll be out the back of beyond on your own. I don't like it."

"Edward, an airport isn't exactly the back of beyond. I'll be fine. And if we split up we'll cover the possibilities that much faster.

Edward considered. He looked into her face, and she cocked her head, projecting unconcern. "Well . . . All right. But you must be very careful. If there's any question, come get me."

She patted his hand.

"Don't worry, I can take care of myself. But we won't get anything done if we don't get a move on."

He started the Land Rover, and they headed back towards Springbok.

At the center of town they checked the map, and turned onto the road that led to the Van Der Meer mine.

After about twenty minutes Edward slowed at a spot with a wide turnout. They studied the place, comparing it with their mental picture of Maggie's corner.

"Let's stop," said Jessica.

It was a dangerous stretch of road.

An enormous turnout separated the road from the precipice. Dry brush lined the edge, but there was no guardrail.

"It's strange that there's no guard rail here," she remarked. "I saw several spots on the way up that had them. Particularly on the outside turns."

"Yes," agreed Edward, "Although it would be difficult to go off here—by accident, at least. This turnout is wide enough to for a pretty good sized truck."

Jessica nodded.

It wasn't a likely spot for an accident.

But maybe for a murder . . .

They got out of the car and stretched. Edward wandered over to the side of the road and looked down.

"My God," he whispered quietly.

"What is it?" asked Jessica, and she came up and stood beside him.

"It's as if I'd been here before. I can remember my father's description, word for word . . . a bend in the road, where the cliff face is sheer . . . a large outcrop of rocks across the gorge . . . and an old, weathered tree. There, see? You can still make out a gouge, after all these years. The car must have sideswiped the tree on the way down . . ."

He stepped over to the edge and carefully made his way down toward the tree.

"Edward, be careful," called Jessica.

She scrambled over the graveled surface to join him. He was staring solemnly at a small plaque under the tree.

"I had forgotten about this."

The plaque read: In loving memory of Margaret, beloved wife of Charles, and our beautiful daughter Lilly, 1963.

Jessica put her hand on Edward's shoulder.

They stood for a long time in silence. When Edward finally looked over at Jessica, he saw that she was crying.

"Jessie?"

She sniffed, trying to hold back the tears. "My parents," she whispered, simply.

"Oh Jessie, I'm sorry. It was thoughtless of me. Your parents, they died in a car accident didn't they?"

She nodded.

"It was a drunk driver. They were on their way home. It was the night of the school concert. I had decided to stay on with some friends for a party.

"I had a special 'friend' there. You know, a boy I had a crush on. Dad had asked me to drive them home. He had been really tired of late, and did not feel up to it. It was quite a drive. My mother never did get her license. But I was selfish, told them I just had to stay, and that I would come home with friends later."

Edward put his arm around her shoulder and drew her to him.

"Then what happened?" he asked quietly.

"There never was a later. The police came by after about an hour, and told me they were both dead. They took me to the hospital firstly, to . . . to see them. Later I went to my Aunt's."

Edward was quiet for a long time, comforting her as she wept. At last he broke the silence. "You were only seventeen?"

"Yes," she sniffed. She looked up at Edward solemnly. "My father was a good driver, or at least I thought so. But he was so tired that night." Jessica squeezed her eyes tightly shut, forced the last tears from the corners. "If I had gone with them, I could have driven."

"There was no guarantee that you would have been able to avoid the other car."

"I know, but Dad had made me go through an Advanced Driver School after I got my license. He insisted, although I thought he was foolish at the time."

"Really? I never knew that. So you're an expert driver, then, are you?"

"Well, I wouldn't say that. I failed the first time, but Dad sent me back. I think it was his reaction to the fact that Mum never learned. He said if I was going to go out into the world, driving around here, there and everywhere, then I was to be prepared for all eventualities, and I was to go back until I passed the test. Which I did, eventually. Then I went on to do Defensive Driving. That was fun, I loved that."

"Your Dad cared about you."

"Yes. Yes, he did. I still miss them both dreadfully."

She looked at Edward and smiled weakly.

"Let's go," he said quietly.

They made their way back to the Land Rover. Jessica automatically sat in the driver's seat this time. She started the car, and they continued on toward the mine.

In only a few minutes they came to a large but dilapidated sign that pointed out the entrance to the Van Der Meer mining company.

Jessica pulled off the road and stopped.

Edward got out and went around to the driver's side. Leaning in the window, he gave her a quick kiss on the cheek.

"Be careful. These sods we're dealing with are likely to get up to anything if we get too close to them."

She nodded, then turned the car around and headed back to the road leading to Springbok.

It's nice to have someone worry about me for a change, thought Jessica, as she drove toward the airport.

She suppressed a sigh. It was the first time she had been away from Edward for nearly a week. It felt . . . strange. Like all of her wasn't there. He had been so kind to her, so patient.

Still, she'd be glad when this was over.

There was no security at Springbok Airport. Jessica asked about the Van Der Meer plane at the administrative office, and then drove her Land Rover directly out to the hanger they'd indicated. On the way she unfastened the top two buttons of her blouse. She had a feeling this encounter was going to require all of her powers of persuasion.

A lanky blond man in a brown leather flight jacket was picking bits of gravel out of the tread of the front landing gear tire as she drove up. He rose and came to meet her as she parked next to the plane and got out.

"You're here early," the man said.

Jessica thought fast. "You were expecting me, then?" she asked.

"Well, I wasn't expecting a lady, actually—not that I'm complaining," he added smiling, "But yes, I was expecting someone from the buyer's office by the weekend. You are from the buyer?"

Jessica quickly realized that she couldn't press on with this line of interrogation, so she decided to shift subjects. "The plane's for sale, then?" She asked.

The man raised his eyebrows, considering her. "It was," he shrugged, nodding toward the jet. "You're too late, I'm afraid. Quite a deal they got. Low hours, good range, a real honey."

"How far is its range?"

"Far enough to get me wherever I've been asked to go."

"London, even?"

The man eyed her, a hint of wariness creeping into his expression. "Sure. I've had her to London several times, just this past year." He leaned against the Land Rover's hood, appraising her openly. "Why do you ask?"

Jessica dodged the question by sticking out her hand. "I'm Jessica. Jessica Farrell."

"Kip," said the man, taking her hand possessively in his. "Dan Kipling, actually, but everybody calls me Kip."

"So, I take it this is the Van Der Meer plane," she asked, walking around the aircraft, swaying her hips as she went.

Kip followed her, watching her with obvious interest.

"That's right. Little beauty, as I said."

"Much room for passengers?"

"Enough," he said. He eyed her, puzzled.

"Look . . . Jessica is it? As I said, this aircraft is sold. Now if you're after a pilot, I'm your man." He leaned against the side of the plane and openly appraised her. "But I have a feeling you're after something else. Wouldn't have anything to do with a kid, would it?"

Jessica froze. She turned slowly to look at him.

"Uh . . . a kid?"

"Yes, a kid. I flew a kid in here, a couple of days ago. It's been playing on my mind ever since."

"Go on," said Jessica. She could feel her pulse pounding.

"She didn't seem to want to be here. It didn't feel right, bringing her kickin' and screamin' into the country. But I did because I was paid to fly, that's all! I had no part in bringing her here. You can blame Winston Van Der Meer for that."

She was stunned. To have the information she was after fall into her lap like this.

"Where is she now?" she asked breathlessly, adding, "I won't say anything about your telling me, I promise."

"I'll show you where she is, but I can't take you there. Mr. Van Der Meer is far too powerful for a peon like me to cross him." He pulled a map out of his flight bag and spread it onto the hood of the Land Rover. Smoothing the map with his palms, he looked her straight in the eye. "And if anyone asks? . . . You've never met me."

Chapter 11

Winston Van Der Meer stood on the catwalk of the tall, brown building at the edge of Pit 23. A new crush had started, his third and final desperate attempt to extort compensation from the wretched hole of Pit 23.

Winston's eyebrows lifted in surprise. He'd been expecting a phone call from Edward Drummond, not a visit. But the man crossing the courtyard below was definitely Edward. And he was heading straight for the separation plant.

Rising some 30 feet above the barren ground, the building was surmounted by the metal catwalk where Winston stood. Directly beneath him was the conveyor belt, which carried the gravel into the giant metal cylinder that emerged from the section below. The crushing cylinder.

Winston watched the endless flow of gravel. He licked his lips. The day was heating up. The air seemed to suck the moisture from his skin, and his mouth was parched. He couldn't hear the sounds of the mining operation coming from the pit, but he could smell its dust in the air. Where he stood, the only sound was the noise of the continuous cascade of gravel pouring off of the conveyor belt into the top of the crusher.

Below, he saw Edward catch sight of him, and quicken his pace. The man crossed to the base of the building and climbed the stairs to the top, then followed the catwalk along the side until he was within a few feet of Winston.

Winston turned to face him. "I assume that it's me you're looking for?" he said.

"It's my daughter that I'm looking for," said Edward.

"How would I know where your daughter is?"

"I won't dignify that question with an answer."

"Surely you're not accusing me of harming a child?"

"Let's start with kidnapping. You'd better not have harmed—"

"Please, Mr. Drummond. I'm a very compassionate man."

"Was it compassion, when you had my uncle's family killed?"

Winston's hand tightened on the railing of the catwalk. The noise of the gravel falling below them was loud in his ears. "Who told you that?"

"A woman named Mary."

Winston snorted. "Her," he said, disdainfully. He shook his head. "Your Uncle Charles always did love the gutter."

"At least my Uncle Charles loved something other than diamonds."

Winston fought for control of his emotions. He remained silent, his bony fingers working themselves over the railing of the catwalk as he pursed his lips, thinking. He turned to watch the gravel cascade off the end of the conveyor belt below them. The gray blur was mesmerizing: a steady stream of base material, concealing the tiniest of prizes. At last he looked back at Edward and said, more gently, "Charles was lucky. He loved deeply—if perhaps unwisely."

"Love is rarely wise," replied Edward.

Winston watched him impassively. "Perhaps not," he said at last. "I suppose I love this company above all else; yet little good it's done me." His tone sharpened, and he turned to face Edward. "You have something I want," he said coldly.

"As do you."

Winston nodded. "Give me the information, and I will release your daughter."

"How do I know she's all right?"

"She's all right," answered Winston. "And even if she weren't, what could you do, hey?"

Edward swallowed, and nodded. He reached into his coat pocket and produced the sheets of Charles' notes, then handed them to Winston. The old man opened them, examined the notations for a few moments, and then looked at Edward. "You own this land, I assume? I'll require the deed."

Edward shook his head. "It's not mine to give."

Winston raised his eyebrows. "Explain."

"Charles had a son," Edward began. "An illegitimate son. By Mary Mogamo."

Winston nodded. "I'd heard as much," he said. He shook his head in disgust. "A bastard Coloured boy. What an embarrassment. No wonder he left South Africa."

"Not an embarrassment," snapped Edward. Then, softer, "And not Coloured, really. The boy was very light-skinned, and was raised as white. He grew up to be a successful executive, and quite a crusader for Coloured rights, I understand."

Winston's eyes grew narrow as he listened. "Go on," he said coldly.

"Charles arranged for the land to be transferred into the boy's name."

Winston felt his pulse surge. The sound of gravel was deafening in his ears. He could feel his face changing, contorting in anger. He crumpled the papers and shoved them into his pocket, then drew forth Jessica's pistol. "Bladdy hell. What are you saying?" he demanded through clenched teeth.

Edward held up his hands defensively. Winston was clearly insane, but he was in too deep now. He thought of Jessica and poor Sarah, and wished that he'd brought help with him. It was a mistake to split up. His only chance was to tell Winston the truth, as calmly as he could, and hope that the man would see how hopeless his situation was.

"Tell me!" screamed Winston. His arm straightened, aiming the weapon at the center of Edward's chest as he cocked the trigger.

"I'm saying that Charles' son owned the land where the diamonds were found," said Edward, evenly. "But the son died recently—that's when the letters were sent—and now the diamonds are owned by Mary Mogamo."

Winston's vision grew red around the edges. The sound of the gravel in the crusher echoed in his skull and his outstretched arm shook in anger. "No! . . . No!" he screamed. "Even Charles could not have been so crass as to give my diamonds to that, that . . . half breed!"

Winston's arm trembled, his finger tightening inexorably on the trigger before him. He swallowed convulsively, his face damp with perspiration.

He would kill this bastard. No. Not a bastard. The bastard was already dead. And Charles was beyond the reach of his anger. But Edward was his last link to the man who had ruined his life. It was Edward who must pay for this treachery.

Winston's face contorted into a savage smile, and he squeezed the trigger just as Edward dodged.

Edward wasn't fast enough. The pistol erupted with a sharp report. The bullet caught him in the side and he spun into the railing of the catwalk.

Winston's voice rose in an almost inhuman growl that began deep in his throat, building until it turned into an insane shriek. He raised his foot and slammed it into Edward's stomach.

Edward clutched at the catwalk railing, but his hand slipped in his own blood, and the force of the blow folded him in two like a broken matchstick. He plunged through the opening below the railing, the back of his head slamming into the top bar as it was forced through.

As if in slow motion, Winston watched Edward's feet follow the rest of his body through the gap beneath the catwalk railing. His limp form landed on the gravel-laden conveyor a few feet below, and was inexorably carried toward the maw of the giant cylinder.

Winston turned away.

He cursed. How could things have gone so wrong?

He stuffed the gun in his pocket and hurried down the catwalk steps.

There was one more witness to take care of. Then he'd head for the airport.

*   *   *

After leaving Kip, Jessica pulled the Land Rover off the tarmac of the Springbok Airport and headed west, retracing her path. She turned north on the road that went past the Van Der Meer mine. In about a mile she came to Maggie's Corner. The road made a wide sweeping curve to the left as it rounded the ridge, then the left curve tightened up suddenly, the right side of the road hugging the chasm. Carefully she eased the Rover across the oncoming lane and onto the turnout, stopping well back from the shoulder. She got out and walked around to the right rear door, opened it, and rummaged in her suitcase until she'd found a pair of jeans and some sneakers.

Using the Land Rover for cover, although there was little danger of spectators here—she'd never seeing another car on this road—she slipped off her skirt and high heels and put on the jeans and sneakers. Securing her other clothes in the suitcase, she walked to the left side of the vehicle, got in the driver's door, and headed on toward the Van Der Meer mine.

In another two miles she passed the mine entrance where she had dropped off Edward, but she continued on, as Kip had instructed. The pavement of the narrow two-lane road was now heavily pitted and potholed. No effort had been made to maintain a centerline marking.

She followed the winding road for another mile. It hugged the rocky cliff, the right side dropping into the gorge. A trail of red dust hung in the air, marking her progress. She could see it when the switchbacks carried her back the other direction.

She nearly missed the obscure turnoff that Kip had described. A tired chain hung across it, suspended from a post on either side.

Affixed to the middle of the chain was of rusty "Keep Out" sign, although the words were no longer legible.

Jessica turned the Land Rover off the road and pulled up to the chain. She got out and examined the nearest post. The chain was simply hooked over a rusty bent nail driven into the top of the post. Gingerly she lifted it off and tossed it toward the other post, where it landed in the red dust with a thud.

She got back into the Rover and slowly eased it up the dirt road. Embankments on either side grew higher until she found herself driving up a narrow canyon. The road avoided the very bottom of the canyon, where a dry ravine evidently carried water during the rainy season. Now the hills were bone dry, the cloud of dust behind her attesting to many rainless months. Dead grasses covered the more accommodating slopes of the canyon, but many of the walls were too steep to support any growth. Torrential rains had scored long vertical grooves in the walls that reminded Jessica of claw marks.

After about a mile the valley floor widened between the canyon walls momentarily. Up ahead she could see that the walls rushed back together to form a box canyon. In the small, flat enclosed space was a tattered steel structure, little more than a shed. Several abandoned pieces of earthmoving equipment were near it, and farther away a stack of dented barrels suggested its former use as a mining base. A rusted flagpole, its pennant long since weathered away, stood incongruously near the structure.

Jessica slowed and approached cautiously. She saw no other vehicles, but they could be in the rear. Carefully, she eased the Land Rover around to the back of the metal shed. Nothing there, either. She stopped her motor and rolled down the window to listen. The canyon was deathly silent.

The knot of fear that had been forming in Jessica's stomach tightened, and she opened the door and silently approached the metal shed. Dark thoughts flickered across her mind, but she pushed them away and forced herself to the small, barred window at the rear of the structure.

It took a moment for her eyes to adjust the dimness inside. Along the opposite wall was a similar barred window that shed a little more light into the dreary interior. A rough wooden table, its surface covered with charts and papers, occupied the center of the shed. On top of them, a cellophane package of doughnuts lay half-eaten, along with several empty soda cans.

To the right of the table was an army cot. Relief surged through Jessica as she spotted Sarah perched on the edge of the cot.

Her eyes scanned the interior of the shed, but there was no evidence of other occupants. Nevertheless, she cautiously crept around to the opposite side, surveying the exterior as she went. Although the surface of galvanized steel was rusty, it was well constructed. There was no obvious way to penetrate it, without some serious tools.

She came to the opposite window and peered in, letting her eyes once again adjust to the dimness. The opposite side of the room contained little more than her earlier inspection had revealed. A Porta-Potty had been set up in one corner, and old magazines were piled along the wall near it. There was no one but the girl in the shed.

"Sarah," she whispered.

The child looked up.

"Jessica!" she cried, running to the window.

"Shhhhh," she cautioned. "We must be quiet, just in case. Now quickly, tell me, is someone coming back?"

"Yes," said Sarah. "That man said he he'd be back as soon as he got more food and soda."

"How long has been gone?"

Sarah thought for a moment. "A long time, Jessica," she said, seriously. "He left this morning."

"All right," said Jessica reassuringly, "Let's get you out of here. Sit on the cot, while I figure out how to open the door."

"Yes, Jessica," said Sarah. She walked back to the cot.

Jessica continued her circuit of the building. When she came to the door she found that it, too, was made of galvanized steel. A metal hasp was bolted to it, and secured with a stainless-steel pad lock. She surveyed the area around the shed. In spite of its industrial nature, there was little in the way of tools or loose material lying about.

Quickly she returned to the Land Rover, and opened the rear. Lifting the cargo mat, she found a tire iron. She grabbed it and returned to the door.

It wouldn't fit behind the hasp.

She tried smashing the hasp with the tire iron, but it only served to blunt the edge of the metal.

Jessica examined the hinges. The hinge pins didn't appear to be removable; they were welded onto the hinges, somehow.

How the hell am I going to get into this thing? she thought desperately. Her mind raced. She had to get the Sarah out of there before someone found her. There was no other way out of the canyon. And she was unarmed.

She scanned the area for something of use.

Her eyes lit upon the flagpole. It stood apart from the shed a short ways, and showed no signs of recent use. But the rope still ran up it, some fifteen feet. She ran back to the Land Rover, tossed the tire iron into the back, opened the front door and retrieved her purse. Pawing through the contents, she found her Swiss Army knife.

Hurrying, she returned to the flagpole and began sawing at the cord, first with the knife, and when that didn't work quickly enough, with the saw blade. Finally she discovered that working the sharp edges of the scissors against the stiff rope was the quickest way to cut through it. As the final fibers parted, the loose end whipped up the pole, as the opposite side cascaded down off the pulley. In a moment she was holding a thirty-foot coil of rope in her hand.

She crossed to the shed and tied one end of the rope securely to the padlock. She played the rope out in a line along the ground, then ran back to the Land Rover. She started it, pulled it around to the front of the shed, then backed it up over the end of the rope, and climbed out. She secured it to Land Rover's towbar and got back in. Easing the vehicle into gear, she slowly pulled forward until the rope was taut, then continued to press on the gas. She felt tires slipping on the dusty ground, then the Rover lurched suddenly forward and she heard the sharp report of the hasp tearing loose, followed by the crash of the steel door as it swung open and slapped against the side of the building.

Jessica slammed on the emergency brake and ran back to collect Sarah. The girl was already stepping through the doorway by the time she caught up with her. They hurried toward the Land Rover.

"Quickly, now, climb in the back," she instructed.

Then she saw the truck barreling out of the ravine walls and into the box canyon. She saw the driver straighten when he caught sight of them, and heard his engine race. It looked like Winston, but she couldn't be sure.

There wasn't enough time to deal with the rope. She pushed Sarah in and slammed the back door, then plunged into the driver's side and threw the Land Rover into gear.

The truck was right in her path. She had to buy time. She floored the gas pedal and cranked the wheel to left, spraying loose rocks in all directions as they careened around the rear side of the shed. Just before she lost view of the truck, she saw it begin to veer in the opposite direction around the shed, trying to cut her off. She spun the wheel to the right, and the Rover responded by doing a quick 180.

Accelerating, she retraced her path around the shed. By the time she cleared the front of the building she felt almost airborne. The truck was nowhere in sight. Pressing the accelerator all the way to the floor, she burst out of the box canyon and began to careen down the narrow ravine.

"Fasten your seat belt, Sarah. Now!" Jessica yelled.

She heard the girl fumbling to comply.

At first she thought that the truck might have had some difficulty. She couldn't see it in her rearview mirror. But halfway back through the ravine she spotted it behind her, large and menacing, squeezing its way down the gully through her cloud of dust.

As they slid onto the Van Der Meer mining road she nearly lost control on the gravel-covered pavement. The Rover fishtailed wildly, but she steered into the skid, even though that was the direction of the precipice. With relief, she felt the tires catch, and accelerated on the rutted pavement. When she looked back, the truck was barely two-car lengths behind.

In only a minute she passed the entrance to the Van Der Meer Mining Company. She glanced down. She was doing almost 100 kilometers per hour.

This is crazy on this road, she thought. But she had no choice. She pressed on, her tires squealing at each turn.

The truck was even closer now, filling her rearview mirror like some metal monster. She felt the Rover hesitate, then fishtail, and she realized that the truck had driven over the rope she still trailed. There was a sinking feeling in the pit of her stomach, and she fought to control the wobbling vehicle.

With a snap, the Rover lurched forward, and she guessed that the rope had broken. Again she tried to pull away.

The truck slammed into her rear bumper with a crunch. Her body was thrown against the steering wheel. Sarah cried out. Quickly regaining control, Jessica pressed harder on the gas, clutching the wheel with one hand while she fastened her shoulder harness. Little good this will do in a five hundred foot drop, she thought.

The truck was pulling alongside her on the right now, traveling in the opposite lane. I hope the bastard hits a cement truck head-on, she thought. But she knew it was too much to wish for. She'd never encountered another car on this road.

Jessica could see that it was Winston in the driver's seat. His eyes were wild, and he grinned crazily at her as he yanked on the steering wheel, scraping the truck against the side of the Land Rover.

Sarah cried out as the car was forced against the left guardrail and sparks flew. She cowered in the back seat.

Jessica pulled the wheel to the right, and managed to force Winston's truck back over the centerline, but it took every bit of concentration to keep the Rover from spinning as it pressed against the larger mass of the truck.

She wondered if Winston had the gun with him, but she was afraid to slow down and find out. And if she sped up, she was afraid he'd get behind her, and snowplow her right off of one of these dangerous corners—guardrail, or no guardrail.

And so she continued to fishtail down the narrow road, hoping for an oncoming car that would force Winston out of the other lane.

The road was beginning to look ominously familiar, and she realized with dread that Maggie's corner was the next outside curve. There was no guardrail to save them, there. If Winston pulled the same stunt again, they'd be at the bottom of the ravine in a few seconds.

She glanced over at the truck. Winston was glaring at her like a madman, all of his energies focused on forcing her off the edge. He knows this is where Margaret and Lilly died, she thought. He knows, and he's trying to do the same to us.

She considered her options. There weren't any. She'd just have to out-drive him.

Pulse pounding, she watched for the onset of the curve. Pushing in the clutch, she dropped the Land Rover down a gear and floored it, dropping the clutch in and letting the car surge forward with an insane lurch. Loose gravel shot out behind her, and the Land Rover pulled ahead of the truck for a moment.

Reacting automatically, Winston floored the truck, leaping back beside her. As they moved into the turn, he slammed his wheel to the left.

But at that instant Jessica was pumping the brakes, slipping the clutch out and madly down-shifting, hoping the car could hold its footing as it began to skid into the corner. It hit the gravel of the turnout, and felt more like it was skipping over fresh ice. But by working the clutch and brake she was beginning to slow it.

Winston, still accelerating, careened to the left, caught off-guard in his rush to force Jessica off the road. The truck fishtailed and slid across in front of the Land Rover, sliding sideways on the gravel of the turnout. The Land Rover slammed into the driver's side door of the truck, transferring some of its forward momentum to Winston's vehicle. The truck's right side bounced over the dirt rim of the turnout as Winston clung to the useless steering wheel.

For a moment the truck perched there, two wheels still on the turnout, Winston's fate hanging in the balance.

The Rover came to a complete stop.

Only a few feet in front of her, Winston stared into Jessica's eyes in terror. She watched him fumbling for the door handle, his eyes wide. Then, in slow motion, the truck disappeared over the edge.

From far below came the sounds of grinding, twisting, crashing metal as the truck careened its way down the precipice. Something compelled Jessica to open her door and slowly walk to the edge. Halfway there, the heat of the explosion hit her, and she retreated back to the Land Rover as thick billows of black smoke poured back over the edge of the embankment.

* * *

Jessica was quiet as she drove back to the Van Der Meer Mining Company. She drove carefully, almost meticulously, ordering her thoughts. Oddly, by the time that she reached the entrance to the mining company, she felt almost elated. She'd accomplished their mission, Sarah was safe, she and Edward had come to an agreement about the future. After all of the turmoil of the past weeks, she was surprised to find that she'd never been happier.

Her light mood dispelled when she saw the emergency vehicles clustered beyond the administration building. Up the road, a dozen people were crowded around the entrance to the tall metal builder with the conveyor protruding from it. An ambulance, it's light still flashing, was backed up to the doorway.

She pulled the car up as close as she dared, told Sarah to stay put, and hopped out. She pushed her way through the crowd, feeling inundated by the babble of Afrikaans. A technician in a white coat was standing outside the entrance, looking in.

"What happened?" she asked him.

"Somebody fell onto the separation plant conveyor," he replied in a thick South African accent.

Jessica's pulse pounded in her head. "Who was it?"

The man shook his head. "Don't know. Nobody knows."

She squeezed her way between two people in the doorway and paused to let her eyes adjust to the dim light.

There was a stretcher on the floor in the middle of the room. A man lay on it, his shirt cut open, and his side covered with white tape and bandages. It was Edward.

She ran to him, and knelt down beside the medics. His eyes were closed. She searched his face for some sign of life.

"Edward," she cried, reaching out to touch his cheek.

Slowly, he turned his head toward her and opened his eyes. "Jessie," he said softly. There was a smudge of blood on his cheek, but his eyes were clear, and bright. "Are you alright?" he asked.

"Am I alright? What about you!" she said.

"I'll be fine. Just a little banged up. But Winston . . . He didn't take the news well. It was stupid of me to tell him. I just couldn't resist gloating a little, I guess. Now I'm afraid he's gone after Sarah."

"She's fine, Edward. I've got her in the car." Edward's smile sent her soaring, far into the heavens. Jessica took his hand and smiled back.

"We must be careful, until the police have him," said Edward.

Jessica shook her head. "Winston's dead," she said. "He went off the road at Maggie's Corner. If I ever doubted that there was a God, I don't any longer. There could be no more fitting end for that monster."

Edward closed his eyes and nodded. One of the technicians lifted his head and began working on his scalp, cutting away some of the hair and cleaning the skin with a cotton pad. Edward winced.

"What did Winston do to you, anyway?" asked Jessica.

Edward grinned at her. "Tried to send me for a ride in his rock crusher. Oh, and he shot me. Just a little. He's a very bad shot."

"Oh, Edward," Jessica cried. "Are you sure—"

"I'll be fine," he said. "Although it was touch and go there for a few minutes." He nodded toward the ceiling. Jessica looked up, and saw where the conveyor ended above a massive cylinder from which huge metal shafts protruded. Edward continued, "I was hanging above the crusher by both arms, seemed like forever. It's so noisy in here, no one could hear me screaming."

"Oh my God. What happened?"

"Help arrived from a most unexpected quarter," said Edward. "She got them to shut off the machine, just before I fell." He turned his head to the other side, and for the first time Jessica noticed someone crouched in the dark on the other side of the stretcher. It was Liz.

The woman's eyes met and held Jessica's.

"Liz, what are you doing here?" Jessica asked.

"I've been asking myself the same question," she said. She brushed the hair from her face and continued. "I guess I just wanted my piece of the action. But it looks like we're all about thirty years too late, huh? Funny, isn't it? All these years I've been your tormentor, Edward, and in the end I wind up as the knight in shining armor."

"You were never my tormentor, Liz. You just never cared about a family. I did."

Liz shrugged. "It's true. I don't really know what's the matter with me, but it's true." She raised her fingertips to his cheek, then drew back. "You never understood me, Edward."

"We could have been happy, Liz. We were, for a time," he said.

"No," she said. "It was impossible." She closed her eyes for a moment, and for the first time Jessica could almost recognize the woman she'd seen in the picture on Edward's mantle all those years ago. "Do you have any idea what it's like to be trapped, your whole life? Like some flower under a bell jar? Unable to breath, to move, always trying to live up to the image that proper society expects from you . . ."

He nodded. "I understand," he whispered.

"Do you?" she said softly.

She looked at Jessica, who slowly nodded.

"Perhaps you do," she whispered. "Perhaps you do."

"What will you do now, Elizabeth?" asked Edward.

She looked at him.

"Disappear again. I can't go back to England. Too many people want me safely locked away. Besides, Sarah doesn't need me in her life." She glanced at Jessica, then back at Edward. "And neither do you." She smiled wanly. "I think I'll stay on here in the Cape. Plenty of money just waiting for an enterprising person like me to come along and talk someone out of it."

She stood, and looked at Jessica. "Don't mention me to Sarah, please. She doesn't need to know."

Jessica nodded. She watched the woman slip out through the bright rectangle of the doorway.

"It's for the best really," grimaced Edward, as the ambulance attendant strapped him down onto the stretcher. Jessica walked out with them to the ambulance. Sarah scrambled out of the back seat and ran toward her father on the stretcher.

Behind the car, standing silently in the shadows of a tin shed, was Liz. She watched her child fuss over Edward, then cling to Jessica for comfort as the stretcher was loaded into the ambulance.

The next time Jessica looked, she was gone.

Chapter 12

Snow was falling gently against the ornate window when Jessica woke to the sound of Sarah shouting delightedly from downstairs.

A white Christmas. She smiled to herself, and snuggled closer to her husband. Husband, she thought, smiling to herself. Edward slept peacefully beside her, still tired out from the late night before, when the two of them had stayed up late to set out the Christmas presents and finish decorating the living room.

She heard the thunder of little feet as Sarah scampered up the stairs and into their bedroom. She ran over to the bed and leapt onto it, waking Edward in the process.

"Come on sleepy heads, Father Christmas has been," she said excitedly.

"We'll be down in a few minutes," she smiled, shooing Sarah out of the bed and through the door. "And you can get some of those Christmas biscuits you were chasing last night, before you tear into the tree," she called after her.

Turning back to Edward, Jessica poked him playfully in the ribs. "Come on, duty calls." He groaned, and began to drag himself out the far side of the bed.

Jessica washed her face in the bathroom. She still found it hard to believe that she was married. The still-recuperating Edward had formally proposed as they were waiting for the plane to carry them back home from Cape Town—had it really been a month ago? She'd seen it coming this time: the intense look in his eyes as he prepared himself to ask her. She hadn't hesitated. She was laughing, and saying yes before he'd even finished asking. Edward had looked at her with pure joy in his eyes. Sarah was thrilled to learn that Jessica was to be her mother. Two weeks later they'd been married.

Edward, wrapping his arms around her from behind, interrupted her thoughts. "Are you ready?" he asked, kissing her lightly on the top of her head.

She turned in his arms and kissed him passionately. "Ready as ever," she said, smiling, then broke away.

"You keep kissing me like that and we will never get downstairs," he laughed.

She giggled and ducked from the room. "Come on," she called, "it's Christmas."

They spent a pleasant morning sitting together by the fire in the library, drinking eggnog, and watching Sarah open her packages.

Around mid morning, they adjourned to the kitchen to put on the turkey for Christmas dinner. It was a large one, because they were expecting Jack and Emma to join them. They'd become quite the item in the past months. Jessica, having known both of them so well, felt that they were really right for one another.

Mac joined them in the kitchen for a short while, before heading back to his cottage to prepare 'something special' for the Christmas lunch.

A car door slammed outside.

"It's them, it's them," cried Sarah as she rushed to the front door. Her father and Jessica were close behind.

With hugs all around, the newly arrived coupled unbundled themselves and joined the family in the library. Sarah sat on the floor by the Christmas tree, unwrapping a present from Jack and Emma.

"Brought this for you to read old boy," said Jack, as he handed Edward a newspaper from his suitcase.

Jessica peered over Edward's shoulder and read the article.

It was a copy of The Cape Argus, from South Africa, dated December 20th. The fourth page was folded back to an article about the Van Der Meer Diamond Company. After losing its founder, an audit had revealed many accounting discrepancies, and the company's creditors had forced it into liquidation.

"Well, I feel sorry for the workers, but as far as the rest goes, good riddance," said Jessica. Edward patted her hand.

Mac came into the room, gesturing excitedly.

Edward rose from the chair. "What is it Mac?"

"This here ring," he said holding up his wife's ring and waving a piece of paper in his other hand.

"What about it?"

"You see, that rascal Mr. Charles, he was a great one for puzzles and so on. You know, cryptograms, word games and the like." Mac surveyed the room. He had everyone's attention.

"I was looking at the paper that Jessie left on my table," he continued, "with the numbers on it from all the rings. Well, while I was waiting for my special Christmas pudding to cook, I did a bit of fiddling around. I wrote down the letter equivalents for each number in my ring, and you'll never guess."

They shook their heads, waiting for him to finish.

"Well, they spell out Drummond."

Edward grinned. "If we'd figured that out earlier, we wouldn't have needed so many rings," he said, shaking his head. "But so what Mac? This is Drummond castle, he was a Drummond. What's the significance? It was just an amusing way for him to come up with the combination to the safe—and the measurements of the flagstones."

"Nay laddie, remember yer Uncle's letter."

He dug it out of his top pocket and smoothed it out on the hall table.

He read aloud, "The treasure lies behind the name in the rings, forged in that year when the combination of events so overwhelmed me that all that was left for me was revenge."

"Do ye not see? The treasure lies behind the name in the rings," he reiterated.

"Go on . . ." said Edward, a hint of interest creeping into his voice.

"I began to think about where I see the name Drummond in the castle here. I get to every room when I clean, so I thought about it. Follow me."

He led them into the great room, stopping before the painting of Margaret and Lilly.

"We already checked this out Mac," said Edward, kindly. "We found that clue."

"Aye, ye did," nodded the old man. "But did ye find this."

With a flourish he swung the entire painting out, revealing a wall safe behind it.

"Well I'll be damned," exclaimed Edward. He stepped forward and tentatively spun the dial.

Taking the paper from Mac, he entered the first set of numbers. When he tried the handle, nothing happened. His shoulders drooped in disappointment. He tried the second. Nothing. "Drat. It would take a ton of explosives to get this old thing open," he sighed.

Jessica took the paper from him and studied it in the dim light of the room. "Hold on a minute," she said, thoughtfully. "It says, 'forged in that year when the combination . . ." that's it!"

"Try this Edward," she said breathlessly, pointing to the 1963 at the bottom of the plaque.

Edward shrugged, and entered the numbers. This time the handle turned, and with a soft click, the lock disengaged. He opened the safe.

Everyone tried to peer around Edward at once.

Carefully, he extracted the safe's only contents: a carved box, exactly like the one that they had found in the cellar. Slowly, he opened it.

It was filled with rough pieces of stone. It took Jessica a moment before she realized that they were diamonds—hundreds of them, some larger than her thumbnail. Many were still encrusted with a dull, white scale, but some glittered back at them temptingly.

They stared at the treasure in Edward's hands. Softly, Jack whistled.

Edward turned, and held out the box toward Jessie.

"These must be worth millions," he breathed. "Look at the size of them."

Jack picked one up and studied it. "That is one big hunk of rock, Edward."

"Let's have a gander," said Mac, from behind.

He picked out a particularly large one, and moved closer to the light, examining it, weighing the rough stone in his hand.

"Yer Uncle showed me this stone once, long ago. He told me it was the largest diamond he'd ever found. Over one hundred carats, he said, before cutting, anyway. He told me that someday he'd have it cut, and name it after Margaret. Said it would reflect her purity, and light." Mac sighed. "I thought he'd long since sold it, to support the estate."

Mac placed the diamond back in Edward's hand.

"Then that is what we'll call it," said Edward, "in her memory." Edward handed it back to the man he'd known since he was a small child. "But perhaps you should be the one to take care of this Mac."

The Scotsman shook his head, but Edward took his hand, and placed the stone in it. "And when it's cut, Mac, I'm sure that my uncle would have wanted you to have the other gems that come off it."

"Sir—Eddie—really, . . . I can't," the man stammered. But Edward just wrapped the man's fingers around the stone and patted his hand.

"Besides," continued Edward, hefting the box, "There are enough stones here to keep all of us comfortable for the rest of our lives."

Jessica watched the others as they excitedly examined the diamonds. How would this unexpected discovery affect their marriage? She was silent as they all went back into the warmth of the sitting room. Noticing her silence, Edward handed the box of diamonds to Jack, and settled down beside her on the couch. He looked at her with concern.

"Are you alright with this?" he asked quietly, barely audible against the background of animated voices. Jack and Emma were excitedly explaining the find to Sarah.

Jessica shrugged.

Edward took her hand in his, and drew it to him. "I'm not unaware of how you felt about me being wealthy."

Jessica looked into his eyes. There was incredible kindness there, and a depth of affection that nearly moved her to tears. In a flash of insight, she realized that he was asking her if she wanted him to give the diamonds away. How could she fail to respond to someone willing to give up everything he had, just to make her happy? She could only imagine how much the diamonds must mean to him. They represented not only their future security, but also his uncle's legacy.

Biting her lower lip, she weighed her response carefully. But Edward's unselfishness made her decision easy.

"You know," she replied thoughtfully, "I married you thinking you were a pauper. The fact that we were equal was important to me. In fact, I rather looked forward to supporting you, for a change. It troubled me that all those years ago everyone thought I was after nothing but your money and position. As a result, the house in London never really felt like home. To me, it was more of a palace, and I some interloper, pretending to be the princess."

"And now?"

"Now, . . . I feel differently. I feel that I have earned your love. Earned the right to be by your side, no matter what. And although the neighbors and servants—and even that house—are long gone, I feel that it would be clear, even to them, that I didn't marry a pauper for his money!"

Edward nodded and waited for her to continue.

She smiled at him, and raised his hand to her lips, gently kissing the ridge of his knuckles. "I don't feel like an interloper anymore. And this castle is our home now. And theirs, as well," she added, nodding at Jack and Emma, who were helping Sarah assemble a doll house on the floor by the Christmas tree.

Edward moved against her, encircling her with his arm. She leaned her head on his shoulder, letting her auburn hair cascade down the front of his shirt.

Jessica continued. "Let's put the diamonds back in the safe, for now. We don't need them. And they'll always be there, if we ever do."

She felt him nodding.

They were both quiet for a while, watching Sarah play. Then Edward cleared his throat, and pulled her up, turning her to face him, with a hand on either shoulder. "Very well," he said, seriously. "We'll put them away—all except a few." He shook his head to forestall her objection. "We'll sell just enough to open an office—in town."

"An office?" she asked.

He nodded. "Downtown. Just a small, ground floor space. With gold letters on the door—I like gold lettering, don't you?"

Jessica looked confused, but he continued, "They'll say 'Drummond Company,' . . . no . . . 'Drummond Associates'—I think that's better. 'Drummond Associates, Architects'." He grinned. "No one needs to know that you're the only architect. And I can do the books, write the proposals, make the coffee, whatever." He was smiling, awaiting her reaction.

Jessica beamed back at him, her heart filled with love. He did understand. "You'll be my investment banker?" she murmured.

Edward nodded. He moved forward, and brushed her lips with his. Suddenly he was hugging her to him, kissing her passionately. But in a moment he broke it off, and held her again at arms' length. "But I must ask you one thing," he said, soberly.

"What?" she asked, still trying to take it all in.

"You don't have any objection to sleeping with the office help, do you?" He was grinning again, and she pulled him to her roughly, and kissed him soundly.

"None that I can think of," she said, laughing.

They kissed until Jack and Emma finally sent Sarah to fetch them to come and play with the dollhouse. Then it was lunchtime, and they all gathered in the dining room, to enjoy Mac's Christmas luncheon buffet.

Mac beamed as they complimented each dish. "'Tis a delight just havin' the house filled with happy people again," he said. "And a young 'un, too" he added, smiling at Sarah.

Later, Jessica sat in the window seat of the library, and watched her new family enjoying Christmas afternoon. Edward and Sarah were using leftover boxes to make furniture for the dolls; Emma and Jack sat on the couch, quietly chatting; Mac dozed in a chair by the fire. She sighed contentedly.

Outside, large flakes of snow were falling, blanketing the fir trees with quiet comfort. Snow in London had always seemed the enemy. Here it was a cheerful conspirator, sealing them off from the demands of the rest of the world.

Jessica looked down at her hand. The gold band caught the warm glow of the firelight. Edward had wanted to buy her a wedding ring, but finances had been tight; she'd told him she didn't want one. And she didn't.

She turned the ring, and the circle of diamonds caught the fire's light, flashing crimson. It meant more to her than any wedding ring. Past and future, love and hope, she saw them all reflected in her simple ring of diamonds.

Authors' Biography

Sharon Stevens is the pen name of the writing team of Steve Alcorn and Sharon Brindal.

Steve Alcorn is the founder and president of Alcorn McBride Inc., a $10M company that designs attractions for theme parks all over the world. Mr. Alcorn's non-fiction work is widely read throughout the themed entertainment industry, and he is a frequent speaker at conferences in both the US and Europe. He is currently working on *Everything In Its Path*, a novel based upon the true story of the collapse of the St. Francis Dam.

Sharon Brindal lives in Western Australia where she is active in a number of writer's groups. She and Mr. Alcorn began corresponding through a writer's forum on the Internet. They collaborated on Ring of Diamonds entirely by electronic mail, and have never met.

9 780738 835310